I0549080

"Pixie"

"A Cheerful Mischievous Sprite"

by

D J McAllister

Copyright © 2016. D. J. McAllister. All rights reserved
No part of this book may be reproduced or transmitted in any form or by any means, graphic, electronic, or mechanical, including photocopying, recording, taping, or by any information storage retrieval system, without the permission, in writing, of the author.

ISBN: 978-0-692-62691-7

Design: Dedicated Book Services, (www.netdbs.com)

DEDICATION

To all the Military Personnel, Veterans, First Responders and Emergency Personnel who save our lives and protect the American People on a daily basis.

Many thanks to Betty, who without her these books would not have been completed.

If you liked this book please post a photo of this cover on Facebook or other media, so your friends and their friends will know where to buy the book.

AMAZON.COM/ BOOKS/ djmcallister

TABLE OF CONTENTS

FOREWORD

This is the story of three women that I was privileged to know and love and will continue to love, probably till I die. I couldn't write "Dear Diary", men don't keep diaries. And "Dear Journal" sounds stupid, so I'll just tell you the story from the notes and scraps of paper I scribbled during the most interesting times. Reading it now, I don't even believe that we did some of these more ridiculous things, and I was there.

My one regret is that I had to lose one beautiful, wonderful woman to find another, but the blessing of the children lives on. I smile every day about some strange or funny incident long past. Until I wrote this, I'm sure the kids all thought I was crazy. As they would walk by, I could hear them say, "Look at him, he's doing it again."

Most men are lucky to find, and love, and be loved by one jewel of a woman in their life, and rightly so. I found three. All three knew me better than I knew myself. They all knew what I thought before I thought it, what I wanted before I wanted it, and fortunately for me they acted on their thoughts.

Woman is the most wonderful gift man has ever received, including life. Life without a woman is a drab, colorless existence. Man can plod through life and achieve many things, but why, if not to share it with that most wonderful of all creatures, woman.

With the right woman in your life, the birds sing for you, roses bloom and their fragrance lifts your thoughts of love and carries them to that one special woman who gently receives and nourishes them, only to give them back to you tenfold.

What is the perfect woman? Her presence lights up the room you are in when she enters, her voice turns on your brain with a pleasant pat, her figure stirs the lion within you every time you gaze upon her, her smile tells you that everything's alright and assures you that her love for you is still burning bright. Her love envelopes you and warms you like a giant handmade quilt wrapped around you.

This, then, describes these women in the story I am about to tell you. I hope you can be as fortunate.

Chapter 1

Sarah, My Love

My first love was Sarah. She was the best thing that ever happened to me. She was everything that I wasn't. She was polished, I'm rough. She could cook and take care of the house, I'd be starving and living in a pig sty. She was a beautiful caring woman.

And now she's gone. A drunk driver crossed the median and hit her car head on. She was pronounced dead at the scene. For me, the only good thing that came out of that whole fiasco was the fact, the lousy bastard that hit her, died too.

Before this tragedy, I used to drink, sometimes when we went to parties and especially when I was on road trips away from home. The team I worked with and I would go out after the inspections and sometimes drink way too much.

Not anymore. Since my beloved Sarah's death, nothing but soft drinks for me from now on. I refuse to be the reason for causing someone heartache like I have had to experience because of my drunk driving.

I work out of town most of the time, and it so happened on this particular day, I returned home from a trip to Denver with the Team. I walked into the house about five thirty and no one was home. But, that's not so unusual because Sarah would take our son, Harry, and go shopping.

So I put my stuff away and walked the three blocks up to Mrs. Johnson's house to say "Hi". Mrs. Johnson has known Sarah since she was born. She has been a friend of Sarah's mother for many years.

She has a warm smile and reminds me of everyone's grandmother. When she saw me, she broke down crying and told me about the accident. The funeral was Saturday, April 28. That's the day I lost my best friend.

All this happened last April and I've been walking around in a fog most of the time ever since. I go to the cemetery every Saturday when I return home. I talk to her, discussing my weeks activities, my feelings, and take her some flowers.

Sometimes I take Harry, but he's only five and still doesn't understand why his mom went to work one day and never came home to him.

Have I mentioned? I'm a member of a team of inspectors, called War Readiness Assistance Team or WRAT for short? (We've been called a bunch of rats more than once.) We travel the fifteen western states and inspect the Army Reserve for readiness. We have an office in the USAR center here. Our team travels to all the major cities and a lot of the minor ones in seven states, the Dakotas, Nebraska, Kansas, New Mexico, Colorado and Utah, on a regular basis.

Our schedule is somewhat strange and is as follows: We are usually out of town for ten to fourteen days and in town for a week. We normally work out the final details of the trip on Monday and leave on a Tuesday. We are scheduled to work that week, the weekend, and the following week and then arrive home the following Friday.

We'll be home a full week until the following Tuesday. That means we are home nine days and out fifteen days. There are also the occasional short trips too. I was just returning from one of these trips when my life turned upside down.

Now the flood of grief is like a river that overwhelms me. Its current has pulled me down into the darkness of despair. I couldn't eat, I couldn't sleep, I couldn't work, I couldn't think. I didn't care about anything except Sarah. I would reach out for her and discovered she wasn't there anymore. The emptiness of my bed a chasm, a crevasse, one so deep I pray it will cave in upon me to relieve my sufferings.

Bill and Linda, two dear friends of mine and Sarah's, came by on several occasions trying to help pull me up out of my depressive state of mind. My parents tried, Sarah's parents tried, even the guys I work with tried, but nothing worked. I couldn't shake this morbid state of mind until I realized my little sweet Harry had lost his mother and couldn't afford to lose his dad too. It took me six months to fight my way back to the living.

It was hard for me to complete those last couple of months of college. It's a good thing I had pretty good grades, because I didn't get much studying done in April and May.

But I did get my degree in Business for whatever that's worth. I didn't think I really needed the degree, but if I'm ever going to make anything with my life, I guess it was important to do the education thing.

When I was a kid, my best friend, Ted Collins, and I went to school together. Ted was much smarter than me, and always got 'A's in everything. I bet he would be surprised that I finally got a degree in something and I would bet he has more than one degree by now.

When I'm depressed, sometimes I think about Sarah and the good times. I met Sarah and her best friend Linda, about six years ago. We happened to meet at the local bowling alley.

I was a fill-in for someone on another bowling team. I went a little early that first night to find where I was going. I was twenty-four years old and didn't have sense enough to come in out of the rain, but I did learn something there.

If I want information, I would rather ask a woman than a man for several reasons. I would rather listen to a girl's voice than a man's anytime. I can follow what she's saying a lot better and there's no ego to deal with. Also, while she is talking to me, I can enjoy looking at her beautiful form as well. Oh, look. Here comes a cute gal now.

"Excuse me, I'm DJ McAllister and I'm the new substitute on the 'Pin Slingers' team, can you tell me where I can find the team?" I asked her.

"Sure, I'm Linda Williams. See there," pointing across the room, "that guy with the glasses talking to the blonde girl, that's them." She said.

Linda is a beautiful statuesque thin woman about five foot nine and one or two years older than I am, with blonde over-the-shoulder length hair. She is small on top but the rest of her body is quite nice and great looking long legs.

I would have asked Linda for a date until I saw the rings on her finger. Out of the corner of my eye I could see another girl walking toward us.

"Oh, here comes Sarah, my best friend, she and a couple of guys are on our team." She said.

Linda introduced her friend. As Sarah extended her hand in my direction for me to shake hands, I realized my whole body has quit, frozen in time, seized up, nothing worked. She was so beautiful that my heart stopped, my lungs quit working, and my mouth went dry. I couldn't talk, I tried but just some weird sounds came out.

Finally I croaked out something and Linda laughed and pushed me toward the guy she pointed out earlier. She was saying something about getting started. I could hear them giggling behind me as I stumbled toward the bowling alley encompassing my team, humiliated.

It took me a couple of months during that bowling season for me to learn how to talk again and to finally approach Sarah to say something. I made it my goal that when our team finally played Sarah's team, I would find some reason, any reason, to talk to her between frames.

Eventually, after several months, she gave me her phone number just before the league year was over. That was the beginning of a lot of wonderful times for us.

*   *   *   *   *   *

This job of mine is pretty good and so is the pay. We pretty much get to set our own hours as long as the inspections get done. We work a lot of overtime when we're on a trip, which means we get a lot of time off when we're home. That part's good, but the traveling gets under your skin after a while. Especially when you have a sweet woman in your life and you wish to be in her presence.

It was like that with Sarah. Her and I spent many long hours discussing our goals in life, wants, needs, and children. I just always wanted to be near her and finally the day came when I proposed marriage. She would be the gift that would complete me. It was a day of celebration and two happy people would become one on that day.

Sarah and I had decided before we were married to have two children and then we would see if we wanted more when the youngest was three years old. We had talked about having another baby when Harry was three, but decided to wait one more year. Looks like we didn't make it.

Before I had met Sarah, I had already bought a small ranch-style home with a basement on Pattie Street in Wichita. It had one medium and two small bedrooms. Once we were married, I tore out walls and made one large and one medium bedroom out of it. I added a fireplace in the living room and built a two car garage back by the alley. We kept her car and my pickup in it.

I did a few other additions that I could actually do. We used to make love in front of a roaring fire in the living room pretty often during the winter months. She thought the house was a castle, pictures of us are all over the walls in every room. There is a big one of her in the bedroom where I can see it every day and every night.

As soon as you walk in, you could tell a woman lived there because of the woman's touches all through the house in the decorating. I didn't change anything after her death, except now there's clothes and junk piled around and the house looks cluttered.

My stuff is still on the shelves around the house. I have always enjoyed designing buildings. I wanted to go to college to be an architect, but the Service thought I was an Electronics Technician, so it never happened. I started building little model buildings a long time ago and now there are a lot of shelves displaying my models all around the house.

Sarah did everything for Harry and I, cooking, cleaning, taking care of the house, paying the bills. She did it all smiling, singing and dancing around the house like she was in a movie or something. And all this packaged in a five foot, six inch, freckle-faced redhead with a terrific figure.

Now, everyone is telling me to get on with my life, but when it's the right time, my life will let me know. Until that happens, I guess I still have the anchor out. I'm still in the grieving process and hey that's okay. Getting over such a woman as Sarah does not come easy. I have a right to feel this way.

Yesterday, one of the guys on the WRAT team was talking about paying his income tax. It's only November, why is he worried about it now? Sarah did all that herself too. I'm not going to try it. Maybe I'd better find an accountant right away before tax season comes.

Chapter 2

Taxes

Sunday at church I was talking with my old friend Walt Fortman. "Say Walt, do you know anyone that does taxes that I can trust?" I asked.

"Go to Hughes, Ingram and Jessup, ask for Denise. She's an accountant and does taxes on the side. Tell her I sent you." He said, slapped me on the back, and then he headed off. "She will help you."

It was Monday, November 12th, when I walked into the offices of Hughes, Ingram and Jessup Inc.

"May I help you sir?" The receptionist said in her clear crisp voice, a forced smile from ear to ear, put on for all who enter the premises. She was obviously more interested in her typing assignment because she barely looked up at me.

"I'd like to see Denise, Please." I said.

"Do you work for the government, sir?" She asked while typing and looking downward.

"Why, yes I do, but - -."

"I'm ringing her," the receptionist cut me off, mumbled in the phone, paused, then replied, "She'll be right out, won't you have a seat?" Pointing to the chairs against the wall, then resumed her typing once again as though I did not exist.

It was only a minute until Denise was standing there. The receptionist stood to introduce me to a beautiful woman with light reddish brown hair and a big happy smile and said, "This is Denise Monroe, she handles all our government accounts. She will be able to help you with whatever you need." Then once again, sat down behind the large desk to resume her typing knowing she had completed her mission in life.

Denise led me back to her desk and asked, "What can I do for you." Her voice had a lilting quality that you don't hear very often. A kind voice that you want to listen to over and over, it made my ears happy. And a smile which welcomed you with sincerity. Feelings I had not expected seemed to bubble up inside me just from the sounds of her sweet voice. I had to tell myself to get a grip and tried to speak.

"Your receptionist must have thought I wanted to talk about government business." I said lowering my voice to a near whisper. "My name is DJ McAllister, and I do work for the government, but what I came to you for is that I need someone that I can trust to do my taxes."

"My wife died last year and she always took care of everything. I was recommended to you by my friend, Walt Fortman, at church yesterday."

Denise looked about twenty-six, and about five foot six, I think, shoulder length almost red hair with a slight curl. She has a very pretty face and her hair is obviously well cared for. Doesn't use much makeup.

She is thin, maybe even skinny. She was dressed in a medium blue suit with a white high neck blouse, black shoes, looked very business-like.

"Oh, you go to Central Christian then. I do too." She said in an excited voice, then continued. "Walter should have told you that I do the tax business at home after work, but if you can be discreet and not say anything to the people here in the office, I can help you now. We can communicate on the phone from time to time, if necessary. Do you have any of your records and receipts?" She asked.

"My wife did all of that and I don't have them put together, if that's what you mean, but I can get most of it in a box by Thanksgiving, I think."

"OK, clip it together by category, like medical, travel expenses, income, home expenses, you know." She said, gesturing with her petite hands making little piles of information she would need for tax filing.

"I should explain my work schedule to you, it's a little unusual." I explained how we traveled and gave her one of our quarterly schedules from my briefcase.

"For the time being, call me on my office phone in the morning when you come back from your trip, and I can talk to you during lunch. Here's my card," taking one from an organized tray on the front of her desk, "I like to know a little about the people that I work for, could you write down some of your pertinent information for me the next time that I see you?" She asked.

"Sure, thanks a lot." I said while stuffing the business card in my wallet and stood up. "I'll get started on this right away." I left thinking that this woman must know the tax business and codes inside and out. She sure sounds smart to me. Her attire and poise both denoted an intelligent woman.

My normal routine when I'm in town, is to get off of work at four in the afternoon and go by Mrs. Johnson's house to pick up Harry. Her daughter, Carol, who is thirteen, usually is playing with Harry when I get there and she meets me at the door.

Mrs. Johnson has been a lifesaver ever since the accident. She had been keeping Harry off and on, but now with me out-of-town so much, she takes care of him like he was her own grandson. Maybe she is, he calls her 'gamm-ma' and has ever since he started to talk. I left her a key to my house in case she needs to get something for Harry.

When our team is home from a trip, I try to play with him for a little while before I make something to eat. We have a lot of soup and sandwiches now. When I was single, I got cases of Campbell's soup and stocked it up in the kitchen.

Well I'm starting to do that again, except now I've found that Dillon's carries a brand called "Food Club", and the soup is about five or ten cents a can less. Over the last year, I've filled up the kitchen with cans of corn, beans, peas, tomatoes some fruit and soup, lots of soup. It's easy to have a can of soup and a grilled cheese sandwich, and I'm definitely not a good cook. I have burnt almost everything you can think of. We usually eat around five or five thirty so Harry can have time to play before he has to go to bed.

This week, the Team and I got back to town on Friday, December 15th, and I called Denise for an appointment. She set a lunch appointment with me for the following Monday. I looked for her, but didn't see her in church on Sunday.

I had lunch with Denise on Monday at a little Mom and Pop cafe just around the corner from her office. I got there a little early and got us a booth on the side next to the windows.

While I was waiting for Denise, my thoughts turned to my first date with Sarah. It was in a little cafe just like this one, that we had lunch and coffee together for the first time. I remember it was in April and she was wearing a light sweater with a scoop neck. She sat across from me and asked me a million questions. I was in a trance with her beauty and all that fiery red hair and freckles. She could have thrown food all over me and I would have loved it. I might not have even known it, either.

Denise startled me when she walked in. I was still caught up in my daydreaming. Denise spoke and shocked me out of my cloudy mess. She was dressed in a dark blue, wool, winter suit with a colorful blue V-neck sweater. We ordered a light lunch and I gave her the biography I had written.

Bio   Devon John McAllister

Age 25, 6', 185 lb., dark brown hair, hazel
eyes, glasses
GS-11 with US Army.
One dependent, Harry Scott McAllister,
3 years old
Own a house on Pattie Street, Wichita,
Kansas

She hurriedly read it and tucked it into her purse
which matched the color of her attire perfectly.

"I left the box of receipts in my car, we can transfer them to your car when we go back, if that's OK
with you?" I suggested.

She told me all about taxes and the government as
we had lunch. She sounds like she is an expert in this
area. After we ate we walked back to my car and got
the box of receipts.

"What is that? That's not like any car I've ever seen
before." She spoke as her eyes perused the car from
different angles and looked inside at the interior.

"It's a '65 Porsche." I said with pride, "I've had
this since it was a pup. Probably the best car I ever
had." I retrieved the box from off the front seat for
her.

"Come on, I am parked in the garage across the
street." She said as she looked both ways at the on-
coming traffic. We walked across the street to the
parking garage and up to the second level where she

led me to a light blue three-year-old Pontiac, four door sedan. She opened the trunk with her key and I put the box of receipts describing my life inside.

"OK, I'll get started on your taxes right away and call you when I have something for you." She said with another big smile. I held the car door open for her, and shut it once she was safely settled inside. Then I waved to her as she drove off, then went to my car, and drove back to work.

December is one of my favorite months and Christmas is one of the two best holidays, but this year Christmas would be a time of sadness for me. Harry and I went to the cemetery Saturday to spend Christmas with Sarah. We both cried a lot. A holiday feels empty without a loved one.

In the winter, the Team either stays close around home or we make plans to visit a warm area of the country. This particular January, we flew to Albuquerque and spent two weeks of wonderful warm weather down there. I have a lot of friends who live there, so we always have a lot of fun, even in the winter time.

The weather that we came back to was below zero in the temperature range and with three inches of snow on the ground. I like to leave my car in my garage at home when I go out on a trip and then take a taxi to the airport. I find it's a lot less trouble and I don't have to worry about scooping snow off my car at night in a deserted airport parking lot when I'm dog tired from traveling.

Today, the cab dropped me off at my house at three thirty on a Friday afternoon. I hurried inside to get the heat turned-up in the house. I had to do all the usual things like putting my clothes away, looking at the mail, and listening to the answer machine. There was only one call.

"Hi DJ, this is Denise Monroe, you know, about your taxes? I need to see you when you get back. Call me at the office. Bye."

Afterward, I went up the street and picked up Harry. We played in the snow on the way back to the house. Nothing like a good snowball fight between father and son.

I spent Saturday gathering up all the latest records and receipts that I could find for November and December. I placed them in a big manila envelope. I figured Denise's phone call was about not having receipts for that the whole year.

Denise had said she went to the same church, but I didn't see her on Sunday once again. Monday, I called her from our office and made an appointment for lunch on Tuesday, at the same little cafe we had been before.

She was smiling as she came in and sat down. As usual she was dressed in a nice-looking suit and sweater but this time with pants because of the cold.

We ordered and she said, "You didn't file your income tax last year! We could ask for an extension but I almost have it all done now so there's no need to do that." She said.

"What? I didn't file my taxes last year?" I felt confused, and embarrassed with that last bit of news. My mind racing over the year trying to remember.

"Yes, and there is usually a penalty for that, it's a good thing that you're going to get a refund, it could have cost you a lot." She said.

"I can't believe it." Exasperation at the oversight turned to relief that no penalty would need to be paid.

"Yes, there are usually penalties to pay." She stirred sugar into her coffee cup as she spoke. "IRS is very strict about non payments of taxes on time. You must not make a habit of that."

"No, no. I can't believe that I forgot to file my taxes." My hand had moved to my mouth to help cover my shame. "My wife always handled these things. It seems I still have much to learn."

"Call me after your next trip, I should have it all done by then and you can send it in right away." She said, trying to reassure me.

"We both seem to be talking, but neither of us is listening." I said. "My mind is in a whirl." I could only sit and shake my head back and forth, then mumbled, "I didn't pay my taxes." It was said softly but she must have heard me.

She giggled at my comment.

Then I told her to start over and I would shut up and listened. I needed her to go through it again to make sure I fully understood everything. As she talked, I noticed that I really enjoyed the sound of her voice. Then to myself, I said, "I'm going to work on a way that I can listen to her more often."

Each year our Team had a New Year's Eve party at the Army Reserve Center. We each invited a lot of the people that we work with to come and bring along their spouse or girl or boy friend. Everyone had a great time. Well, almost everyone. Yours truly had another tough time of it.

Monday when I went in to the office, there was about six inches of snow on the ground and it was still coming down hard with little signs of it letting up. There weren't many cars on the streets, nothing seemed to be moving. If it wasn't for that wonder car of mine, I'd have been snowed in.

I made a pot of hot coffee and sat down by the window, soon I saw a cloud of snow moving down the street, how strange. The cloud turned into the parking lot on the north side of the building where our office is.

There aren't any cars in the parking lot yet and it's after seven thirty. The cloud stopped in the middle of the parking lot. I chuckled and said out loud, "Oh, it's Gene in his VW Baja Bug." He's doing doughnuts all around the parking lot and those immense tires he has on it are throwing snow everywhere. He plowed up the parking lot pretty good so I guess now he'll come in now.

"Hi Mom, I'm home." Gene said loudly. It was his usual spiel to get a response from anyone who may be inside.

"In here, Gene." I yelled to him.

Gene and I sat in the office and drank coffee and talked until noon. We've been good friends since I came to town. He was one of the first people that I met here at the Reserve Center.

There were only about a dozen people in the whole building that morning, so we went home at noon. Our next trip was canceled. With all the snow on the ground, I didn't go to see Sarah. I spent my birthday at home with Harry and I bought a cake and some ice cream at Dillon's. It was a pretty depressing day, but I put on a good show for Harry so he wouldn't be depressed.

After Harry went to bed I sat there and visions of Sarah came to me, she was dressed in white at our wedding. Then I could see her loveliness when she was pregnant with Harry, then we were in bed making love. I fell asleep on the couch dreaming of her.

That following Sunday, I saw Denise at church. We talked for a few minutes back in the hallway. We decided to meet for lunch on the Thirtieth.

There was that same smile, that same lilting voice, but a different dress this time. She's bundled up pretty good for the cold, but it looks like I see a bruise in a place where I am sure there shouldn't be one. Hard to tell in this light, but it concerned me.

"Here's your tax returns for last year, all you have to do is sign them down here at the bottom on both copies and send this one to Federal and this one to State. The addresses are already on the envelopes. Don't forget to put enough postage on them." She giggled a tiny, happy noise and smiled up at me.

I didn't waste any time getting the tax returns in the mail. You know how the IRS can be.

In February, the team went to Denver and we had really nice weather for that time of year. It was sunny and in the forties the whole time. I drove down to Colorado Springs to see my dad and the family on Sunday. We all had a good time together.

All of us on the team enjoyed being away from the cold for a couple of weeks. We got back on the seventeenth and I called Denise just before closing on Friday.

I saw her that Sunday in church and once again we chatted in the hall. She really is a beautiful woman, a lot more than I first thought. I met her the following Tuesday for lunch. It had warmed up a little to 35 degrees. "Wow, heat wave."

"I'm sorry, I won't have anything done - -." For the very first time since I met her, the smile disappeared.

I interrupted her, "I didn't call you to talk business, I just enjoy talking with you and besides you're beautiful and nice to be around." There, I said it! I hope she isn't offended by me being so forward with her.

"Well DJ, I really appreciate that, I don't hear that from anyone anymore. You really think I'm beautiful?" The smile is back and bigger than ever.

"Of course I do. I'm surprised that there aren't guys telling you that every day." I said.

Well, she didn't get up and leave anyway. That was progress. She was silent for a few minutes as she finished her lunch. I could tell she wanted to say something. It played across her face. I wanted to ask, but fear of being pushy kept me silent. I decided when she was ready to speak and trusted me, she would tell me what troubled her.

"It looks like it's time for me to get back to the office, but call me on Friday after each trip as soon as you get home, I'd like to talk to you more about this." She said. Her words were spoken positively, but her eyes seemed tormented. Her actions spoke that she just wasn't ready to trust completely.

Each time that I've seen her, I've noticed more than one bruise on her face and arms. When I asked about them, she quickly dismissed it as nothing or had some lame excuse for how it got there. Today at lunch, I noticed what looked like another bruise in a different place that was partly covered with make-up, but I didn't say anything this time. I've got to find a good time to approach her about it. She is so beautiful that I can't imagine someone hitting her, but that's sure what it looks like.

March was still really cold and we went to Tucson to help the other Team with an Armor Battalion there. It was cold and windy at Fort Huachuca. All four of us on the team bought sweaters at a store in Sierra Vista, but it didn't help. I was glad to see that trip end.

I called Denise as soon as I walked in the door Friday afternoon. We spoke for a few minutes and decided to meet for lunch at our favorite cafe on Monday.

I went to the cemetery alone to talk to Sarah the next day. "Hi Sarah, I brought you some flowers. I met the most beautiful woman I have ever seen since I met you, the other day. She's smart, dresses well and even has the kind of red hair like you. She's doing my taxes now. I hope I can see her after it's all done. It'd be nice if we had some things in common."

I see Denise in church almost every Sunday now and when I can, I talk to her for a few minutes, but last Sunday she was with another woman so I just waved and she waved back to me.

I was sitting in our usual booth in the cafe and it was a 'Raining Nicely Monday', but here comes Denise with an umbrella and raincoat.

She put up the umbrella and took off the raincoat showing a nice green summer suit with a really low cut green blouse and a large gold pendant necklace hanging down the middle. We ordered, but I couldn't take my eyes off of that necklace and the surroundings. She is pretty small there but it sure looked good from where I sat.

I asked her, "How has everything been going?"

"It's been a really busy season for me. I'm swamped every night when I get home." She said, after all it is tax season.

Well, that sure kills any ideas I might have had about asking her out. For a few minutes we both sat enjoying each other's company. We placed our orders and took sips of our cold drinks after the waitress left. Then out-of-the-blue she nervously asked, "Last month you said you thought I was beautiful. Do you really think so?"

It startled me, but I spoke up energetically. "You bet, and you are the first woman I have said that to in over a year." I must have looked at that necklace, because she looked down at it when I said that.

"Do you like my necklace? I wore it especially for you today." There's that smile again. She leaned forward in her seat to give me a good look. I, of course, took full advantage of the opportunity to get a closer look at her necklace and I absent-mindedly cleared my throat.

I blushed, "I didn't want to be so obvious where I was looking."

"That's OK." She laughed that sweet glorious laugh that lifted my soul. Inwardly, I sighed a relief that she was not put out with me.

We talked and laughed until she had to go back to work. She smiled a big one for me, covered the necklace with her coat, opened her umbrella and charged out into the rain. It's time for me to go back too, and since she's gone, there's no reason to stay.

In April, the team went to Utah, and worked in Salt Lake City. We had a great time. I have a good friend, Paul Hawthorne, who lives there and we went all over town together seeing the sights. He took me to some very unusual restaurants. He is a big fan of the railroads, so we, therefore, had dinner in the cafe at the Rio Grande depot. There I learned more about the Rio Grande and the Union Pacific than I thought possible.

After our supper, we waited around the station for the Rio Grande Zephyr to arrive, coming in from Denver. Sure enough, here it comes pulled by engine 5771. We both got on the train after all the passengers got off. The engine pulled the train cars up north of town and turned on the 'wye' so that the train would be headed in the right direction to go back to Denver.

I followed my friend through the train and listened as he told me everything about the appointments and the cars. Paul really knows his stuff when it comes to talking about these trains.

I've known Paul ever since I came to Salt Lake for the first time and we've been good friends ever since. But he can really be a pain sometimes.

"How are you holding up since Sarah died?" He inquired with interest. Turning his head in my direction to see in my eyes how I would respond.

"It's been tough, especially since I had to do a crash course on how to take care of a small child. But Harry is a good kid and he helps me the best that he can."

"How long has it been now?" He asked as they continued through one train car to the next, exploring their surroundings.

"A year on the 25th. And I still miss her." I fought to not sound sad. He was my friend, but some things still ached too much to share even with a close friend.

"Have you been out with anyone?" He was still drilling for information.

"No, but I met someone." My head started to ache and I was searching for a way to change the subject.

"Did you ask her to marry you?" He asked.

"Paul! I've only known her for six months. And it's been all business up till now." Now that got under my skin, big time. He can be very exasperating at times.

He laughed, knowing he was treading on sensitive nerves, but continued anyway. "What's she like?"

"A lot like Sarah. Kind of reddish hair, smart, she's an accountant, and really good looking."

"Did you sleep with her yet?" He asked and there was no denying the humor in his voice.

"No! Man, you get right to it don't you?"

"What are you waiting for?"

"I don't want to rush her, besides I've seen bruises on her. I think some guy is beating her up." My memory quickly recalled the bruises and the thought heated my blood.

He turned again to face me and bluntly asked, "Do you love her?"

"I don't know, but it wouldn't take much." Wow, Paul has me really on edge thinking about this.

He laughed. "Don't forget, I'll dance at your wedding." Paul just loves to screw around. He got married when he was eighteen and he thinks everyone in the world should be married.

I got back early in the morning on Friday the 10th and called Denise right away. We met at the usual place for lunch. She was dressed in the usual suit and blouse. But this time she is wearing a pink blouse almost up to the neck that is buttoned all the way up.

"Here's your tax returns for this year, you should get a small refund this time from both Federal and State." She handed me the documents and then in a separate envelope, she handed to me and said. "Here's my bill, I'm sorry it's so much, but there was an awful lot of work to do to straighten out these two tax years."

She was apologetic, but I knew she had to do a lot of extra work to pull me out of my tax bind. I took out my checkbook and wrote her a check for the whole thing and gave it to her.

Then out of curiosity, I had to ask, "No special necklace this time?"

She looked down at her feet and her tone of voice lowered. "I didn't have time to prepare, but maybe next time. Tax season is over now, so maybe my life can get back to normal now. As normal as that is."

The smile disappeared for a minute, but is starting to come back slowly. I'm beginning to think that I'll be able to read her just by the smile. It's something I'm going to follow to see if it actually does work.

"Is there something wrong?" I asked with concern in my voice.

"No, I just had a little pain, that's all." She said, but her face showed the hurt and grimace she had made. I noticed another bruise just at the collarbone. I'll bet that's why she 'didn't have time to prepare'. I have got to find out what that is all about. I'm going to say something right now.

"I - - -." I was starting to ask the question but was cut-off.

Hurriedly, Denise gathered her belongings, stood up, and said, "I've got to hurry back to the office, call me as soon as you get back next time, bye."

And she was gone.

It had been a year since Sarah left when I went to the cemetery Saturday. I talked about how well Harry is doing in kindergarten, and Mrs. Johnson, and finally about Denise. I confessed to Sarah, "I think I could love her if it weren't that I still loved you, my sweet Sarah. What do I do?"

Chapter 3

The First Date

In May, the temperature warmed up a little. The days are getting longer, we've got Daylight Savings Time now and that results in an extra hour. The flowers are starting to bloom, I see people starting to wear lighter clothes and short sleeves, soon the grass will be long enough to cut. Looks like spring is here. I really like spring.

I dialed the telephone and heard that lovely voice. Lovely is not in my vocabulary, but it's the only word I could think of to describe it. "Hello, Hughes, Ingram and Jessup, Denise speaking. May I help you?"

With eagerness I said, "Hi, it's DJ. I'll have some time off around Memorial Day and I thought you might like to go to dinner with me on the weekend before the holiday." My mind says, "*Please say yes!*"

"Yes DJ, that's very nice." A slight pause and she continued: "I would like to go, but it will have to be an early dinner right after work on Friday." She said.

"OK, I'll pick you up at your office at four thirty, Friday afternoon." Oh, how I wish I could speed up the calendar until Friday.

I picked Denise up promptly at four thirty that Friday and took her to the Scotch and Sirloin. It's a really nice place that serves prime rib and all the fixings. Since this is our first date, I wanted to impress her a little.

My memory had to revisit that second date with Sarah for just a minute. We went out with Linda and Bill to The Old Mill for a nice dinner. Sarah had invited them along because she was a little scared, I think. I smile at that memory. Sarah was wearing a blue business-like dress with no jewelry. Funny, I can't tell you what either Linda or Bill were wearing.

The four of us talked and the women went to the powder room often. Bill and I got along very well and have been friends ever since. I didn't know it then, but Sarah told Linda that night that I was the one she was going to marry. *I wonder if Denise has such thoughts about me?*

Because of the warm weather, Denise was wearing a knee length skirt and jacket in a maroon color with a light burgundy blouse with a nice round neckline. She wore matching high heel shoes along with cute earrings and a small gold necklace. I noted to myself what a stunning woman. One who meets me smiling. Always smiling. I really like that.

I can tell that she hasn't been out to a fancy restaurant like this for a long time because she had a hard time ordering. I decided to try to relieve the tension.

"Why don't we both have the prime rib with a baked potato and salad?"

"Sounds good to me." She said in a voice which denoted a hint of thankfulness.

"How would you like the prime rib cooked, ma'am? The waiter asked, looking at Denise. Apparently he too knew beauty and it wasn't wasted on him. The waiter was patient with us as he took the order and I took great pride in the fact that she was with me.

"Medium, please." She said, unaware of the looks she was given by the waiter.

"I'll have mine rare, thanks." I answered before he asked.

"Would you like something to drink before dinner, ma'am?" The waiter asked her with keen interest.

She looked at me as if to see if it was all right. "Why don't you have something fancy, Denise?"

"Yes, I'd like to have something light and maybe a little sweet, I don't know much about this." She said.

The waiter smiled and suggested: "May I suggest a Strawberry Daiquiri, ma'am?"

"Fine, that sounds good." She said, and handed him back the copy of the menu she had been fidgeting with for ten minutes.

"I'll just have Pepsi if you don't mind." Then handed him back my menu as well. I was glad to see the back of the waiter by that point.

"You're not going to have something too?" She asked.

"No, I don't drink at all when I have to drive. Pepsi will be fine."

During dinner I noticed another bruise just peeking out from the side of the neckline facing me. With her sitting on my right, I could see the bruise very clearly and asked about it.

Clearing my throat, I began to approach the topic which has been on my mind for several days. "I've noticed bruises on your body before and now I see another one."

"Oh, you mean this?" She pulled her blouse open so I could see it better. Revealing much more, to my surprise, and at the same time I noticed the smile dropped right off her face onto the floor like a stone.

The bruise was about the size of a man's fist and just above her right breast. It didn't seem to matter to her that I could see down inside her blouse at all her fine attributes.

Of course we were interrupted at that moment when the waiter brought the drinks and salad. We slowly started to eat without the answer to my question, but I knew she was thinking about the question because of the water in her eyes and her pink cheeks.

"I'm married." She said through her tears, "and he goes out with his friends every Friday night. He comes home drunk, when he even comes home at all, and he uses me for a punching bag all weekend."

She was crying as she told me this. My mind began to reel as I thought, "*I just don't get it, why would a guy do something like this?*" My temperature was going up, just the thought of it made me hot! "Man., what I would love to do to him in return!"

Denise fought to control her tears and continued to explain. "He won't be home till late, so I'll pick up the two girls at the baby-sitter and go to one of my girlfriends' houses until I think he might be asleep before we go home. Sometimes he would be passed out on the floor. Sometimes I have to stay the night at their house if I feel too threatened."

The waiter once again interrupts, this time with the main meal. It sure looks and smells good. I'm going to start to eat and tried to find a way to ease her tension some.

"I didn't know you were married. I didn't see a wedding ring on your finger."

She glanced down at her ring finger. "Oh, I took that off a long time ago. I was too ashamed to say that I was married to someone like him. I never go anywhere with him." She said, as though that answered all the questions swimming around in my head.

"How could you marry someone that beat you up like this?" I'm still hot under the collar at her husband and probably sounded astounded to her, and rightly so.

"He wasn't always like this. Well, he always had a temper before we were married, but nothing like this. It started about a year ago when he got laid off from his job."

She paused between bites of her entree, then continued. "He got back to work about four months later, but he didn't stop drinking and running around. He seemed to get more violent a couple of months later. I don't know if he has a girlfriend, but I don't care anymore." She said.

We sat there and talked for an hour and a half. She got her composure back and we finished the meal. The prime rib was delicious, but I pretty much lost my appetite. I'll bet she did too because she left most of her dinner on the plate.

We decided not to have dessert, so I got a doggy bag for the remaining meal and we left. I took her back to get her car. We're going to have to go back to that restaurant under better circumstances again.

I followed Denise to the baby sitters and then to her girlfriend Jean's house. She took the girls and the doggy bag inside and came back out to my car and sat down.

She looked like she had a lot on her mind as she approached the car and I patiently waited for her to open up to me.

She began by saying, "I don't know much about you and I think I'd like to. What do you like to do? Do you have any hobbies?"

"Yes, I do some woodworking. I make furniture and clocks and stuff. And I build little buildings."

"You what?" She sounded intrigued by the notion, "I always wanted to do woodworking." The smile is back after a couple of hours of the somber look. She encouraged the conversation to continue by adding,

"The idea of making something out of just some old pieces of wood is somehow appealing, but what was that other thing you mentioned?"

"I wanted to be an architect, but didn't, so I design and build little scale model buildings out of wood and plastic and cardboard." Encouraged by the expression on her face I continued, "I'd be happy to show you my workshop sometime, if you want, and provided it does not cause you any problems with your husband."

"I'd love to." After she convinced me she would not be in any additional trouble with her husband, she gave me her address and phone number and Jean's number. "You might need these."

I took one of her cards and wrote my address on the back and handed it back to her. She laughed and said, "Did you forget that I have all that information from your taxes already?"

As she started to get out of the car, I leaned over and kissed her. It just happened and felt the natural thing to be doing.

"I'll be glad to help you with a possible solution. You just tell me what you want me to do." She kissed me back without saying anything more and left.

The next trip with my company team was a short one. I got back on Thursday, I called Denise at the office and we made a date to have a short dinner and dance on Friday.

As usual, I picked her up at the office at four thirty sharp. She was dressed in a classy, light cotton dress with a scoop neckline. She was wearing high heels, small earrings and necklace. Her customary smile appeared as she sat down in my car.

We went for dinner at La Chinita. I ordered the 'Mexican Plate Special' for both of us. It is a big meal with refried beans, rice, an enchilada and a tamale with lots of salad and salsa on the side.

After dinner we went to the Ace of Clubs for a drink and some dancing. It's just a bar with a jukebox and a dance floor, but it works for me. The booths are in the back corner where it's dark and that's one thing that I always liked.

She picked out about six songs together and I put the quarters in.

"I like this." She said as we walked out into the middle of the floor for the first tune.

She was light on her feet, she looked good and smelled good too. "I love the smell of you tonight."

"Thank you, it's Chantel." She said.

We danced the first two songs without saying much, just holding each other.

I would kiss her neck and hold her close, and run my hand up and down her back, she responded by doing the same.

During the third song we kissed for the whole time, and when it was over we both laughed about it.

We sat down in a booth across from each other. When the waitress came we ordered a Pina Colada for her and Pepsi for me. We held hands and talked like a couple of kids while we had our drinks.

"What am I going to do?" She said with a frown.

"Do you have a lawyer?"

"No, but it looks like it's time I got one." She said.

"I can recommend one if you want."

"The company where I work has a lot of contacts, so I'll be able to find one easy enough. I can't take it anymore and I have to get him away from the girls and me." She said.

She talked about a restraining order from the court, a divorce, reconciliation, criminal charges and anything else she could think of.

I told her that I didn't study law and didn't have any of the answers.

She looked sullen as she said, "I think that a divorce is the only answer."

I took her back to her car at her office and followed her to Jean's house just like before, except this time she came over to my car and sat down with me.

"Don't worry, I'm going to finally get it taken care of." She said.

She kissed me goodnight, it was the kind of kiss that leaves you breathless, and went inside.

When I got back to town after my second trip in June, I called her at her office.

"I'm so glad to hear from you. I went to see Mr. Buchanan, a lawyer the company uses, the next day after we talked and I filed for a divorce. Tom had to move out of the house right away." She said.

That was the first time I had heard his name.

"My lawyer told him that he would not file criminal charges against him, as long as he moved out immediately and agreed not to try to see me or the girls. Mr. Buchanan said the divorce would take sixty to ninety days before its final. It was a bluff, but it worked." She said.

Chapter 4

Simon Says

June really started to warm up. The temperatures are into the eighties and nineties. I have to cut the grass every time I get home now. I don't know much about flowers, so I don't cut anything that has blooms on it.

June is tornado season here in the plains and we've had a few scares and some big rains. Denise helped me plant a garden recently, and I hope there'll be some vegetables from it this summer.

But, with all that rain and warm weather comes fruit and vegetables, and there are vegetable stands along the roads south of town. There is a particular orchard called Nickleson's that has the best peaches I have ever had.

I remember when Sarah and I would take our baskets on a Saturday and spend most of the morning picking, and eating peaches. We always got sticky and messy, but we had a great time together. We usually ate more than we picked, and we always paid extra for that.

"Hughes, Ingram and Jessup, Denise speaking."

"Hi, we're going out to North Dakota on Tuesday and I wanted to ask you if you'd like to go pick some peaches with me when I get back from this trip?"

"Sure, it sounds like fun. Is it OK to bring the girls?" She asked.

"You bet! This is the kind of thing that kids always like to do. We could make a picnic of it."

"OK, I'll come over to your house. What time do you want me there?" She asked.

I wanted to tell her that I wanted her right now, but I took hold of myself and said, "Why don't you come over around nine or nine thirty Saturday morning?"

"OK, see you then." She said.

The Team went to Bismarck on the seventh of June and returned on the sixteenth. I called Denise as soon as I got into the house and we talked on the phone for about an hour. Her voice is somehow soothing and it makes me feel good. Just to hear her talk. She said the weatherman predicted the high temperatures to be in the high nineties and low hundreds.

She arrived in her Pontiac at nine thirty Saturday morning. When she came to the door there were two girls with her. Denise was wearing shorts, really tight shorts, and a thin shirt. I had noticed the first time I saw her that she had a nice behind, but standing there right in front of me in those shorts, I would say it's a lot better than I first thought.

I had only seen her legs from the hemline of a skirt down, but now there is all of them to see. And I like it. Boy, do I like it! Rounding out this vision of love-liness were the customary white sneakers and her beaming smile.

"Hi DJ, these are my daughters, Melissa and Jennifer, girls this is DJ." Denise said.

"Hi – i – i - i." They said in unison.

"Melissa is seven and Jennifer is eight." Denise said.

"Hi girls, nice to meet you. This is my son, Harry, he's five."

"I have two half bushel baskets to take. I dug around in the basement and found these." She said holding two plastic containers that looked like they were ten years old.

"OK, let's go."

We went out to get into her car.

"Here, you drive." She said throwing the keys to me.

I wrestled her big car down the road and after I got that thing parked at the orchard we all had a look around.

"It's a big orchard. Look at the trees. Peach trees as far as you can see with beautiful pink and red peaches."

There were many people in the orchard with the same idea as we had. Everyone listened to the spiel that the guy from the orchard gave, and we all loaded onto a trailer pulled by a tractor and went riding through the trees.

When you want off, you just holler and the driver stops. We all piled off in the middle somewhere and everyone got a basket or something except Harry. He doesn't pick peaches anyway, he picks them up off the ground and throws them. He can only throw one a few feet though.

"Look at all of this. I didn't even know it was here." She said.

Delicious peaches were waving at us from every direction. We picked all of the baskets full and everyone ate their fill. Denise and I agreed to pick at the same tree and try to watch Harry at the same time, which wasn't very easy to do.

As we were talking and picking I stretched to reach for a nice juicy peach when Harry distracted both of us and she moved her right breast right into my outstretched hand as I squeezed my hand to pick the peach off the tree. She stopped in her tracks and so did I, but I didn't lose my grip.

"I don't think that one is a peach." She said.

"Oh, yes it is, and it feels like the best one I've picked in a long time."

We both laughed and she moved to another part of the tree to work. She's not as flat as I thought.

Harry hit me with a couple of juicy peaches off the ground. He got her once too. I pushed her arm while she was eating one and it squeezed juice all over her face. It ran down her neck and onto her shirt. I knew there was no way that I could get away with that. I would pay, and pay big.

A few minutes later, I was minding my own business picking peaches and when I wasn't looking she sneaked up behind me and squeezed one into my face. We had an all-out snowball fight with peaches off the ground for a few minutes and all of us including Harry got really into the fun.

We were all standing there laughing when the tractor came. It was time to go, so we all went back to the office. Everyone went to the bathroom to get some of the sticky juice off. I paid for the peaches, we loaded them into the trunk and we were on our way north back to town. On the way back, we stopped at a park for our picnic. Fried chicken and cheese strips. Oh, wow!

"Did you have fun, you look like it. You've got peach juice all over your clothes."

"Boy did I? This has been more fun that I have had in years." She laid her hand on my thigh as she said, "How 'bout you girls?"

The girls and Harry all said they had a blast.

I took this opportunity to lay my hand on her thigh. It was warm, firm and smooth. She made no motion to move my hand, nor I hers.

When we got back to my place, I took one of the baskets out of the trunk and into the house. Everyone came in and the girls went back to Harry's room to play.

"How would you like to have dinner with me tonight?

"I'd love to." She said.

"Can you get someone to stay with the kids at this short notice?"

"I'm sure Jean or Linda will be glad to help." She said.

Did she say Linda? No! It couldn't be.

"What time is good for you?" I asked.

"How about seven?"

"OK, I'll pick you up at seven." I said.

"Come through the alley to the back door, I'll be out on the back porch waiting for you." She said.

They left and I went up the street to see Mrs. Johnson. She told me that Carol would be glad to come down and watch Harry while I went out tonight.

I messed around the house and played with Harry till five. Then I made mac and cheese for him and I got showered, and put on a thin dress shirt and pants. At least the restaurant will be air conditioned.

I pulled up in the parking area at the back of the house and there she was, on the porch swing. She came running out and jumped in the car. She had on a thin pink cotton sundress that really looked cool.

She leaned over and kissed me lightly and we took off.

I drove to the Canton Restaurant. Some light Chinese food after all those peaches this morning should be OK. I had cashew chicken and she had Moo Goo Gai Pan. We laughed and talked about the kids and her divorce.

When we were done she said, "Why don't we go to the Ace to dance?"

"Sure, let's go." I had visions of holding her in my arms.

It didn't take too long to get to the Ace. We found a booth and I scooted in next to her. I had my usual Pepsi and she had a Screwdriver. I put some money into the jukebox and we got up to dance.

She hugged me real close and I responded. I love feeling her body against mine. I let one hand slide up and down over her back. I'm having visions again. Holding her is great.

While we were dancing I noticed a guy at the bar that is staring at us, I can't let any one see what I'm doing so I put my hand back on her waist.

"Didn't you like that?" She asked.

"Of course I liked it, but I thought people might see. There's some guy at the bar staring at us." I motioned toward him.

She turned to look, "Oh, maybe we should go sit down then." She said.

We went back to the booth. "You said you liked it?" She asked again.

"Yes, I've wanted to squeeze that ever since the first time I saw you."

"Hey mister," she said in a little girl voice that I hadn't heard her do before. "Want to play a game with me?" She twirled her finger in her hair like a girl of ten might do.

I laughed at her 'little girl' voice and she did some more for me. "Sure, little girl, what game did you want to play?"

"Its called 'Denise says'." She said still twirling her hair with her fingers.

"Sure."

She pulled up the hemline of the dress to just below the middle of her thigh. "Want to see more?" She asked.

"You bet!" I exclaimed. I don't know if this is going to be good or bad, but I'm in for the duration weather I like it or not.

"I'll show you mine if you show me yours." She said holding the hemline with both hands.

"What would you like me to do?" I asked.

"Denise says, you unbuckle the belt and I'll raise this a little."

I unbuckled the belt and her hands moved up a little.

"Denise says, unbutton your pants."

I did and she pulled the dress all the way up to her waist. What a sight!

"It's red!"

"Of course its red, the hair on my head is red too. Well almost, with a little help." She said.

I reached for the prize, but she intercepted my hand in midair.

"Denise says, no touching, only looking." She giggled that little tinkling noise as she said it.

"What do you think?" She asked, still holding the dress up.

"I think I would like to make love to you right now." I said.

She laughed and said "Would you now? That was what I was hoping." She dropped the hem and I felt a twinge of disappointment.

"And I think I'd like that too, but we can't go to my house, and you said the girl from down the street is at your house, and it's a cinch that I'm not going to try to get into the back seat of your little car." She said.

"Then what's the answer?"

"We can sit here or I can go home." She said.

"That's not a very good choice. Why don't we dance and fool around some between dances?"

"OK, that sounds like fun, let's go." She said.

The first dance I looked for the guy that was staring at us earlier and he wasn't there. "I don't see that guy."

"Good." She said.

We danced all of the dances in that set with both of us having fun. She told me more than once that she enjoyed the feeling she got when I caressed her.

We danced and fooled around till ten and she decided that we should be going. I took her home and we sat in the car and she kissed me so hard and long that we both got out of breath.

I'm going to have to learn to breathe and kiss at the same time if I'm going to be around her very much, and I sure hope I am.

As she got out she said, "You make sex fun for me and you let me do something tonight that I have always wanted to do. Thanks."

Chapter 5

Let's Play Hide and Seek

The Team went out to Cheyenne Tuesday and we returned on the following Wednesday. The trip to Wyoming was a good one, but it is still nine days away from families for the rest of the guys and I do miss Denise.

I called her as soon as I got home. She said that the repairman came and fixed the washing machine Tuesday, and it didn't cost that much. I told her that I had to do some yard work tomorrow, and if she would like to stop by, I would like to see her.

Saturday in the summer is my day for yard work. No matter what else gets done, I have to cut the grass and try to trim up everything as best as I can. And if I don't do some of it during the week, I usually can't finish it all on Saturday, so tonight I'm starting on the grass. Denise called and said that she had some running around to do but she and the girls would be here later.

I got the grass cut and went in to get a shower before I started dinner for Harry and I. Something simple and quick.

Denise has filed for her divorce and Tom has moved out of the house, now we can spend more time together when I'm home from a trip. I've seen Denise almost every day that I've been home since we went picking peaches. But because the kids aren't in school, there are less chances to do anything fun unless we do it covertly.

She cooked dinner at her house a couple of times and she brought the girls and I cooked at my house. They all decided that if there was any cooking to be done, I shouldn't do it. I'm hurt. I thought I did pretty good.

It was about six o'clock when she arrived. I was just finishing getting dinner ready. I made macaroni and cheese with hot dogs, even I can't screw that up. Denise brought a cake. After we ate, her two girls went out to play with Harry in the back yard.

It was a hot night and we were all dressed in cut-offs and loose shirts. She had on a shirt that showed her flat midriff. Damn, is she ever good looking!

I got some ice cream out of the freezer and we all had cake and ice cream after dinner. By the time we finished eating, it was just starting to get dark.

One of the girls said, "Let's play hide and seek."

So we all went out into the back yard and the girls decided that mom would be "it".

I asked the girls if one of them would stay with Harry.

"He's only five and I don't want him to get lost."

So we all ran to hide while Denise hid her eyes and counted, "One, two, three, four - - -."

I ran into an old garage at the end of the alley and stood in the shadows. Soon she came slowly down the alley peering around everything.

"Psst," I hissed, "in here."

She immediately looked around to the garage and moved slowly to the open door. As she stepped tentatively inside still looking for a sign, I stepped out of the shadow behind her and wrapped my arms around her, turned her around and kissed her.

It was hot that night, but that wasn't the reason that I was sweating now.

"Do you like what you found?" She asked.

"I couldn't tell, you moved my hand away so quickly the other night."

"I'm not moving it now." She said.

"And I'm taking advantage of that."

There I stood, hugging and kissing her.

In her mocking little girl voice she said, "Hi mister, do you like me?"

"Well little girl." I said. "I sure do like you. Is there anything I can do for you?"

"Gee, thanks mister, I'd like for you to do something for me right now." She said.

"We don't have much time, the kids will be looking for us."

She gave me directions and I followed them to the letter. It had only been a minute or two when suddenly we heard the voice of one of the girls calling,

"Mom, where are you? Mom m m m?"

"Damn, I knew it! I never get to have any fun!" She said.

She turned and kissed me and ran out of the garage leaving me standing in the shadows.

We played hide and seek for another hour and they had a lot of fun, although it was hard for me to continue. Harry said he wanted to go in and get something to drink. So we all went into the kitchen for some juice, by that time I had calmed down to nearly normal.

As we sat around the kitchen table talking, Denise said, "I need to go over a few things with you, why don't you call me tomorrow. Say at ten thirty, sharp. Well, we better be getting home guys, let's go."

"I'll walk you out to your car." I said.

She got in on the driver's side and the girls both got in back, with my son talking to them through the window. The window was rolled down and as I leaned over to rest my elbows on the window ledge of the car. She took my hand in hers and held it to her cheek as we talked nonchalantly about nothing at all.

"There now, doesn't that help?" She asked in a coy little voice.

"Oh yes, that's something that always keeps me up." I said.

"Don't forget to call, it's important." She said as she removed my hand and started the car. We waved to them as they drove off.

I usually go in to the office at seven fifteen in the morning. This morning though, I couldn't get my head to work, all I could think of was her wonderful body. I worked and worked, trying to accomplish something, but just couldn't. I labored through the morning till Gene said, "Hey DJ, it's ten thirty, I'm going out to the shop."

Wow, it's ten thirty! I grabbed the phone and whizzed through the buttons.

"Hughes, Ingram and Jessup, Denise speaking."

"Hi, it's me."

"Hi, me. We need to go over something together, I'll meet you at your house at eleven forty five, we can have lunch together if you stop and get something on the way, OK?" She asked.

"Sure." I said. "I'll see you at quarter till twelve."

"See ya." She said and hung up.

For the next hour, I tried to finish up as much as I could. I left the office at eleven twenty, stopped at Long John Silvers for two fish dinners and got home about ten till twelve. Her car was on the street in front of the house, and when I came in the front door she was sitting at the dining room table.

"How did you get in here? The door was locked."

"You never lock the door on your back porch." She said.

I went over to the table and spread out the food and sat down.

"Boy am I ever hungry, this looks good." She said as she got up and came over to me and kissed me lightly on the lips. "Let's eat."

"You didn't tell me what was so important that you wanted to see me about."

"In a minute." She said.

When I finished my lunch, I took the bag and other stuff to the garbage can in the kitchen.

I came back through the door and extended my right hand to her. She took my hand and came over to me and our bodies fused together.

I took her into my arms and kissed her as passionately as I knew how. "You have a bra on."

"Yes silly, it's daytime, I don't want anyone to see - - - except you." She said.

I stood there kissing her for a minute until I started moving slowly over to the couch. We sat down without losing any contact.

"By the way, this is what I wanted to see you for." She said as she giggled.

"Ohmygosh, look at the time, I've got to get back to work."

And she flew to her feet and gave me a kiss and started for the door.

"I don't believe this."

"We'll finish this tonight, See ya." She said as she ran out the door.

That's the second time she's done that. It's a terrible feeling to be left making love to a vision. So I got up and went back to the office.

I was sitting at my desk that afternoon daydreaming about Sarah, when I remembered the first time I felt her.

I picked her up in that little yellow Datsun pickup. She was wearing a black nylon dress with a black jacket, black bra and probably black panties too, black stockings and shoes and a black net thing over her bright red hair.

I stopped at a light and leaned over to kiss her. We went to a place for a drink and dance and it wasn't what we wanted. So we drove to another place. It wasn't what she wanted, either, so we went looking for a place that would work.

All of a sudden she said, "Stop here." I pulled into the parking lot and stopped. We sat there for a few minutes before going into the club.

I reached over to kiss her and put my hand on the side of her cheek and caressed it as I kissed her. She kissed me back, and we sat there like that for a few minutes, and she sighed an agreeable sigh. After a few minutes she said it was time to go in.

We took a seat in a booth in the back and when the waitress came we ordered a drink. I had a bourbon and water and she had a Tom Collins. We sat down and talked and drank.

I put my arm around her waist and she cuddled up close. My hand found a button on the front of her dress, so I opened the button. My hand moved up and opened another. My hand moved up and reached in to find a bra and put the squeeze on it. All of a sudden she said she had to go to the bathroom.

When she came back, she took up the same position, the buttons were still open, but the bra was gone. My hand found something special to squeeze. We both sat there for a long time without moving anything except my hand.

I shook my head to try to clear away the memories. It's time for me to go home. I'm not going to get anything done as long as all I can think of is Denise and Sarah.

Chapter 6

An Interesting Evening

It had been an unusual couple of days for me, so I decided to take it easy for a while before I made us some dinner.

"What would you like for dinner, Harry?"

"Can I have a hamburger, Dad?"

I made us a couple of hamburgers and fried potatoes in the skillet. Just about the time we finished eating the phone rang, it was Denise and she wanted to speak with Harry. Harry doesn't get many phone calls, and this was grown-up Denise asking to talk to him.

He loved it, "Denise asked me to go to a party Dad, can I go, huh?"

"Sure son, tell her yes."

He was smiling as he handed me the phone to hang it up.

It was seven o'clock when I heard a car horn beep outside.

Harry ran to the door and on the way out shouted, "Bye, Dad."

And off he went. About an hour later, I was watching TV when the doorbell rang. When I got to the door, it was Denise standing there, dressed in knee length shorts, a nice silk blouse and the usual sneakers.

"Hi, come on in, I'm really glad to see you."

"Hi, sorry I'm late but the kids took a little doing." She said rushing past me.

"What?"

"Well, I told you I'd see you tonight, and I didn't know what to do with the kids. Maryann is having a party at her house and my girls and Harry got invited. You're welcome." She said with some amount of finality.

"I thought you were just saying that."

"One thing that you need to know about me right now. If I tell you something, I mean it, unless I'm in one of my ornery moods." She said.

She giggled after she said that. Her giggle sounds like a tinkling little bell, I think I could listen to it all day, or all night, I hope. She dropped her bag on the end table on the way in and sat down on the couch with me.

"And how do I know that?"

"You don't. That's what is so much fun for me." She said. More giggling.

I got some Pepsi and chips and we sat and talked and watched the TV and laughed at some of the jokes for about half an hour or so. Until she decided to move in for a close encounter of the best kind.

"What did you have in mind, little girl?"

She explained in great detail what was on her mind. I had no choice but to succumb to her will and agree to this torture.

"I've never done anything like that before." Denise said.

It took her all night to complete her torture of me, and of course, I resisted every move she made.

As you might expect, after a short rest she was out of bed, singing and out into the kitchen to fix coffee and who-knows-what for breakfast.

"Your breakfast is getting cold." She called.

"OK, let me wash up a little first." I called back.

"OK, but hurry." She said.

After a very fast shower, I went to the kitchen where she had made coffee and a breakfast of potatoes, eggs, bacon and toast. The breakfast was on a plate on the kitchen table with her sitting at the table directly behind it smiling.

"OK, let's eat." I said.

While she was in the shower she yelled to me, "I have to pick up the kids at nine, so when we get back here, you need to have the place picked up so they don't get any ideas, OK?" She said.

She left at eight thirty and I got started cleaning up the house. When she got back just before nine thirty, it was presentable and the kids went back to Harry's room to play.

But first all three of them had a lot of fun telling us all about the party and what they did and how Harry fell asleep in the middle of the floor and had to be carried to one of the beds.

Denise and I sat down with a cup of freshly brewed coffee in the living room. I felt absolutely wonderful, nervous, proud and excited that she allowed me this occasion to enter into her life and, I hope, her love.

"I'd really like to see your workshop now, OK?" She said.

"Really? OK."

As I was about to say "let's go out to the shop", she climbed onto my lap and gave me a big hug and kiss, that gal sure can kiss.

We went out to the shop where I showed her each of the power tools, the wood bins, the shelves and cabinets. She even looked at some of the projects that I had in work.

"How long would it take for me to learn to run all these machines?" She asked.

"Not that long, but I'd want to take it slow with you. I don't want anything happening to you."

In her little girl voice she said, "Why mister, huh?" She pointed her finger under her chin and rolled her eyes at me.

"Could we start now? It's hard enough for me to keep from grabbing you every time I see you, without you making it harder." My hands were starting to shake again.

"I must admit it sure was hard." She said and laughed uproariously at her own joke. She doesn't make that many jokes.

"Let's start with the radial saw here."

I explained everything that I knew about the radial saw, how to run it, the safety features and what not to do. We even cut some wood with it.

Once I got started, I concentrated on settling the nervousness down. We spent nearly the whole day in the shop and back and forth to check on the kids when she said, "I really like this, I think I could enjoy it. I've never had the chance to do anything like this. I was never treated like a real person before."

"You're a lot more than a real person to me." I don't think that came out right.

We finished our first class and cleaned up the shop, and headed toward the house.

"I want you to meet Mrs. Johnson, she takes care of Harry and lives just three blocks up the street." I said.

The evening air cooled me down as we walked up the street together hand in hand. By the time we arrived at the Johnson's house I was beginning to feel a little more under control. She really shakes me up and I've never had these kind of feelings before.

"Hi, Mrs. Johnson, this is Denise Monroe, we have been dating and I wanted you to meet her, she might come to pick up Harry sometimes."

"Hi Denise, I'm so glad DJ has found a nice girl." She said.

We talked for a few minutes when Denise said, "Let's go back, the kids are probably getting hungry."

"Come and see me sometime Denise." Mrs. Johnson said.

When we got back to the house, Denise made all of us lunch and took the girls home.

"I'll see you about seven. Bye." She said.

I had a lot of work to do around the house and after a big lunch, I wasn't hungry for supper. But Harry wanted a grilled cheese sandwich, so I made us a couple, then he went into his room to play around six thirty. Denise came at quarter after seven and we sat on the couch and talked.

"I've been married for twelve years and I've never done anything like we've done in the past few weeks. That time in the bar was so much fun, and watching your face when I pulled my dress up was worth it all." She was giggling about it.

"Last night was the best night I've had in years. You made me feel important" She said.

"That's because you are important to me." I said.

It didn't take me two minutes before I was back on the couch. We grabbed each other in a fury and in no time at all she was on my lap wiggling and bouncing like she did before.

I had my hands full again and we did that for quite a while before the long day took its toll on both of us. It wasn't long before we were both too tired to continue.

"I can't believe that I'm so tired. I think that I'd better go home and get some sleep." She said. "But first, get the kids picked up."

She got up and left. I decided that it was time for me to get some sleep too. I dragged myself across town and brought the kids home and we were all of to bed.

She called Saturday about noon to say that her washing machine wouldn't work when she tried to do the laundry.

"I'll come over and see if we can fix it. If we can't, we can do the laundry together." I said.

I called Harry and we drove to her house, Harry went running in the back door like he lived there and I knocked on the door.

She came to the door, "You don't have to knock when you come to see me. We're all ready, let's go."

I don't have to knock, that means there's no one else. That's a relief.

We worked on the washing machine for an hour and got nowhere. I tried everything I could think of, but I don't have the training or the skills to fix one of these.

She left the kids with Linda while we went to the laundromat. I've never liked to do laundry. That was the reason the first appliance that I bought after I got moved into the house was a washing machine. We spent four hours doing the laundry counting driving time and lunch across the street at a fast food place.

Saturday isn't a good time to call any kind of repairman, so we looked through the yellow pages together and she picked out one to call on Monday.

"If we have to, I can take it to the shop in my pickup." I said.

We stopped at Linda's on the way back. Linda came out with Denise and said, "Hi DJ, stop over when you get a chance."

I can't believe it, it is Linda. I've known Linda for years, and I didn't know she knew Denise. I didn't say anything, just nodded my head.

By the time we got back to Denise's house, it was time for supper, so we went into the kitchen and she whipped something up. What a woman! She never stops. I kept the kids occupied so they wouldn't get in her way in the kitchen.

When Harry and I finally got ready to leave, she walked out to the back porch with me and kissed me for a minute or two before Harry came running. I can't seem to get enough of her.

Chapter 7

The Prowler

The Team went out on Tuesday and returned home on the following Wednesday. The trip to Wyoming was a good one, but it is still nine days away from their families for the rest of the guys and I do miss Denise. I called her as soon as I got home. She said that the repairman came and fixed the washing machine Tuesday, and it didn't cost that much.

I can tell that it's going to be a hot one this summer, it's only June and already it's well into the nineties. It's a good thing I have air conditioning in my house, I'd really melt without it, and because the heat gets to me so much, I sleep with nothing on at night in the summer. The phone rang at three am Saturday morning.

"Yeah?" I'm not too cordial at three am. I was dreaming about last week and doing my laundry with a naked girl. But there was that lilting voice I love so much on the phone.

"DJ, could you come over, Annette is spending the night and we thought we heard a prowler. Be sure to come to the back door and be quiet." She said.

"Be right there." That woke me up!

I jumped up and pulled on a pair of old raggedy cut-offs and slippers. I called Mrs. Johnson and asked her if she would watch Harry for the rest of the night if I brought him up there. She agreed and we were off and running and I raced over to her house.

It was a hot night and the air was still, that always makes it seem even hotter. There was a full moon out that made it look like I didn't need my lights. When I got out of the car, I could hear the crickets.

I ran to the back door and tapped lightly. She appeared in the living room and walked toward me. The moonlight coming in the window behind her made her nightgown light up like a halo around an angel.

She moved slowly toward me almost as if she were floating, and her silhouette became more and more definitive and distinct as she neared the kitchen door where I was standing. I was frozen in my tracks with anticipation observing the fine lines of her figure as she moved.

But, as she entered the kitchen, only ten feet from me, the moonlight faded as did the silhouette and the gown became opaque. She had all the lights off in the house as she let me in.

"I heard something outside and it scared me, would you look around and see if there's anyone out there?" Her voice trembled slightly.

I went outside and slowly walked all around the house and the house next door on both sides and didn't find or hear anything. I guess I spent about fifteen minutes walking around the alley and the street in front and both sides of the house and when I came back to the back door, all the lights were still off.

She met me with a cup of hot coffee and a kiss and told me to come in and sit down. We went into the front room and I sat in an overstuffed chair. One of her friends, Annette, sat on the couch also dressed in a nightgown.

Denise came over and spread out her gown so she wouldn't sit on it and sat on my lap, and her tush was really warm on my bare legs. As she sat down I put my hand on her thigh, her skin is so soft and smooth I want to touch all of it all the time.

Denise introduced me to her girlfriend, Annette, and explained that Annette was staying the night with her because she was mad at her husband, Mike. It seems they have a problem.

When Denise sat down on my lap I noticed that she didn't weigh very much. "You feel awfully light, how much do you weigh, anyway?"

"Ninety nine." She said.

"Ninety nine pounds? Is that all?"

"Mike and I only made love when we were trying to have a baby. He didn't want to do 'that' any other time just for fun, it was to be reserved for having kids." Annette said.

"Has she been drinking? She sounds and acts like she's drunk."

"Only a little, I thought. But we finished a little bottle of wine that I had and she brought a bottle of Chablis. But she sure sounds like she's loaded." Denise said.

"Well Annette, I don't know what Mike is thinking or what I can do, but why don't you tell him and show him what you told us and see if you can't get him to feel your way?"

"Do you like what I have on? I really like what you have on." Denise said. "It would be better if it was nothing."

"That might be a lot of fun, but you have company."

She almost vaulted up and did a pirouette around with her arms outstretched in front of me so that I could get a good look at her. Her hands came together at the top of her head and that immense smile appeared, and she still had not spoken.

I thought she was good looking before, but nothing could compare to the view I had right then. She is so beautiful, it gives me a headache, and I know she was quite certain that there was enough light for me to clearly see everything she wanted me to see.

"See you tomorrow, DJ."

She turned around and walked to a position with a window directly behind her and stopped and slowly turned halfway around and looked over her shoulder at me.

"What do you think? Is everything OK?" She asked with a coy little smile.

When I stood up and went toward her, I said. "Everything is beautiful. I hope to see it – you - again - soon."

She kissed me once and pushed me out the back door and said good night. I didn't want to go, but I got into my car and went home. I slept like a log the rest of that night.

It was late Sunday afternoon when I thought of Linda, and decided to go visit her and Bill. She and Bill have been married for ten years I think, and Sarah and Linda were best friends. I don't think that Denise knows that I know Linda.

I knocked and she let me in to the living room and gave me a hug.

"Hi Bill, hi Linda, how's everything? You still paying the bills, Linda?"

"You know me, all I ever do is take care of the bills, seems like everyday, although it's fun most of the time, come on in and have a drink." Linda said.

I sat down on the couch and Linda brought me a Pepsi, Linda has always known about the alcohol thing.

We talked about his job and her job and mine and houses and cars. You know, all the small stuff.

Then Linda said, "You sure are lucky. Sarah was a gem. She was such a fantastic girl, and she fell in love with you. Now it looks like Denise is falling for you too."

"I loved Sarah with all my heart and would have been content to spend the rest of my life with her.

But now that she's gone and Denise came along, I think I'm allowing myself to let go of Sarah and fall in love with Denise. It's really tough."

"Do you still go to the cemetery?" She asked.

"How did you know about that? Yes, I do go to talk to Sarah, about once a month now."

"Denise tells me everything, especially now that she is rid of that creep. Sarah and Denise were my two best friends, but I don't think they ever met. Sarah was outgoing and happy while Denise was repressed by that crud she was married to." Linda said.

"All she was allowed to do was cook and clean. And she better cook only what he said to, and she better clean the house constantly. No time for fun or relaxation unless it was his idea.

"Repressed is the best word to describe her. But then you came along and put a crack in her shell. And for the life of me, I don't know how you did it, she wouldn't let anyone in. All of a sudden, I'm hearing about DJ. I knew it had to be you, how many people are called DJ?" She said.

"I don't put any strings on her. If she says she wants to do something, then that's what we do. I don't feel like I'm giving up my manhood by being nice to the one I love. Oops."

"I heard that!"

"Well, keep it to yourself." I said.

"DJ, I know that you have always been ornery, well watch out, Denise is too." She said.

"I'm beginning to find that out."

"She has said something about sex with you. It must be good, she gets all red faced about it." She said.

"Yeah, it's good. Maybe the best I've ever had."

"Are you going to marry her?" She asked.

"Probably."

"Of course! You are crazy about her!" She said.

The Team is scheduled to go to Cheyenne and Casper on Tuesday. We'll be back the following Wednesday and have the week of the Fourth off.

Chapter 8

Independence Day

Sunday July 1

I got up early and made coffee and some breakfast. Harry always wants some kind of cereal for breakfast. In order for us to make it to Sunday School at nine forty five, I need to be at Denise's house by nine.

Harry is always hard to get going in the morning, so I have to start early with him. This morning he surprised me, we were both ready to go before eight. So I decided to get to Denise's house early.

I always park in the back by the alley and go in the back door of Denise's house. When we walked in, there weren't any sounds to be heard so I left Harry downstairs and went up to her room.

There, in a lump under the covers, was the girl of my dreams, asleep. I reached around to find which end was which, and found a foot. By carefully measuring and examining, I found her butt and reached under the cover and pinched it. She screamed and her head popped out from under the covers.

"Good morning, are you ready to go to church?" I asked in my most patronizing voice designed to give her as much guilt as I could heap onto her.

She looked at me as if she had seen a ghost.

"What time is it?" She asked.

"About eight o'clock, my dear."

She jumped up like she was shot from a cannon, forgetting that she had nothing on at the time. She ran around the bedroom dressing on the run. Then she woke the girls and got them dressed as well.

While all that was going on, I retired to the kitchen where I made a pot of coffee and put the cereal and milk on the kitchen table just in case, and chuckled a lot. Believe it or not, we made it to Sunday School on time. I couldn't stop laughing all morning, she kicked me every time I laughed or chuckled.

After church was over, we had lunch outside in her back yard in the afternoon and I nursed my sore legs.

"I'm taking next week off, I have a lot of annual leave and I've got some things to do."

"Good, we can have lunch together, I'll come to your place." She said.

"OK, I'll cook it and get it all ready, all you have to do is eat it."

"I'd better go shopping then, do you want to go?"

"Sure, we'll drop the kids with Linda, let me call her first." She said.

While she went in to talk to Linda, I just got a thought. After that fabulous night Friday, it looks like Denise is going to be around for a long time. Maybe we should have a vehicle that we all could ride in together.

I'm sure not going to give up my car, but that pickup has been sitting in the garage for a long time since the last time I drove it, and I know a guy in the reserves that's a car dealer. I think I'll call him tomorrow.

"DJ, are you awake?" She said.

"Huh? What?"

"I've been standing here for five minutes waiting for you to come back from dreamland. What were you thinking about?"

"Oh, just some plans for the week."

"I'm ready." She said.

We went to Dillon's and I got hamburger, hot dogs, two steaks, Pepsi, M & M's and Butterfingers. "OK, I'm through, let's go."

"You're joking aren't you? We ARE going to make another pass around the store and I'll put the stuff in the basket, you push it, and no complaining." Denise said.

I don't know what's the matter with women, I had enough for the week. She really went wild. Milk, eggs, butter, cheese, tuna, bread, buns, lettuce, tomatoes, radishes, onions, salad dressing, ketchup, mustard, pickles, noodles, spaghetti, macaroni. What am I going to do with all this stuff? Good thing she didn't pick out some soup, I've got lots of soup.

"OK, now we are ready. We'd better take this to your place and put it into the refrigerator and the cabinets right away." She said.

After paying for the groceries we drove to my house.

Sometimes Denise is more helpful than I would like her to be, this was one of those times. She opened the refrigerator to put the stuff away.

"What are you doing here, science experiments? I can't put anything in here till it's cleaned out." She said.

After completely emptying the refrigerator and cleaning it way too clean, Denise put everything away, but not without several caustic comments.

After everything was put away, she sat on the couch and laughed for a long time about how I am living now. I had seen her giggle, but she was laughing, holding her sides. It's embarrassing.

"DJ, I do not understand how you do it. It's a wonder that you and Harry aren't sick, eating food out of that refrigerator. I can see I'll have to keep an eye on that too. But, no matter how dumb you are about cooking and cleaning, I love the way you treat me. That's the first time I've laughed like that in years." She said and laughed again.

"You deserve to be treated far better than I have been doing." I said and she smiled approvingly.

Soon she was ready to go home. I picked up Harry at Linda's house, she kissed me a long wet one and Harry and I went home for some well deserved rest.

Monday July 2

This week is a short one with the holiday in the middle, so I'd better make a list of the things I have to do.

At nine I called Leonard at the car dealership. We talked about me trading my old Datsun pickup for a van. He said he had a three year old Dodge van that he could make a good deal with. I met him at ten with the pickup. We looked at the van and gave it a test drive.

"Look DJ, here's what I can do." Len said.

After a short time of negotiating back and forth, he handed me a few papers with our deal on them.

"What kind of deal is that? Come on, I can get that anywhere. This van isn't anything special, it's a drab tan with brown carpet on the floor everything else stock except seats, besides there's only two seats in it."

He agreed and we finally made a deal. I get the Dodge Van 318 V8 automatic, and he gets the pickup and topper and five hundred dollars with tax and title fees included.

"I'll pick it up first thing tomorrow."

"Great! That'll give me time to get all the paperwork done, are you going to transfer your plates?" He said.

"Sure."

"It will all be ready around eleven." He said.

"Better make it one thirty."

"OK, see you then, DJ."

I just got back to the house in time to make some grilled cheese sandwiches and chicken noodle soup with iced tea and set the table. It was all ready when she walked in. She was dressed in a beautiful business suit in blue. I had my same old jeans and shirt and boots on.

"This is really great, I didn't think you had it in you." Denise said. "If soup was something special on the menus around town, you might win an award."

She watched the clock, she had to leave at twelve forty five to be back to work at one after plotting and planning for the future.

I'd like to put another bedroom on and a deck along the rest of the house. I worked on some preliminary drawings and put them down till later, there's a lot I want to do to update the house.

The rest of the afternoon, I began to pack Sarah's clothes in boxes and pushed the boxes into the back of the closet. There's a lot of clothes, so I'll do a little each day. That left me in a gloomy mood. I should have started this a long time ago.

Tuesday July 3

Tuesday started with cereal and milk again, I wish I had bought some bananas now. I checked my list to see where I should start. I packed some more of Sarah's things. Boy there's a lot more clothes here than I thought. I got some ideas yesterday for the room, so I added them to the drawings.

Denise doesn't know this, but there's a nice old lady up the street that knows all about cooking, and I'm going to take a walk to see her. Harry went with me before Denise got here so he can be with Mrs. Johnson while Denise is with me.

"Hi Mrs. Johnson, could you help me with a little problem?" Mrs. Johnson is such a life saver.

"Sure DJ, what is it?" She said.

"I told Denise to come over for lunch and I want to make a mushroom and cheese omelet, but my omelets always come out hard. How do I make it fluffy like Sarah always did?"

She began to laugh and explained it in "great" detail so that I understood it.

"But I don't have any of that stuff."

"Sure you do, look on the first shelf in the cabinet on the left of the stove, it's all there." She said.

Sure enough it was.

I timed the omelet like she said to be done at eleven forty five, the toast was in the toaster and the table was set with glasses of iced tea.

Perfect, here she is. She's dressed in a cotton skirt and blouse of yellow, she looks like a happy little flower.

"Look at this! And it smells so good." Denise said.

She sat down and tasted the eggs and looked as if she couldn't believe it.

"It's delicious!" She exclaimed in a surprised voice.

"You sound surprised."

"After cleaning your refrigerator, I am. I'm the only thing keeping you alive." She said.

She's probably right.

We sat there and she giggled and talked till it was time for her to back to work. She is the giddiest woman I have ever run across, and I have known a few.

"What are we going to do tomorrow? It's the Fourth you know." She said.

"You come over tonight, and I promise you a surprise that will answer that question."

"OK." She said and left.

It's a good thing I didn't have to be at the car dealer's lot right away, because I needed some time to recuperate, my legs weren't working very well just then.

I met Leonard at one thirty to get the deal completed. Titles, plates, keys and a check were exchanged and I was driving the van back to the house. I put it in the garage. I'll show it to Denise later.

I packed some more of Sarah's things and worked on the room design till it was time to go get Harry. Denise would be here right after work.

Her curiosity wouldn't let her wait till she picked up the girls and had dinner. Sure enough at four forty six she drove up.

I stalled her and messed around for a few minutes till she said, "Come on, come on, tell me what it is. You're really loving this aren't you?"

"Yes, actually, I am. Follow me."

We went out to the garage with Harry trailing along behind. I opened the side door and turned on the light and stood aside so she could go in first.

"Oh, look! It's perfect! When can we start on it? Denise said.

"Right away."

"Let's put in lights and little storage places, a bed in the back, waste baskets and drink holders, a radio in front and back with separate speakers, and air conditioning. You can paint it can't you DJ?"

She's like a kid in a candy store. She went on for quite a while. Then suddenly she stopped.

"You really do love me, don't you?" She said.

I didn't say anything, I couldn't get a word in with her talking as fast as she could, I just shook my head.

"Let's take this to the park tomorrow and have a picnic. Do you have plates on it? I'll call Linda, maybe they can meet us there. Let's go to K Mart and look at what they have to put in this. I always wanted a van, you know." She said.

"No kidding, I never would have known."

About halfway across the yard on the way to the house, she jumped up and hugged me. Finally she settled down and went to get the girls, she made a quick dinner and we all went out shopping for van stuff.

I bought some window black to tint the windows in the back and side doors so people couldn't look in. She found a book with lots of pictures and drawings and some wooden drink holders.

She said, "Oh, look at this." at least a dozen times during our short shopping trip.

"I'll start on the inside layout right away. This is a good chance for you to teach me how to use all the wood tools in your shop." She said.

Wednesday July 4

Today is the Fourth of July, Independence Day in America, we celebrate it with picnics and fireworks. After cereal for Harry and I, we got in the van and drove to Denise's.

As usual, Harry ran in ahead of me and disappeared into the house. Denise met me at the door dressed in a green short sleeve pullover and tan shorts and white sneakers with a big kiss and some ear nibbling. I am so lucky I can't believe it.

"I've fixed a lunch to take to the park with us, I hope you remembered to bring your cooler." Denise said.

"I brought two coolers and four lawn chairs, they're all in the van."

"Linda and Bill will meet us at the park around ten."

I helped do whatever I could. The kids piled in back on the carpet and we're off.

We started to cook everything around twelve and ate till two I think. Every one had their fill of hot dogs and hamburgers, Linda brought some killer potato salad and a cake and we polished it off along with a great watermelon.

Around four in the afternoon, I was laying in the grass and Denise had the side doors of the van open sitting in the doorway talking to Linda, when she said, "Come on over here there's something I want to show you."

I walked to the van and crawled inside. It's a good thing the roof vent and all the windows are open or it would get stifling in here. Once I got myself seated, she pulled up her top and she had nothing on under it. She giggled when she saw the look on my face.

The door on the side of the van didn't quite get closed and it swung open just as the awesome sight was presented, both to me and those outside the van. It would be an under-statement to say that I was shocked, not surprised though.

Bill and Linda were sitting in their chairs about fifteen feet way sipping their drinks and laughing.

Denise's face got red and she turned and looked at me, so I looked out over her head to see what's going on and they completely cracked up.

We climbed out and went to sit in the two lawn chairs next to Linda and Bill.

"You're just jealous that it wasn't you, Linda." Denise said.

It was Linda's face that got red this time. Bill cracked up again and almost fell on the ground this time.

"I see that you and DJ have sex a lot, why so much?" Linda said.

"I'm trying to perfect my technique." Denise said with a bit of aloof in her voice.

Everyone cracked up again.

"I think it's perfect now." I said.

"Besides how else am I going to keep him trim?" She reached to rub my belly.

We all laughed until we hurt. We sat there and chuckled and made all sorts of lewd and crude comments for some time after that.

We all got on Bill's case next with good bills, bad bills, unwanted bills, overdue bills, unpaid bills.

"You know Denise, you could do worse, I've known DJ a long time and Sarah was one of my two very best friends, and I went to their wedding." Linda said.

"You did? You never told me that. How long have you known him?" Denise said.

Linda forgot to mention that she was Sarah's maid of honor at our wedding.

"He really is a sweetie! She said, avoiding the question.

"If you are going to talk like that, I'm going to move over here with Bill where I won't get any more compliments." I said.

"Tell me about Sarah." Denise said.

I moved my chair on the other side to talk to Bill. We talked for a while then he wanted to see inside the van.

Linda and Denise talked in hushed tones for at least half an hour, then broke it up as quickly as it started.

"You know DJ, I have a friend that does upholstery. His name is Mike, and if you call him tomorrow, I'll bet he could do this whole van for you, and he's very reasonable." Bill said.

I wrote down the number on a scrap of paper I found in Dee's purse and put it in my pocket.

It was starting to get late, I moved slowly behind Linda and Denise. First I kissed Linda on the cheek, then I put a big one on Dee. "We should be going, Dee."

We wanted to get home so the kids could set off their fireworks. Denise and I made sure we explained all about them and how to be safe with fireworks. The four of them went into the street in front of the house and had a great time till all the stuff was gone.

Denise came back and sat down in the yard with me and watched the kids have their fun.

"This is my Independence Day, you know. You have given me my freedom. I don't have to do anything that is harmful to me or my kids anymore and I have you to thank for that." Denise said.

She sat and cried. I felt so useless right then.

Thursday July 5

The temperature is supposed to be a hundred ten today so everything will be in slow motion today.

I called Mike about the upholstery in the van and he told me to bring it to his shop so he could look at it and give me an estimate. We set up a time for this afternoon.

I took some of the pictures down off the walls but not all of them.

The living room couch is a hideaway bed, so I pulled it out and set it up in the middle of the room for later. I had to get clean sheets and pillow cases on it. I want it to be ready when she arrives.

I begged Mrs. Johnson to help me to fix a tuna casserole. I made a salad and put out the dressing on the table.

Denise arrived right on time wearing a thin dark blue cotton dress. I was sitting at the table with a glass of iced tea.

"Hi darling." Denise said as she kissed me and sat down.

"Nice dress, Dee, it looks cool."

"Like it? It's my easy off, watch."

She stood up and reached around back of her neck and did something and the dress fell to the floor all in one motion. She stood there completely naked except for shoes and a thin veil she had in her hand.

"What do you think? OK?" She said.

"Is it ever!"

When she is standing in front of me completely naked, and enjoying my nervousness. She molded into my arms and we kissed for several minutes, then she went back to a chair and dressed as if nothing had happened. She really loves to tease me.

I spent the rest of the day finishing up the drawings for the addition. It has two cozy bedrooms now.

Denise came over with the girls after dinner and we all played Monopoly till late.

Friday July 6

I got all the things on my list done so today is just lunch for Denise and anything else I can do for her.

I'm not going to try another thing like that tuna thing yesterday, there's a Chinese place that has take-out. I'm going to get one of their big lunches for two and keep it hot in the oven till she gets here. I'm so smart.

I set the table like I did every day, I called ahead and left to get the food at eleven. As soon as I returned, I put each box in a bowl and popped them all into the oven, the cook at the Chinese restaurant told me how to set the oven.

It's quarter till twelve now and everything's ready. The first time I have ever done that.

And she's right on time, as usual. As she walked in, I took it out of the oven and put each bowl in the center of the table.

I didn't do this to impress her, but it appears that it did.

"Oh DJ, it's beautiful and it smells so-o-o good." She said.

"It's just take-out from the Chinese place on Oliver."

"But look what you've done with it." She said.

She sat down and she ate and talked till almost all of it was gone. Usually she eats only a small portion during lunch because she has other things on her mind. But today she ate everything in sight.

She had another dress on like she did yesterday, and I'll bet it is an 'easy off' too. She went to the couch and sat there with a big smile on her face. This is becoming habit forming.

"I had every intention of having a light lunch and some heavy sex for lunch, but you spoiled my plans. I don't feel like doing anything right now." She said.

"Nothing wrong with that, let's sit here and talk."

"You mean it?"

"Sure."

"Seriously, I don't think I tell you often enough how beautiful I think you really are."

She sat on my lap and she talked and I felt very good, she did too. We both loved it.

"It's time for me to go, what if I come tonight and stay the night? OK?" She said.

"You think I'm going to say 'No, don't come to my house and spend the night with me'? That'll be the day."

She gave me a promising kiss and left.

Since she's coming tonight, I'll heat up the tuna casserole we had yesterday.

Denise opened the door at six and the smoke was so thick, I couldn't see her come in.

"DJ? Are you alright? Where are you?" She yelled.

"In the kitchen!"

She must not have seen me because she ran right into me.

I had opened the oven door and she saw the smoke pouring out. She shut off the oven, pulled the casserole pan out and put it into the sink to run water over it and we ran out into the back yard. She was laughing all the way.

"What did you do?" She asked.

"I heated the tuna casserole we had yesterday."

"What did you set the oven at?" She asked.

"I only had twenty minutes before you came, so I set it at 450. I guess I forgot it." I said with a foolish feeling.

We went back in with her laughing all the way. She took it out of the sink and we scraped it into a bag so I could take it to the trash.

We opened all the windows and put a fan in the door and went out to eat.

We had a good dinner and after cleaning the smoky house again, we settled down for the night. The house will probably smell bad for a couple of days now, I guess. The things I won't do in the name of love.

Chapter 9

A Ride in the Sun

Saturday July 7

Harry and I went to Denise's house at nine in the morning, he went running into the house and I pulled out the lawnmower. I got started on the front yard right away.

The weather forecast is for another hundred degree day today. By nine thirty I had the front yard cut and she met me as I came around the side of the house with a big glass of iced tea.

"Hi, thought you might need this. I'll start on the flower beds, the girls are playing with Harry." Denise said.

When she finished with the flower beds, she decided to take the girls to Linda's house on the way to my place. We're going to cut the grass and do the weeds there too.

"Why don't I take Harry up the street and you and I can go for a drive? We can finish the yard later."

The three of us walked up to Mrs. Johnson's house.

"Good morning, Mrs. Johnson."

"Good morning, DJ. Hi Harry. Hi Denise." Mrs. Johnson said.

"We're going to go out for a drive for a while, I wonder if we could leave Harry here?"

"Sure, I like taking care of Harry." She said.

"Thanks, we'll try to be back around noon."

Denise and I walked back down to the house, got in my car and left. There are fields all around the city in all directions, but what was I going to do? I drove aimlessly toward the west, until it came to me.

I drove out to a dirt road on the west side of town out around Maize and turned north toward what looked like wheat fields. After a few minutes, we were surrounded by flat wheat fields. I can see a small knoll ahead on the right, I pulled the car up to the top of it and shut the motor off.

"What are you doing?" She asked.

"It came to me while we were driving out here, we can combine two into one. You wanted to do it in a field and in a car too. This is your chance."

I reached back and raised the jump seats into the upright position so the front seats would recline, then I got out and went around and opened her door.

"Look here," I said pointing to a knob on the side of her seat.

"What?" she said.

I moved it.

"Now lean back."

She leaned back until the seat was in its lowest re-clining position.

"Is that comfortable enough?"

She looked at me with a look of disbelief. I took off my shirt and shorts and stood there naked in the sun for all to see. There probably was no one for miles around.

"You don't mean you want to do it out here, do you? We don't have a blanket." She said.

"Not here. There." I said pointing. "In that seat. In the car."

"Are you kidding? She said.

"This was your idea."

She got into the car and laid back in the seat. I followed. Even with the seat all the way back and re-clined, it was still tight.

We had only been at it for a few minutes when she began to laugh.

"I can't believe this, here I am making out in a car that's barely big enough for us to ride in. With the doors open. In the middle of almost nowhere. It must be a hundred degrees. And the worst part is, that I'm enjoying it." She said.

We exercised with such fervor that we worked up a sweat in no time and soon were out of breath.

"I hate to say this, but I don't think I can take it anymore." She said.

"Wait a minute, is the human sex machine pooped out?" I said.

She laughed. "I guess I'm not as tough as I thought." She said.

"Does that mean that you're done?"

"Yes, I give up." She said.

We rested in place for more than a few minutes until I could muster up the strength to get out of the car.

We must have been a sight, standing there putting on our clothes and sweating so much you'd think we had been lifting weights all day.

On the drive back I stopped to get a bucket of Finger Lickin' Chicken, then we went to Linda's house to get the girls.

We packed them into the jump seat in back and then home for some lunch. On the way past Mrs. Johnson's house, Denise jumped out to get Harry.

I had everything on the table at about the time that she walked in with Harry.

The kids ate and ran outside to play.

"Don't even look at me, I'm beat!" I said.

She leaned over and gave me a tiny kiss on the cheek.

"Thanks, that was a lot of fun. I don't ever want to do it again, but I'm glad we did." She said.

Later after we had rested enough to move, she went back to the garage to take measurements on the van and while I cut the grass, then she went inside to work on the interior design of the van.

We worked all afternoon on our various projects.

After I finished, the kids went to play in the back yard. I had just walked in from putting the lawn-mower away when she called.

"Come on kids, It's time for dinner." Denise said. "Here's a glass of iced tea. You look red, are you OK?"

"Yeah, I think I just overdid it a little today. I need a little air conditioning."

I sat down and drank the cold tea, and felt much better after the tea, the rest, and the cool breeze from the air conditioner.

We spent the rest of the afternoon together with the kids, Denise and the girls went home about seven. "I'll pick you up for church in the morning."

The next morning, I got up early and made coffee and some breakfast. Harry and I had cereal for breakfast. It seems like that's all we ever have for breakfast. We arrived at Denise's about nine and we were soon on our way to Sunday School.

After church, Denise and the girls went to change and come over later, Harry and I went to the house.

Denise and the girls showed up about half an hour later. She fixed dinner and the kids went out to play. She really wanted to get that van finished.

Denise was at the dining room table and I was watching the Cardinals play the Pirates on TV, when the doorbell rang. I looked at her and she shrugged, so I answered it. It was Sarah's parents.

"Hi, we thought we'd stop over and see you and Harry." He said as they walked in.

Almost on cue, Denise came in from the dining room in her thin cotton blouse and shorts, and she froze in her tracks. There was a strained silence as the two opposing teams surveyed each other.

"Denise, these are Sarah's parents, Mr. and Mrs. O'Connor."

Dee said "Hi" and looked at the floor.

"Folks, this is Denise Monroe." I said.

They said "Hi" and sat down.

"Well, to what do I owe this visit?"

"We hadn't seen you since the accident, and we just wanted to see how you were doing and say 'Hi' to Harry." She said.

"I'll go get him." Denise said in a strained voice.

Harry came running in to 'Gamma' and 'Pa'.

We all visited for about a half an hour and they left. Denise was on her best behavior, but I could tell it was a strain on her. In fact, it was a strain on all of us.

About an hour later Denise said she was finished with the design for the van.

"Come on over here and look at this." She said.

"Hey this is really good, I like this. Let's start on it right away." I said.

She was pleased about the design and that I liked it and was ready to start on it right away, but I guess seeing Sarah's parents took a lot out of Denise. She just sat around for a long time in silence and watched the game with me, she didn't tickle me or anything. She just sat there. Usually she is so frisky that I couldn't finish watching anything.

She got the girls and left about six. I walked her out to the car and she gave me a kiss.

"Sorry, I didn't think it would affect me like that. I'll make it up to you. I love you." She said.

Back to work tomorrow.

Chapter 10

Office, Office
Who's Got an Office

Our Team arrived very late on the plane last night. There was some kind of engine trouble or something. They don't tell you anything when you're flying. There was only one cab available at the airport when we arrived at eleven thirty, so we all took it to the office. All of us just dropped everything on our desks and went home. Gene took me home and I dragged in around midnight.

I went in to the office at eight in the morning to find two of the guys already there. They were trying to put things away so they could get on with their weekend. After about an hour the others had left and I was getting close, when the phone rang.

"WRAT Team, McAllister."

"Hi honey, I haven't seen you in two weeks. Are you busy?" There was that voice again, that wonderful lilting voice.

"I'll be here for about another half hour, then I'll be over to your place right away."

"OK, see ya." She said.

I hung up and got back to it. About twenty minutes later there was a knock at the door of the office. No one knocks at this door, who could this be?

I opened the door to see Denise standing in the hallway in front of the door wearing a raincoat and holding an opened umbrella above her head. I admit that it rains here in September, but it isn't now and hasn't for a few days, besides it never rains in the halls of this building.

"May I come in? It's raining out here." She said.

I stood there with my mouth hanging open as she slinked by me. The raincoat was buttoned all the way up to her neck. She was wearing brown pumps to go with the brown coat.

"Well, come on in and sit down. I'll be done in a few minutes." I went to my desk and sat down. She came to the front of the desk and began to unbutton the raincoat, slowly and deliberately from the neck down. When she opened it, there was nothing under it. At all. Just all that beautiful skin.

"It's been two weeks since I've had you at home. I think it's time, don't you?" She said.

"Here?? Now?? But, we can't - -!"

"OK." She never even heard me.

She moved around to the side of the desk and sat up on it. The raincoat opened up like an old dictionary as she sat down.

I may not be the smartest guy around, but I'm not dumb enough to pass this up. I locked the door and put the key in from the inside and turned it halfway around.

"DJ, I really love you. But I love to tease you even more. We should go home right away." She closed up the old dictionary and opened the door. Then she began to laugh.

This is one of the silliest things that I have done yet. You always go along with me on all of them to the bitter end. I really appreciate that." She said.

"I've only known you about a year, but you have given me my life back. You see the fun in nearly everything. I think I can honestly say that I love you.

"I have a question for you."

"What is it my knight?" She said.

"Will you marry me?"

It must have come as a shock to her, because her mouth dropped open and she was speechless.

"Y-Yes I'd love to marry you, but tell you what, if you're really serious, then ask me again. I love you more than anything in this world, but I want to know that it's not because of the sex." She said.

It looks like it is time to buy that ring I want for her. I have been looking for the right one for weeks. I finally found it at Jared. It was a little expensive, but all diamonds are. I have been carrying it with me every day.

We met at my house, she parked at the curb in front. We went in and she went back to the bedroom to get changed into something more appropriate. I turned on the radio, made coffee and sat in the living room to wait for her to finish dressing.

A couple of months ago I went through the dressers and closets and packed up Sarah's clothes to give to a charity that could make use of them. I packed dresses, blouses, skirts, delicates and boxes of shoes. Everything is in boxes in the back of the closet she used.

Denise came out dressed in a beautiful green silk dress that I hadn't seen before. It fit as if it were made especially for her. Her reddish brown hair was a nice contrast to the green. She was wearing shoes to match and hose.

I stood up as she entered the room and gasped at her beauty. "You look like you've stepped off the cover of a magazine."

"Thanks. I hid this in your closet last month to surprise you with, if the opportunity came up. I guess it has. The closet is empty except for a bunch of boxes in the back. There's a lot of clothes in the boxes back there, whose are they?" She said.

"I packed up Sarah's things a couple of months ago. I didn't know just what to do with them, so they're still there in the closet."

"I know exactly where to take them. I'll help you do it if you want." She said.

"Sure thing, when?"

"Let me make a call Monday, and I'll tell you then. I'll call you at your office."

"OK. Now back to the question that was brought before the committee earlier in the day. It's time to decide where we will live for the rest of our lives." I said.

"I haven't said yes yet." She said with an indignant look on her face.

"Oh, yes you did. You only said to ask you again. Come and sit down here next to me."

She glided over to the couch and lighted there like a butterfly. I knelt in front of her and took her hand in mine.

"If you ever had any questions whether I loved you or not, put them to rest. I do! I always will! Now, Denise Monroe, I am asking you formally. Will you marry me?"

She looked dumbfounded. She started to cry and fell on top of me. "I never thought you would ask, we have been making love all these months, I thought all you wanted was the sex. I was getting used to that. This is a perfect surprise." She said.

"I take it that is a yes?"

"Oh yes, it's a yes!" She said.

"Does that mean that all the wild and crazy sex is over?"

"Not hardly Kemosabie, put on your seat belt, it's just starting." She said as she jumped to her feet.

It's a good thing that Harry was up the street, because she tore my clothes off right there on the living room floor and practically raped me. Not that I minded, of course. I might add that she was very careful with the dress.

We were laying there on the floor entwined like a pair of vines growing on the same trellis.

"It's almost noon, where would you like to go for lunch, Dee?"

"Nowhere till we're done here. But I'll be ready in a few more minutes." She said.

I thought she was finished, but I held up my end till the end.

She wrings me out like an old dishrag. After I recovered, she thought it would be nice to get the kids and go to Belle Plaine to see the arboretum there.

At this time of year, the flowers are almost finished, but she and the girls liked it. Harry was pretty bored with the whole thing.

We all walked around a lot and saw everything there was to see. We'll go back in the spring when everything is in bloom.

By the time we left the arboretum, the kids, especially Harry, were saying they were hungry. I found a pizza place in Derby on the way back and we all went in and pigged out on pizza and Pepsi.

Monday morning the phone rang.

"WRAT Team, McAllister."

"Hi, here's the address of the Battered Woman's Shelter where we can take the clothes. I'll be over to help as soon as I get off work. Love ya. See ya." She said.

Later Monday evening I loaded the boxes of clothes in the van and we delivered them.

During that week, I went to her house or she came to mine every night, and we found a way to make love each time. By Saturday, I was glad to get to sleep in that morning.

She is always talking about doing it in odd places and times. She says it turns her on in a funny way. I made breakfast for Harry and I and he went up the street to Mrs. Johnson's.

I just got an ornery idea and I love it.

I cleaned up the house and did laundry the rest of the morning. At noon I drove to Denise's house and walked in the kitchen door as she was fixing lunch. Today was a busy day for her, something about quarterly taxes.

The girls had a sandwich and went back to the living room to watch TV. Denise and I went to her office, where she went right to work.

She had a small radio playing, books lying around the room, some open, some not. I took a seat on the couch and we talked as she worked. She was dressed in cutoffs, a man's shirt and sneakers.

"Why don't you sit here, pointing to a chair next to her desk, I have to turn around to see you." She said.

I knew that she would say that when I sat on the couch, but I wanted this to seem like it was her idea. I moved to the chair she indicated. We talked for half an hour as she worked, she was really into it.

Now, my plan begins.

I have learned that I can parade around all day in front of her with nothing on and it doesn't even faze her. Looking at my nude body holds no apparent interest for her, but with the slightest touch in the right spots on her body, I can turn her into a seething volcano. That's what I'm going to try to do now, here in her office. What a rotten thing to do. Ha. Ha.

I moved the chair a little and put my hand on her thigh. That didn't seem to bother her. I reached under the shirt and tried to fondle her. She brushed my hand away after only a minute.

"What are you doing, stop it! I can't think while you're doing that!" She said.

"I know, I thought I'd return the favor from last week in my office."

"Where are we going to go?" She asked.

"Nowhere, we'll do it right here in the office."

"What about the girls?" She asked.

"We'll close the door and if you don't make any noise, they won't be the wiser."

"But the door doesn't have a lock on it." She said.

"I'll push the couch over in front of it."

"Oh - - Kay, let's move the couch. I give up." She sighed.

"There's another one of your fantasies fulfilled, my love."

She was grinning a silly grin that says, "I'll get you for this."

"You know you will have to leave now if I am going to get anything done around here." She said.

She only pronounces her words very slowly and distinctly when she is trying to get a point across.

"I'll see you later, I'll bring the girls over and we'll all have dinner together, then I'm going to kick your butt. Get a roast or something out to thaw right away." She said.

Since I already did my ornery trick, I figured it was time for me to get out, quickly.

On Sunday mornings now, I go to her house and we all go to church in the big car. Back to her house for lunch, the kids play together and we watch a ball game, movie or play cards with some friends.

Saturday Denise invited Linda and Bill and the kids to come over for lunch after church. Linda went right for the kitchen to see if she could help, and Bill found a chair in front of the TV to watch a football game. I sat down with Bill and we talked as we watched the game.

We finally got to sit down in the living room and eat, the kids had a little table over by the office.

After lunch, the four of us sat at the dining room table and played Cribbage for a couple of hours. Denise and Linda jabbered the whole time about a wedding and all the details. We all had a good time and they decided that we should do it again the next Sunday that I'm back in town.

I had to go with the team on Tuesday and it was another long trip. We arrived the following Friday on the plane at ten thirty in the morning.

When I got to the baggage area, Denise was standing there dressed in a short above the knee teal green dress with a scoop neckline showing some cleavage with matching shoes and jacket, waiting with open arms. We hugged and kissed there till the baggage arrived.

She drove me home, all she could talk about was how much she missed me and would I sit a little closer. I revealed the ring that I had purchased to her. I had planned to give her in a more appropriate setting. After she was finished jumping around and being completely excited, she left to go back to work wearing her new ring and I took a nap.

She also reminded me that we would be going to Linda and Bill's house after church on Sunday. Another ornery idea is beginning to form in my demented little head.

Sunday we got back home after church and we changed into some comfortable clothes to go to Linda's. After lunch, I told them that Denise and I were going uptown.

There's a park by the river right there next to Century One, and we "just happened" to be walking by the building where her office is located. "Let's go in, I don't remember much about your office." I said. "I'd like to see it again."

"You rotten thing, you arranged all this, didn't you?" She said as I maneuvered her onto the end of the desk.

"Yes ma'am, I confess, I'm guilty of maneuvering, a HANEOUS crime indeed." I said.

"You silly ass, we could have got caught in there." She laughed.

We stood on the street in front of the building and laughed about what just happened for ten or fifteen minutes.

"Now you know what you did, don't you?" She said.

"No, what?"

"You got me all excited and turned on and now you can't deliver." She said.

"Me? You're the one that jumped up and ran out!"

"Doesn't matter, you're going to have to finish what you started." She said.

When she talks that way, I know her mind is thinking up some devious plan. And usually it means trouble for me. Here it comes.

"Come on, let's go home." She said.

"What? She did all this to me and then nothing. That's not fair. When do I get my chance?" I thought.

I have no idea what's going on yet. She whistled around the house all afternoon, had dinner, and about eight, the girls went up to get their bath and went to bed, and Harry went up and laid down on her bed.

And what of the pixie? She sat down on the couch and was asleep in five minutes.

Chapter 11

The Pixie Emerges

Friday

The Team had been out of town on a regular trip to North Platte and Grand Island. Nice weather, good food, lots of work, lots of fun, but it's not the same as being home.

I called Denise at the office as soon as I walked in my door, and she said she would come over and fix supper for me tonight. I really appreciate that. I really appreciate almost everything she does for me.

Sometimes we like to sit close and just talk about current events and what's going on. We sat on the couch together for a long time. When we sit close like this there's a lot of touching and nibbling and kissing going on at the same time. Once in a while one of us actually did say something.

"I would do anything for you, if I could, no matter how ridiculous it is. Murder and treason excepted."

"Would you get me a new refrigerator?" She asked.

"What kind of a question is that? Of course I would, when do you want it?"

"Right after the wedding." She said.

"OK, but can we pick it out together. Have you thought about where we will be living."

"Here, in your house, I'll sell mine. There are too many bad memories there." She said.

"So then, why don't we get the fridge now and put it here so we can be using it?"

"That sounds like a good idea. By the way, we're going to visit my parents across town tomorrow. We'll take the kids, and mom and I will make supper for all of us. Be ready for a lot of questions from my parents." She said.

During this whole afternoon, she has been sticking her finger in my ear and tickling me and every other thing that she could think of. Even while we were kissing and stuff.

"You know, I think I have found the perfect nickname for you."

"What?" she asked.

"Pixie"

"Why pixie, I'm not that short."

"More for your demeanor. The dictionary says pixie means a cheerful, playful, mischievous sprite, and boy I couldn't have come up with a better description of you."

"Who? Me?" She stood up and did an imitation of a shy little girl who has been caught with her hand in the cookie jar.

"Not only that, I got to thinking that you looked like a pixie with your clothes off. I first thought of it on the Sunday before the Fourth when you were running around your bedroom before church."

"Do you really think so?" She said.

She decided to go into the bedroom and take her clothes off and dance around for me with a veil in her hand, waving it like Salome. She likes to be silly if it's just the two of us.

She danced around the living room, and when I grabbed for her, she jumped away. She would touch me and kiss me, but when I tried to touch her, she would jump away again. She is really enjoying this. All of a sudden she landed on my lap and said, "Take me you fool!"

Of course, when I tried, she was up and gone again. This girl has more energy when she's doing something ornery than any ten people I know.

I told her I was going to call her pixie as her special pet name when we were making love or she was being "pixieish".

"OK, that's great with me, but you have to be a 'pixie catcher'." She said.

"Here I come."

I finally caught her and we found more than one thing to do that we both liked to do. But it took us all night to do them too.

I'm sure that Pixie is the perfect name for her.

Saturday

We arrived at her parent's home just before ten. They live on the west side in a roomy-looking older brick and frame house that Denise and I couldn't possibly afford to buy.

Denise and the girls all went in ahead and hugged and said hi, then Denise introduced us. "This is DJ and his son Harry."

We all shook hands and Marion and Bruce Monroe made all over Harry, and he loved it. The women went to the kitchen to make lunch while her dad and I sat in the living room and talked.

As Denise had predicted, her dad had some questions. When it was just the two of us, the conversation was light.

"What do you do, DJ?" Bruce asked.

"I work for the Government on a team of traveling inspectors. We travel the fifteen western states."

"What do you inspect?" He asked.

"We inspect the Army and Army Reserve to see how ready they are if there was a war."

Just then, Denise walked in with a tray in her hands.

"Hi dad, hi love, I brought you some Pepsi. It'll be a little while till lunch is ready. Everything OK?"

"Everything's fine Denise, we'll call you if we need you. Now where was I? Oh yes, you were telling me about your job." He said.

"One thing that Denise doesn't know about me is how much money that I make. We have never talked about it."

"Denise was never interested in money, even as a kid. If you can tolerate her impudent sense of humor and orneriness, she'll do anything for you. And from what I've heard from her in the past few months, you are 'the one'." He said.

I smiled and didn't say anything.

"Where do you live?" He asked.

"I have a little house on Pattie."

"Nice place?"

"Yeah, we like it."

"Where do you come from?"

"I was born and raised in Colorado Springs, and my folks and brother and sister still live there."

"The biggest question of all, how did you meet Denise?" He asked.

"My wife was killed in an auto accident out on the bypass two years ago and when it was time to do my taxes I didn't know how to do them. A friend at church recommended her."

"What church do you attend?" he asked.

"The same one she does."

"Well, great!" he said in a fatherly satisfied kind of way.

Now that all the big stuff was out of the way, he turned on the TV and we watched WSU play a football game.

We had sat there for about forty-five more minutes when one of the girls came in and told us that lunch was on the table. He turned off the TV and we found a seat at the dining room table.

During lunch Denise announced that we were going to be married and she decided the wedding should be in May, because that's when our first date was.

The girls sounded like they are happy about it, but Harry didn't look like he was. He had a frown on his face and suddenly he jumped up and left the table before he finished eating.

Denise left the table to see what was wrong with him.

Now it was mom's turn to ask a few questions.

"Well DJ, How long have you known Denise?" Marion asked.

"I met her last November at her office. She did my income taxes for me."

"Where does your family live?" She asked.

"We're from Colorado Springs, and all of them are still there."

Denise came back with Harry, and he sat on her lap. He still had the frown on his face, but she was holding him close and tickling him, so he seemed content for the time being.

"Was it love at first sight for you, DJ?"

"Yes, I think so. I loved her the first time I saw her. I didn't know it then, but looking back on it I guess I was afraid to love anyone because of my wife. I guess I still love her."

"Your wife?" Marion said. She was quite shocked to hear the word wife come from me.

Denise popped up, "I'll tell you about it later mom."

Mom nodded OK to her. "What about you, Denise, was it love at first sight for you?"

She said no, and she told the story about the gold necklace.

"I laughed about it later, you should have seen the look on his face when I took off my coat and sat down in front of him with that necklace hanging there right in front of his face.

I tested him a lot. He didn't touch me or grab me or insist I do anything. He didn't want anything from me except his taxes figured. The funniest part is that when I did make an offer, he waited.

He treated me with respect and admiration even though I was really ornery with him. I think I fell in love with him because of that. I guess I knew it for a long time I just didn't want to admit it." Denise said.

"I would have known it sooner except for Sarah. I'll probably always love Sarah in that special way that's reserved for your first love. Besides, she is Harry's mom."

"I had him do a Bio for me before I took him on as a client. He thought it was for taxes, but it was really for me." She laughed and looked at me and winked and wrinkled her nose and her parents laughed at her.

"Mom, I talked to Linda about Sarah, she told me everything, I'll tell you about it when we're alone." Denise said.

After lunch the kids found some toys that grandma keeps there for them, and ran out to the back yard. The four of us played croquet and decided to sit on the deck and play Mahjong. We sat at a beautiful round wooden table with wooden chairs and big cushions. The table was already set with glasses and silverware.

As we were playing I called her "Pixie", and her mom looked up.

"He must be talking to you, Denise. You're the only one here that name fits."

Mom and Dad both laughed about that.

"Do you know what she was like when she was a kid, DJ? She would torment the other kids constantly, especially her brothers and her sister. She was always like this."

"Mom!"

"I agree."

"Dad, not you too."

"Don't get us wrong, we're not trying to scare you away, but 'Pixie' is more than a handful."

"Marion, you couldn't scare me away, no matter what you told me." I wanted to tell her that I had already had a few handfuls of my pixie girl, but I kept silent.

Mom told us about her as a kid and some of the mischievous things that she did. With each story, Dee's face would get to another even brighter shade of red.

"Look," her dad said, "her face matches her hair now."

He laughed and her mom and I joined in and her face grew even redder.

"But the funniest thing was, that she told us that all her friends had black or brown hair except her. Even the ones with blonde hair on their heads." He said.

Mom and dad both laughed at that.

"You see, her grandma came over from Ireland, she had red hair and green eyes and a mischievous spirit. Denise is just like her. That's the reason for her almost red hair, too." He said.

"Oh, did she show it to you too? When she was young, she would show it to everyone." Marion said.

I couldn't help but laugh. But there's no way I was going to answer that one and tell her mom that her daughter has enrolled me in the "Nymphomaniac of the Month" club with Denise as the only NOTM for the past several months. Again I kept silent, all I could do was laugh.

"I think that's why Tom wanted her, she was only eighteen when she married him. I think he thought she was different. Turns out he was right, just not the way he thought." Marion said.

Denise began to laugh and told them about the game called 'Denise says'.

"I knew you were the one by then, I just wanted to shock you to see what you'd do. You passed and I loved you for it." Denise said.

"DJ, I'm convinced that you are the right one for her. She hasn't laughed and talked about anyone before like this, like she has about you. It's obvious that you love each other. Mom said.

"I hope the two of you have a long life together. Bruce, don't you think it's time to get that charcoal grill going?" Her mother said.

We finished the game of Mahjong and her dad and I got the grill ready. In about half an hour we were putting steaks and hamburgers on the grill.

The rest of the afternoon was spent eating, playing horseshoes, lying in the hammock, sitting in the lounge chairs and generally being lazy, all except Pixie.

She was lying on the hammock as I walked by, so I leaned over and whispered into her ear.

"I will always try to do all the best for you."

She immediately grabbed me around the neck and kissed me and we both fell on the ground.

"You'd better!" She said.

She immediately began to laugh and her mom said, "I told you, you were the one." Her mom and dad began to laugh again.

Just then the phone rang and dad picked it up. "OK, I'll be right there." He said. "It's Buzz. He needs some help. I'll be right back."

Mom decided to get things cleaned up while dad was gone and Denise took me to her old bedroom to watch a movie with her. The movie she picked out was an adventure story with the biggest stars in Hollywood. Midway through the movie she grabbed me and said, "I don't much like this movie, let's go home and make love."

So we did. When she grabs me like that and says something like that, it's always time for me to listen. And I always do. Since the kids were staying over with Linda, we went to my house by the shortest route. Before this, I thought I knew everything about her. Little did I know.

"I don't think I'll ever understand you."

"Yes, but don't you love trying to figure it out?" She said.

She decided that the old ways are still the best ways.

"You know that we are required to return to your parent's house. Your mom has a meal waiting for us and you know what kind of trouble you'll be in if we miss it. Besides, your dad won't be gone for very long."

She decided that I was right for once and we hurried back to Mom's house.

Chapter 12

Watching Me Watching You

Mike the upholsterer called me last week and told me that the van was finished, so I took my checkbook and went to his shop to pick it up.

"Nice job Mike, that's exactly what she wanted, you must read minds as well as you do upholstery."

He drove it back to the house for me and helped put it into the garage.

Monday after work, Denise and I stopped at Sears and picked out an Amana side by side refrigerator with ice and water in the door. It all came to about seven hundred dollars.

"Could you deliver this next Wednesday afternoon? I'll take off work and he won't be home to get in the way!" Denise said.

"Yes ma'am, what time would be good for you?" the clerk said.

"Could you make it around one thirty? OK?"

I paid for it with a check and we stopped for some carry-out food on the way home.

Tuesday night we worked on the colors for the van and the design. Denise came up with a good idea with chocolate and gold with an interesting stripe design. I wanted to stay with the browns so I didn't have to paint the door jambs and the roof.

Wednesday we cleaned out the garage and hosed it down in preparation to painting the van. I inventoried all the tools I'd need, cleaned them up and put them out on the workbench.

Thursday the team and I went on a short trip to Sioux Falls, Mitchell and Aberdeen. Even though this is a short trip, it's always a tough one. Long distances to cover between towns, big units to evaluate and big reports to write.

When I get back home this time, I'm going to mask and shoot the van colors. We'll tape it off for the stripes after the paint sets up good.

Another short trip to Kansas City. The trip to KC this time won't be anything close to the trip we made last time.

I was working in the unit with the rest of the team, when James, the AST, came in and asked if any of us liked jazz and Count Basie and looked right at me.

He knew I'd say yes because we had talked about it on many previous trips. It seems that the Count and the whole organization would be at Twelfth and Vine this afternoon with Ella Fitzgerald.

"Would I like to go? Does a wild bear sleep in the woods? I wouldn't miss this for anything!"

The others thought I was crazy. My friend James said that I would be the only white face for thirty blocks in any direction, which turned out to be true. But when you get this kind of chance, you take it, no matter what.

James and I got there right at noon and we were able to get close to the flatbed trailer that the bandstand was setup on. This was some of the finest music I had ever heard and I got to see it all in person. I am so lucky!

And you know what the best part was? It was free! Everyone really enjoyed it. We were there till around five when James said, "Hey man, it's time for us to split. You're too bright to be around here after dark."

The rest of the trip to Kansas City was uneventful and thankfully a short one. I hope I get to see Count Basie again.

Denise said to be sure to call her as soon as I got back home. I got back to my house Friday about four in the afternoon so I called her at her office.

"Hughes, Ingram and Jessup, Denise speaking. May I help you?"

"Good afternoon ma'am, I'm taking a survey of accountants to find one who is beautiful and loves me. Do you fall into that category?"

"Hi you silly guy. Yes, as a matter of fact I do, it seems like I am getting that way more each day. And if you come to my house at two forty five in the morning, I'll fix you right up. Be prompt. I love you. Bye." She said.

She must have been busy, she always wants to talk for a while the first time I call when I get back.

I parked in the driveway in back at two forty five am sharp. When I got to the door, she was waiting for me in another see through nightgown with nothing under it.

Boy do I love that! There wasn't much moonlight, it seemed to come and go, so I only caught brief glimpses of that wonderful body.

"Come on in." She said. "Won't you sit here?"

I did as I was told and sat and she sat on my lap.

She began to kiss me and said. "Everything OK now?"

"You bet."

"Do you have to get up early tomorrow? How long would you like to do this?" She asked.

"No and forever."

I kissed Denise good-bye and started for the door. I didn't get much time to sleep, but it must have been deep sleep. I felt good when I woke at seven am ready to fight the day.

Tuesday I called Denise at her office to ask her if she would like to have lunch with me. I parked the van next to her Pontiac in the Hughes, Ingram and Jessup parking lot.

I picked up a Big Cheese pizza on the way and brought Pepsi and some fruit. She popped out the door of their building right at noon and ran to the van.

"What is that wonderful smell?"

I pointed to the box on the floor.

"Oh, you got pizza." She said.

She wolfed down a piece and looked around at the appointments in the van. It has a big "U" shaped couch that makes up into a bed. I had it all ready to go.

There is a table that sets up in the middle of the "U". Behind the driver is a cabinet with an ice box, sink and water available and storage for dishes and utensils. There is a radio and a cassette player in the back and drink holders all around. Storage under the couches for blankets and pillows. Finishing it off is a rear area heater and roof air conditioning.

"This is perfect, I hope you'll tell him how much I like it." She said.

"Already taken care of, Pixie my love."

Later that night we enjoyed a movie together and on the way home in the van she wanted me to stop for a Dairy Queen sundae, but before I could get to the window to order, she said. "Get your butt back here and take care of your future wife before I find someone to sub for you."

Naturally I didn't want anyone subbing for me, so I got my butt back there. She giggled the whole time. I'm not sure if it was for the performance or for the joke she tried to make.

Thursday we started to make the list of people to invite to the wedding.

"I'll call them off and you write. Ready?" Dee said.

I got the pencil and began to play secretary to the CEO of this company.

"My parents, your parents, Linda and Bill. Do you think she would be my maid of honor? Mike and Annette. By the way she called and said that he is after her every day now. Just shows you what a guy will do once he gets a taste. Jean and her husband, the guys on your team, people from my office, and your office. Who did I miss?"

Chapter 13

The Halloween Party

Back in April, Denise and I planted a garden in my back yard with all the necessary vegetables to make a pizza and a few extras. Denise helped all the way from planting to cheering me on. Rah! Rah!

Now it's finally time to finish the garden. It's been a hot dry year, but we've had a few vegetables from it off and on during the year. I hate to admit it, but usually when Dee would take care of the garden, is when we picked something edible from it. But now it's October and we can clean it out for next year.

Yesterday, the weatherman predicted a big snow for the first of October and Denise came over this morning to help pick, clean, cook and freeze all the vegetables. Denise said the TV said the big snow would be Tuesday, but you know you can't believe those weathermen. I just hate it when they're right.

"By the way." She said. "Did you notice that there doesn't seem to be any peppers here?" As she said this, she giggled and acted cute.

No peppers could be found. Of course, she already knew this because when I was out of town, she would tend to the garden from time to time. I have never been able to grow green peppers. I don't know why, but I just can't seem to get it right, and I've told her this before. Just then, I spied a little brown bag behind her on the ground.

"What's that?" I said pointing to the bag.

"Oh, that's nothing." She said.

I had to do a football type running play past her great blocking skill and on to victory and the bag.

"Peppers! I might have known. You were going to let me think you had to go out and buy these weren't you?" I said in a scolding tone. There were only two in the bag anyway.

We had just got started when the wind started to pick up. The longer we worked, the harder it blew. By the time we had finished, the sky was brown with dust. It got in my nose and mouth and I coughed a lot till we finally went inside.

"Are you all right?" She asked.

"Yeah I'm OK, let's get a Pepsi and get this stuff put away."

I wheezed and coughed the whole time till she made me go and sit down. By noon I was coughing and snorting like a wart hog. She called the doctor, but his office was closed till Monday.

Denise had picked up the girls and was there all night and all day Sunday with Harry and I. I got worse as the day went on, and Sunday was a terrible night. I woke Monday to find Dee nudging my shoulder.

"Come on, wake up."

"What? Who?" It was Denise, I was feeling bad, but I began to moan and groan and cough for her benefit. I must have made some of those coughs a little too phony sounding because she began to stroke my head like you would a little dog and said, "Oh, you poor baby."

"I'm taking you to the doctor, get dressed." She left no doubt that she was in charge and that she didn't think I was very sick.

I stumbled around and threw on what clothes I could find on the floor. We arrived at the doctor's office for a nine am appointment. I felt like a swarm of bees had made camp in my sinuses and were out exploring the area.

"Well DJ, you've got yourself a good one this time." Doc said.

"What is it doctor? Will he be all right?" She did all the talking, I was busy blowing my nose and coughing.

"He probably should be in the hospital, but because you said you would take off work and be there around the clock, I'll send him home with you. He has a good case of bronchitis. He must have been a little weak because it is starting to develop into pneumonia. He'll only be down for a week or so if we can get it in time. Go get these filled and get me a progress report on Wednesday." Doc said.

For October it sure seemed to be cold, Dee insisted I get to bed as soon as we get home. She must have picked up the prescriptions, but I'm not sure when. Monday and Tuesday disappeared, when I woke up I found someone in my bed and I had a boob in my hand but I know it's not mine because it's talking to me.

"Good morning, lover, how are you feeling?" It said.

I can't get my eyes to focus. "Who is this," I said to the talking boob.

"DJ, up here, it's Denise, are you OK?" She's tapping me on my head.

Denise? Wow, what do I do? I can't find her. Suddenly I saw her face in front of me and her hands are holding my shoulders.

"Are you OK. You've been asleep two days." She said.

"No, I don't think so, if I was, I'd be grabbing you and I can't find you."

"Here take this." She said.

I swallowed, Wednesday disappeared too.

Thursday I woke up to find Denise sitting in a chair by the bed.

"Hi sleepyhead." She said.

"Are you an Angel? You sure are pretty. Am I in heaven? Have I told you that I love you?"

I was starting to get the clouds out of my head and my eyes are starting to focus. Denise is sitting there dressed in jeans and a sweatshirt looking like she has been there all night.

"I know you love me, but it's nice to hear, even if you are delirious. How do you feel?" She said.

"I can see and hear you, my head hurts, my throat hurts, and probably everything else, I'll let you know."

I got out of bed and she helped me get some clothes on so I could sit with her in the front room. We had breakfast and watched TV till Harry and the girls came in the front door. The wind and cold blew into the room like a tornado.

"Boy is that cold!"

"It's been snowing for two days and the schools are closed. Where have you been?" She giggled as she said it.

"Hi Dad, we're building a snowman." Harry said.

"What time is it anyway, they can't be up this early building a snowman, can they?"

"It's just after four in the afternoon, lover." She said as she went to the door to see the snowman.

"You mean I missed another day?"

"Looks that way." She said.

The kids got a drink and right back out to play. Denise made a great lunch, or supper, of chicken noodle soup and grilled cheese sandwiches, and in an hour, I think, I was starting to feel pretty good.

By the time we went to bed I was walking around without any help and when she got undressed to get in bed, things were starting to look up. I grabbed her and pulled her close and squeezed that talking boob.

"Are you sure you're ready for this?" She asked.

I gave it everything I had and my brain is saying "Oh boy, oh boy, let's go" but my body still has the emergency brake on.

"I give up. Nothing wants to work but my desire for you."

"It's OK, it'll be here when you want it, you just say the word." She said.

I've noticed that she sure is giggling a lot these last few days.

It took till the following Friday for the driver to get the emergency brake released and get the motor started. Unfortunately I never got it out of first gear. Damn!

"Well Tarzan, even you need rest after a bout with the big bug. Let's give it a few more days." She said with a smile and another of those giggles.

"Oh, OK." I said grudgingly. She is so beautiful and always willing to do anything I want and here I am unable to do anything.

Denise and the girls stayed with us till I was able to go back to work, the first day we walked up the sidewalk at the same time, she picked up the mail and gave me a kiss and I held the door for her.

"Look at this." She waved one of the letters and handed it to me.

"You are invited to a full dress costume party on Halloween night at the Crown Hotel beginning eight PM. Donation four dollars per couple to pay for the ballroom."

"That's only eight days to get ready." She said.

"I've had a nice vacation, you think I could help?"

"Now that the snow's gone, you can go to the store and get candy. Here's a list. Do you have any money?" She said.

"I did, but I haven't seen my wallet since the first."

"I'll do the costumes." She said.

I took the list to Dillon's and filled her order. On the way back, I stopped to see if Mrs. Johnson would watch the three kids on Halloween night.

"Sure, be glad to." She said.

I paid her in advance and gave her the candy to pass out for us.

Dee ran all over town for several days trying to find the right costumes for us, I didn't know what the right ones are, but it seemed that she did. She still didn't find them. She did, however find costumes for the kids and herself.

"What are you going to wear to the party."

"I'm not going to tell you, you're going to have to find me before you get a kiss." Dee said.

"Maybe some of the other girls that are there will kiss me."

"Fat chance, I've told them all that you're a lousy kisser, so none of them will touch you." She said and laughed.

"We were going to go as Little Bo Peep and a sheep with a long leash around your neck, but when I got to the costume store, it was gone. You'd have looked good with a leash around your neck." She's giggling again.

All five of us went "Trick or Treating" Friday about five thirty. We walked all around the neighborhood talking to everyone and watching the kids collect bags full of candy. Dee left the girls at home and I left Harry with Mrs. Johnson and we both went home to change for the party.

"I'll see you there. Your costume is in the bedroom closet. See ya." Dee yelled to me as she drove away.

She had already arrived and left me a note with the girl at the door. "Pay the two dollars and catch me if you can. All my love, Pixie."

"What's she wearing?"

"She swore me to secrecy." The girl said.

There were about twenty couples there when I walked in. I could see the only way to find her is dance with the girls and ask questions. The first one was Marilyn Monroe.

"Yes, Dee and I talked for quite a while when she first came, but I haven't seen her since. She wanted me to meet you, I'm Carolyn. We went to school together, by the way, she looked awfully tired."

Marie Atoinette told me, "Dee has been going strong for months now without a break and is really tired. You take care of her DJ." Marie said.

"You know I will, Linda."

Annette was dressed as Dolly Parton, she sure has the equipment for it, and Jean was Martha Washington. They both said the same as the others.

"Oh look there she is. May I have this dance." I asked the wicked witch.

"And what is it you're dressed as?" The witch said.

"I'm the Wookie from Star Wars, do you love me?"

"I might if you get a haircut". She giggled.

"I'm looking for Denise, have you seen her?"

"She's here, I talked to her earlier." She said.

I knew it wasn't Dee right away, the giggle was all wrong. I thanked her and went searching again.

I searched the rest of the night for her, I danced with most of the women there. It seems like they're all conspiring together to not tell me anything, I'm sure Dee put them up to it.

About midnight after almost all the people had left the party, I saw a girl asleep in a chair dressed as Princess Lea, how convenient. I peeked under her mask and sure enough, it was Denise, fast asleep in the chair.

I picked her up while she was still asleep to carry her out to the car. She woke up and screamed and fainted in my arms. I drove her home in her car, I'll pick mine up in the morning.

I carried her upstairs, wheezing and panting all the way, "Boy, 99 pounds is sure heavy at one in the morning."

Did you ever try to undress a woman who is completely out of it? No fun. She must have had a couple drinks besides being extra tired to be this unconscious.

I undressed her and put her to bed then crawled in beside her and fell asleep with her all cuddled up in my arms.

There was not a sound, the room was dark and my arm was asleep. I did my morning ritual and as I climbed back into bed beside her, she woke and rolled over.

"To what do I owe this nice surprise? I see you're dressed and ready to go." She said as she smiled up at me.

"I'm dressed and will be ready soon, I see you're dressed too."

She looked at herself for the first time. "What happened here, did I miss something? I'll be right back." She was back in just a minute, still dressed the same as before. "OK, now I'm dressed and ready to go, but first, tell me how I got here and everything." She said.

"I saw this hairy monster carrying you away and I fought him valiantly and finally overpowered him before he could carry you off to his cave."

As I was telling her the whole story, she got up and walked around behind me.

"You mean this hairy monster?" There's that giggle again. She was holding the Wookie's head high in her hand.

"The kids are at Mrs. Johnson's house."

"Then we have time for a good one." She said.

"Yes, a long, slow, good one."

There's that giggle again.

Chapter 14

Christmas in the Mountains

The Team is going to San Francisco for the semi-annual conference at Fifth Army headquarters this month. I asked Dee last month if she would like to go with us. Of course, she said yes, since he had never been there before.

We were discussing what our plans were when the Colonel called and said. "Could your team stop on the way to the conference, at Las Cruces and have a look at that unit? It's a Transportation unit and they have had a big change in personnel. I'd like to see how they are doing." He said

Well of course when a Colonel asks a question like that, the only answer is always. 'Yes. We would be glad to."

When I got off the phone, I told the rest of the guys and we all had s good laugh. There were plane tickets to change, motel reservations to make, a van to reserve at the El Paso airport and a lot of other little things to change, but we have a week to do it in.

The unit's drill is on a weekend before the conference, so we'll have a couple of extra days out this time.

Mrs. Johnson was overjoyed to say that she would watch the girls and Harry for the week that we would be away. Harry thinks she is his grandma anyway and he always likes to go see her. I gave her a handful of money to buy groceries for the group. I hope it helps.

Denise packed several different outfits, some for cold weather, some for not so cold. The weather forecast for San Francisco said high forties with a cold wind blowing in from the ocean. She always takes too many clothes, but one thing, all of the clothes she is taking are sexy and sharp.

She was nervous about not being able to go, so we arrived at the airport an hour ahead of time, at six am. Yawn! An hour later, when the rest of the guys found their way in, I introduced everyone around.

"Denise, this is Gene, George and the Major, we don't know if he has a real name, just 'The Major'."

"Hi, Denise, I'm Nick Nichelson, we've all heard a lot about you, and it's all good, which is surprising knowing DJ. Ha, Ha, got you back." He said.

She shook their hands.

"I know your names, now I can put a face with each name." Dee said.

"What we really want to know is this, why would an obviously beautiful and smart woman like yourself ever be seen with a guy like this?"

"Well guys it's like this, he saved me from being run over by a speeding train when I was tied up by Snively Whiplash." Dee said.

Boy did they love that! She has been immediately accepted by them as a charter member of the "Harass DJ Club".

The plane left at seven thirty on the dot. It's a direct flight to El Paso, get the van at the airport and a short drive, just about half an hour up I-25 to The Crosses. On the way up, one of the guys spotted a huge sign that said 'What-A-Burger". None of us had ever heard of What-A-Burger, so we all voted to go there for lunch.

We had to find the motel, then the unit, and finally the burger joint. By that time everyone said that they were ready for lunch. You won't believe those burgers. They should serve them in a washtub. They were huge. And by the way, delicious! The guys each got one with fries and a drink. Denise and I decided to cut one in half and no fries. Way too big for us.

Saturday morning the inspection went well. The AMSA Shop Chief told us about an open-air market that was open downtown that day and we all went together. I stopped to pick up Denise at the motel and we were at the market in only five minutes.

There was every kind of thing that grows around there and plenty of others available. Since tequila is made from cactus, it was for sale too. But none of us dared touch it. Most of us pieced through for some special candy and things like that, but the Major said that he and his wife just loved the hot red peppers.

He bought a shock of dried red peppers hanging around the tent. The vendor wrapped them in a plastic bag and put it in a paper bag. Then did it again to be sure.

It's another early flight, but a direct flight to Los Angeles. And with a short layover, we arrived at the San Francisco airport at ten thirty.

The rental van that I had set up was waiting for us. George got behind the wheel and we're off. We were checking into the Sea Captain Motel at eleven fifteen. We should be able to make the conference by noon.

"OK, whadayathink? Lunch across the street at the IHOP in fifteen minutes. Don't you two start anything now, we have to be alert." The Major said.

They all laughed and Pixie's face turned red.

We walked into the conference room at twelve thirty.

"Well look here, the team from Wichita have graced us with their presence." Mike De Stefano said.

There's always one in the crowd, and he's always the one.

We had only been there for an hour or so when the General said loudly, "What's that smell?"

We all had noticed it, but none of us were going to say anything about it. We're the out-of-towners!

Someone found the smell was our very own Major. It seems that he had packed the dried peppers into his suitcase for the flight from El Paso. Now all of his clothes smelled really bad.

"Sergeant!" He said to the Sergeant Major in the back of the room. "Take the Major somewhere and get him cleaned up. And get everything cleaned up."

Once they had left the room, someone began to laugh. It caught on and soon all of us were laughing.

It was a long afternoon, but we finally slipped out of there at four thirty. That's sixteen thirty for you military fans. With the two hour time change it seemed like eighteen thirty to us.

I walked into the motel room and fell on the bed, she was right behind me. She must be a witch, she can always read my mind. My back and legs were sore.

Without asking, she took off my shoes and socks and helped me with my jacket and tie. Then she straddled me and began to rub my back.

She had been doing this for about ten minutes when the Major walked in without knocking followed closely by the other two.

"Boy you two are really good, you've learned how to do it backwards." He said. They all laughed.

She must have been embarrassed, because I could feel her starting to get down.

"Don't mind us Denise, we know how much trouble he has with his back. But, we wouldn't ever pass up a chance to needle him. He has told us how much he loves you and it's all in fun." He said.

"What we came for was to tell you that we worked out a tour of the Bay Area for you, and you can even take him too, if you want." The Major said.

"I don't know, sometimes I think I can't take him anywhere." She said.

They all liked that one.

"I'm OK now, she always rubs the right spot for me."

"Yeah, I'll bet."

We all piled into the car with Denise in back in the center and Gene and I beside her. As I expected, she was dressed in a short skirt and tight blouse of mint green with a very warm looking jacket.

George drove us down Union, all through the Marina district, past Ghirardelli Square, through the Embarcadero, and up Market Street to the cable car stop, explaining each spot as we passed it. We all paid our fare to the end of the line and George left.

"I'll meet you at the other end." George said.

The cable car took us to Fisherman's Wharf, where George was parked waiting for us. We drove down the Crooked Street back to the wharf area and because it was after six, back to the motel.

He dropped us off at Scott's Seafood on the way. Parking is a premium here so it's better to put it into the motel parking lot and walk to the restaurant.

We had a forty five minute wait to get a table, so we all went to the bar. While we waited we finally got the Major to tell how he got cleaned up.

"I had to buy a new uniform, then drop off all my clothes at a dry cleaners, then back to the room and shower and put on the new uniform and here I am. Good as new. I'll not do that again." He said.

"Did you get rid of the peppers?" George asked.

"Not yet." He said.

"Hey Max! Have you got a box we can have?"

Mac brought us a box and we all went to the Major's room and packed the peppers in it and we will take it to the post office tomorrow. No more stinky stuff!

We all had another good laugh about it.

"Go ahead DJ, have a drink, you're not driving tonight." Rod said.

Pretty soon George walked in. We had all ordered, and there was one waiting for him.

We had finished a couple of drinks when they called our table.

"Order anything you want Denise, don't even look at the right side of the menu."

She ordered a big special. It has all the good stuff, lobster, king crab, giant prawns, rice pilaf and salad.

When the food came it smelled wonderful. She made a fuss over each item. She tried the lobster first.

"I've never eaten this before, boy this is good. Then she picked another strange looking piece. "What is this, DJ?" She said.

"King crab legs, here let me help you."

"Do you guys eat like this all the time?" She said.

"Yeah, that's why we like the homemade stuff so much." George said.

After dinner we walked the couple of blocks to Bachelors Two, a bar owned by a friend of ours. We have been coming in to see him since the teams were formed in the beginning.

He stopped in his tracks when he saw her. With the short skirts she wears and the great legs she has, it's no wonder.

"Hi, guys". He said. "Well, well, well, one of you must have miraculously grown some good taste since I saw you last." He said.

"A beautiful lady. A very beautiful lady. Good evening ma'am, I am the lowly bartender, Max. How may I help you, and why are you with this group of bums?" He said.

She laughed at Max's patter and played the straight man for his jokes. Max laughed and had a good time at our expense the rest of the night.

Pixie nudged me in the side at eight thirty.

"I'm really tired, could we go back to our room?" She said.

I made our excuses and we walked down Chestnut and back to the motel. I went to take a shower while she sat on the bed and undressed while watching the TV.

She was flipping through the channels when I got into the shower. I was just getting out of the shower and toweling off when she called to me.

In the morning we were up at six, shower, dress and go to breakfast across the street at the IHOP. She had the day to herself while we were at the conference. She brought plenty of money for shopping and there's plenty of busses and streetcars to go around town. I told her that we would meet her back at the motel at four.

After work we went to Sears Point for the great view and Sausalito to see the town, shopping, dinner and the turtle races. We shopped and had a great time as usual. Just like last night, the guys wanted to go to Bachelors.

Of course Denise and I had to make an appearance if only to show her off. She was dressed in another stunning outfit with a short skirt, this time it was blue. I like showing her off, and watching guy's faces when they see her.

"Are you still with this guy, pretty lady? You could do a lot better, you know. I would like to volunteer to make your life better." Max said.

"Thanks Max, but I guess I'm stuck with him now." She said.

The guys just eat it up when she is cute and witty.

We stayed about half an hour and walked back, this time by a different route to see different shops. But like last night, see found that channel and we were off to the races again.

The next afternoon we went to Oakland and Jack London Square. We spent two or three hours there shopping and sightseeing, then we all had dinner in a nice Polynesian restaurant.

By this time she knew which channel to turn the TV to when we returned to the motel for the night.

Thursday is the last night we have here, and Chinatown and North Beach are on the agenda. George is still the chauffeur this week, he drove through the tunnel and parked on Stockton street near the corner.

We walked down one side of the street in Chinatown and up the other, looking in all the shops. Some places we would enter and browse and make an occasional purchase.

After a wonderful dinner in a Chinese restaurant there, Denise and I walked hand in hand down Broadway through the North Beach area.

The five of us are strung out on the sidewalk, and a girl came up to me and asked if I wanted a date.

"Are you kidding? I can't handle this!" I said pointing toward Denise. "Look at her, she's beautiful! What makes you think I'd be interested in you anyway?"

"Up yours, buddy." She said.

She gave me the one finger salute as she walked away and Dee was giggling the whole time.

North Beach has X rated movies, live sex shows, bookstores and anything else that fits that mold. Suddenly Denise stopped and turned around.

"Listen." She whispered.

From where we were it looked like another girl had stopped the others, I couldn't hear anything.

"It's a guy dressed like a girl." She said.

"Are you sure? How can you tell?"

"Yes. Look." She said.

"What do you mean look? Don't tell me to look. We're half a block away."

I don't know what she saw, but I couldn't see it.

They talked for a few minutes and the girl left. We waited for them to reach us.

"Tell him guys, that was a guy talking to you." Dee said.

"What?" George was surprised that she said that. "I thought it was a girl."

Gene asked, "How could you tell from here?"

"I just knew."

"Damn!"

The rest of the tour was uneventful. On the way back, George told us, "That girl looked as good as any girl I've seen." We all laughed at him.

"Hey DJ, maybe your date is a guy." George said.

"No, I can vouch for her, I've looked very closely, and I try to check every day, honest."

"Dee Jay!" She hit me as she shouted my name.

"Dee Jay!" The others all said in unison, mocking her.

Friday at two p.m. we left to catch the plane for home. This one isn't a direct flight, there is a plane change in Denver.

We arrived in Denver five p.m. local time and Wichita at eight p.m. With the baggage and a cab ride, we were walking in the door at nine p.m.

"I see what you mean about the traveling, it sure is tiring. I'm going to stay here tonight, is that OK with you?" She said.

"Are you kidding?"

During the next two weeks, we settled down and tried to get everything ready for the drive to Colorado Springs on Saturday. It's a long drive. Out highway fifty-four from Wichita to Dodge City, then highway fifty to Pueblo and I twenty-five to home. Maybe twelve hours or so.

We are taking the kids and the van and a whole lot of Christmas gifts. Pixie has been busy for the last few months, buying gifts for me to give to Mom and Dad and my brother and sister.

She went with me shopping once in October. I picked out some pretty nice gifts for my mom and sister, I thought.

"You don't do well at shopping do you? Look, we're going to put all this back. I'll pick out the gifts, all you have to do is pay for them." Dee said.

Now they're all wrapped and in the van ready to go. It's a good thing we have the van in the garage. It's a lot easier to get ready with the bad weather we've been having.

We left early in the morning Saturday and I drove for two hours and stopped for breakfast and gas. Denise drove for two hours and stopped again. We did that the whole way.

When we finally arrived, we weren't as cranky and tired as we had been on other trips. I was driving when we were coming up Interstate 25 from Pueblo. I turned off at the Fountain exit and into town toward the house.

"OK, here we are."

It was warm for December, probably in the fifties. I used my key to get in the back door.

"Where did you get a key?" She asked.

She walked in and found all the furniture in place, food in the refrigerator and the beds made.

"What is this? Whose house is this anyway and why is it empty, or not?" She asked.

"Oh, this is my house, I bought it a while ago. I pay the payments and my sister lives here."

"She pays all the utilities and taxes and keeps up the place for me. She's staying with Dad while we're here. Let me go call Dad and tell him we're here."

"How much are the payments?"

"Eighty three dollars."

"You're kidding." She said.

Mom, Dad and Doreen arrived at five. I handled the introductions.

"Mary Ann, Charles and Doreen McAllister, I would like to present the love of my life, Denise Monroe and her daughters, Melissa and Jennifer."

"My brother Sean and his wife will be along later, he had to work today. And this is my little man, Harry. Harry this is grandma and grandpa and your aunt Doreen."

They all made a fuss over Denise and the girls, but especially Harry and he loved every minute of it.

"DJ contacted us ahead of time, we knew you were coming. I'm so happy you could come." Mom said.

We all hugged and everybody talked. Mom and sis just loved the girls and Denise, they went upstairs to show them their bedroom. Dad picked up Harry and took him out to the back yard where they could run and play together.

A little later Mom and Denise started dinner and the rest of us talked. I tried to help but they threw me out. I've been thrown out of some pretty fancy kitchens over the years, but never my own.

Sis and I set the big table in the dining room. Walking between the kitchen and the dining room, I could only hear parts of the conversation between Denise and Mom.

"We've always liked this house." Mom said.

"Don't forget the glasses, DJ." Dee said.

"Would you take this in and put it on the table, honey?" Mom said.

After dinner, Denise and I sat and talked with Mom and Dad all night. She had a lot of questions for them. I think they both wanted to just hug her all night.

Sean and his wife arrived just after dinner, and I introduced Denise to them. Sean was hugging Denise for what seemed like a long time, his wife had to break it up.

"Come on now Sean, let her go." She said.

"I see it runs in the family, DJ does the same thing with me." Dee said.

They all laughed and Sean just stood there with a stupid little grin on his face.

Harry took to the family right off, especially my dad. Harry has been troubled ever since the wedding announcement, but now he is the center of attention and is loving it.

It was midnight when they all went home. The kids will sleep upstairs, all the beds are made up. We'll sleep in my bed in the master bedroom. Denise was asleep as soon as her head hit the pillow.

Sunday morning, we set the alarm early and all got ready for church. After church we changed our clothes and had lunch at Dad's. He wanted to drive us around the area and point out things that they might not see somewhere else, we all rode in the van with Dad driving.

Later that day we all put up the tree at Dad's house and everyone helped with the decorating. Dad lifted Harry up to put the star on the top, and everyone made a fuss about it, Harry really eats it up. We didn't get home quite so late this time.

Monday was destined to be a long day, we drove up Gold Camp Road to Cripple Creek. Mom took two coolers of food to have a picnic in the park at the end of Bennett Street.

We rode the train, had taffy from the little store, ice cream from another store and walked up and down Bennett and Myers Streets looking in all the shops.

When everyone was thoroughly tired, we drove to Victor and down Phantom Canyon Road to the Royal Gorge to see the bridge and feed the deer.

It was three in the afternoon by the time we started back up highway 115 to the Springs. On the way back they were all talking at the same time as usual, but I could tell the kids and my Pixie liked it.

Christmas Day is one of the two best days of the year for me, the other is Easter, but not for the gifts. Everyone met at Dads house to exchange presents.

I am going to have so much fun today, it should be unlawful. I have gifts for the kids, but Denise took care of that for me. But what I have for her will knock her socks off, and she doesn't wear socks very often.

Sis played Santa, fishing a box out from under the tree and giving it to the person named on the tag. I didn't put Denise's presents under the tree, so I could hand one to Sis when it was her turn to receive a present.

The first was a microwave for her kitchen. She was unimpressed, but pretended it was OK. The smile faded slightly.

The second was the title to the van. That one got her. The smile came right back.

"Oh DJ, you shouldn't have." Dee said.

Next a wristwatch with a gold nugget band. Her excitement level was rising. She was smiling that extra big smile now.

"This is wonderful, thanks so much."

Next a series of brightly wrapped boxes, all the same size and shape.

The first contained a picture of a TV set with the caption, "New TV, see next box."

The next contained a photo of a VCR, saying "New VCR, see next box."

The next, "New stereo, see next box."

Last was, "New entertainment center to hold it all." with a photo of all of it in the last gift with the caption, "All in your new bedroom, see it when you get home. Love, the Pixie catcher."

She was smiling as big as I've ever seen her. Wait till she sees what's coming.

"You are too much, I don't know what to say."

Only two more gifts for her, and Sis knows which one is last.

The next one was a nightwear set consisting of a nightgown, pajama set, gown, teddy and slippers all in blue mist. She broke out in a giggle, and all the women began to giggle and laugh with her. No words this time, just a wink.

Last of all was a box big enough to hold a couple of loaves of bread. She ripped the paper off in a fury, she must have known something. Inside the box was another, only smaller, and so it went till the last box, the size of a roll of scotch tape.

In it she found a marquis cut half carat diamond ring. She broke down crying. Mom and Sis went to her and between the three of them there were shouts of joy and crying for several minutes. Dad held up his hand with the thumb and forefinger in a circle. This time it was Dee's turn to hug me.

"I love you so much I could just hug you all night." Dee said.

"Sounds good to me, don't let me stop you."

Funny thing about women, you give a woman a diamond ring and as soon as they get it on their finger, their whole left arm becomes a trailer hitch, stuck out there in front.

All you have to do if you want to have her follow you is take the trailer hitch in your hand and lead. The whole evening Pixie had that hand out in front of her admiring the ring. That night, she gave me a present that made me as happy as the ring made her.

Wednesday was a tour of the Air Force Academy. The chapel there is the number one tourist attraction in the state, and I didn't want her to miss it.

Even though it was cold we saw almost all of it. I drove back to Dad's by way of Academy Boulevard so she could see all the places for Dee to go shopping.

Around noon it cooled off and the wind came up. We piled into the van and hotfooted it for home, the forecast said snow. By three it was downright cold and the snow started to fall, gently at first. By six, it was coming down pretty hard.

We slept in on Thursday, it had already been a long week. I went out for the paper to find snow up to my eyeballs. I turned on the morning TV news show for the weather.

They were reporting ten inches of snow last night. I called Dad to tell him we wouldn't be visiting today. Denise made hot chocolate and I made a fire in the fireplace. We sat around in our pajamas and played board games with the kids.

They brought out their presents and had them all over the living room. The kids told Denise that they were hungry, so she made a brunch. I went to the kitchen.

"How can I help?"

"You go on back into the living room, your mom and sister told me about some of the things you have burned up when you help." Dee said.

"Gee whiz! One time you put a hamburger in a little skillet with a cover and set the fire on medium, and they never let you forget it. That was the problem, I forgot it."

I could hear her laughing in the kitchen.

After lunch all three kids wanted to go out and play in the snow. They made snowballs and threw them at each other, they worked on a snowman for a while.

The snow was too deep too make a good snow angel, but they tried. After an hour or so they came in and went up to their rooms to take a nap and play. The cold and the high altitude must have got to them.

Denise decided it was a good time for us to take a nap and snuggle while the kids were napping.

On Friday, it was an adventure to go to Manitou, but we did it. We slogged through the snow to the shops that were open. Denise bought some things to take back. We stopped at Dad's house to say our goodbyes before we left.

Saturday morning we left at seven am to drive back. We said our good-byes yesterday and last night. The snow was mostly off the streets and it was halfway clear till we drove into snow at Pratt.

The rest of the way it was coming down pretty good. The closer we got, the worse it was. The ten hour drive became twelve and still going. Harry and the girls were asleep in the back of the van when we pulled into the driveway at Pixie's house.

We carried the three of them into the house and put them to bed. I kissed her and went home to put the van in the garage.

I slept in. I didn't realize what day it was. She called at nine.

"I think the kids and I will stay at home today. They wanted to sleep in their own beds, so I haven't even woke them up yet. It has been a long month for me and I'm beat.

I need to recuperate from both trips, but if you want your back rubbed or anything else, I'll be here waiting." Dee said.

You don't have to tell me twice.

Chapter 15

The New Years Eve Party

December 31

It's New Years Eve and there are parties all over town. She got dressed in her evening gown and high heels, I wore a black suit and we went off to the New Years Eve party at the Royale.

When we walked in we heard the band and walked to the dance floor for a turn around the floor. As soon as I put my arm around her I knew that she had dressed for success.

"What's this?"

"I knew that you'd want to play around tonight, so I'm ready. And don't you forget this! I don't care where we are or what we're doing, at midnight you're mine!" Dee said.

We had been there for about half an hour when she looked around the room and said, "This is going pretty slow, let's go somewhere else."

I had no idea where the parties were located, so I began driving aimlessly, I was driving down Broadway when she saw a sign saying New Years Party.

"Pull in there. The Crown Motel." She said pointing to the sign.

We walked in to find a woman at a table with a sign above saying, "Welcome SINK."

"It's four dollars. Would you take a tag and put your first name and age on it. Thank you." The woman said.

We filled out the tags and pasted them on our left shoulder where she said.

There's a band playing on the bandstand, and there must be fifty couples in the room, the place is jumping. We were enjoying the music and I was especially enjoying her body pressing against me.

Denise and I found a table and sat down to listen to the band. I noticed there were no waiters to be seen.

"I see drinks all around, it must be serve yourself. I'll go get a couple of drinks. Back in a minute."

When I got back to the table, there was a woman sitting with Dee.

"DJ, this is Sandy. She's the one I gave all of Sarah's things to.

Sandy and Dee talked like they were old friends, so I got up to walk around and see if I knew anyone here.

By the time I got back to the table, Sandy was gone and replaced by two other pretty women.

"DJ, this is Mary and Laura, we're going to get a drink, we'll be right back." She said.

Mary and Laura took Dee by the hand and they walked away. Dee looked back at me with a questioning look, then a little smile appeared.

We had food and drinks and danced with many of the people there. I was a very exciting night.

At quarter till twelve, the M. C. announced the time and said, "Please return to your partners, it is almost midnight. We have the room all night and you may continue to mix and mingle till dawn."

Denise didn't bother to ask, she just plopped on my lap and hugged me so hard I got a crick in my neck.

"I told you I'd see you at midnight." She said.

"Sandy and Mary both gave me their card and Sandy asked me to come to her office next week so we can talk about something important."

The card showed their name, address and phone number and "SINK".

"Do you want to stay, Pixie?" I asked.

"Hi, DJ."

I looked up to see the only familiar face I had seen that night. I know my mouth must have dropped open again.

"Well. I never would have thought I'd see you here."

"Are you and Dee members?" Linda asked.

"Of what, we don't even know what this is."

"Why don't you and Dee come to our house on Friday for a little more of this?" She said over her shoulder.

"This has been the most exciting night of my life. We would be happy to visit with you at your house, I'll call you when I can." Dee said.

"Look, we would like you to come to the house for dinner and some explanations on Friday, say six thirty?"

"OK, we'll be there. DJ, I think it's time for us to go home." Dee said.

January 1

There are a lot of new things in my life, new year, new decade, soon to be new wife, new family, new van, new addition on the house, new surprises like the one last night and more sex than I can keep up with. It looks like it is going to be a fun year for us.

We have talked about doing the addition on the house but not about hiring a contractor.

"I know a really good one, my brother, Buzz Monroe." Dee said.

"Wait a minute, I thought your married name was Monroe."

"No I took my own name back when I took my ring off." She said.

"Why do you call him Buzz?"

"I'm the youngest, he's six years older than I am. He flew model airplanes when I was a kid, and they go 'buzz'." She said.

She contacted him for a preliminary meeting at my house.

He must have been close and dropped everything, because it was only a few minutes before the doorbell rang.

"You called, Oh Sister Dear?" He said as she opened the door.

It looks like the 'smart ass' quality runs in the family. We went over the plans and she made some suggestions, so did he.

The addition will be two bedrooms and one bath with a basement playroom. There will be inside stairs to the basement for the kids to use. Completed by a covered deck along the rest of the back of the house and we will convert the back porch to a mud room.

The kids can enter their room from it and we can enter rest of house. The deck will have a railing and steps to the yard. A large undertaking by any standard.

"It must be done no later than the wedding." Dee said.

He brought a contract with him. He filled it out right then, we both read and signed it. He said he will start as soon as the weather permits.

"We'll be done on time, Sis. Don't you worry." Buzz said.

"You can't come to the wedding if it's not finished, Buzz." She said, and giggled about that.

"OK Sis, you know that I'll do anything for you." He turned to me. "I love her you know." He said.

"Me too." I said.

Friday night, we dressed in our best clothes and drove across town to an address well known to us by now.

It was six thirty when I rang the doorbell.

"So tell us, my very best friend, what is Sink and why didn't you tell me about it long ago." Dee said.

"Well Dee, or is it Pixie?" Linda said.

"No, Pixie is the name DJ calls me when we're being ornery or sexy or really close." Dee said.

"OK, Sink means 'Service in Kansas'. It's something like the Red Cross, but on a smaller scale. We have three Nutrition Centers, two food pantries, a Battered Womens Shelter, and a couple of clothing and furniture recycling centers here in town." Linda said.

"Sandy is the Regional Director, Mary is the manager of the Nutrition Center right down the street, and you've already met some of the other managers."

"We stumbled into a New Years Eve party just like you did seven years ago. We only joined to go to the parties, but we got involved with all their work too." She said.

"It's not for everyone, but it has done miracles for us. We don't get hung up with many others, but we enjoy a party a couple times a year."

"They have a party like that at all the major holidays. I never told you because that guy you were married to was such a turd. The parties in warm weather are a lot more fun, too." She said.

The Team left Monday for El Paso and Las Cruces. It used to be that I didn't call her when I went on the road much, till that special evening. I've been calling her more and more ever since. I called her every day during this trip and she kept me up to date on what's going on.

Denise set up a birthday party for me at her house for Saturday after the trip. All of our friends, Linda and Bill, Mike and Annette, Jean and her husband, Buzz and his wife and the guys on the team were there.

After everyone arrived, Denise and Linda carried out a big sheet cake with white icing. The picture on it is a girl in flesh colored icing that looks like Dee. There are only three candles, one in each nipple and one in the middle of the patch of red.

When they cut the cake I said, "I want the red piece where the candle is."

Denise replied, "You get that piece every night."

The girls all laughed.

They brought out the gifts next. The first was a nice gift, an 8 x 10 photo of her, dressed in a beautiful evening dress, signed "Love, Denise" with a note marked "Pass around".

The second was marked "Personal, DJ only". She took the girls into the kitchen and showed them, I walked in behind Linda and looked over her shoulder. It was a picture of Denise on a couch, up on one elbow. It was signed "I will always love you, Pixie".

"I had a girl photographer I know, do both of them." Dee said.

Just then she saw me in the back and began to move toward me. The girls moved apart to let her through.

"We'll put the photos in the bedroom so you'll always be able to see who or what you love the most." She said.

She hugged and kissed me passionately. I really like that.

Next Denise had an ornery gift, a inflatable doll. She brought it out of her room already blown up. She walked it out like a real girl.

"Meet my friend, Marie." she said.

Marie is Denise's middle name, and she only uses it when she's talking about herself and wants to be cute about it.

She had dressed it in one of her old really short skirts and a blouse.

Everyone was howling with laughter by then. I took it and hugged it and said, "Marie, would you like to go to bed with me?" In my squeaky voice, I said, "Yes DJ, I love you." They were laughing so hard they couldn't stand up.

"One last thing, I would like to announce that I won't be doing taxes anymore. It was a lot of work, I needed the money, but it took a lot of time away from my family. Now I won't need the money and I can spend the time I want with my family."

"Most of you already know that the accountant for SINK is leaving and Sandy has offered me the position. I have accepted it and will be starting there on the first of the month."

"In May I'll have everything I want, him, pointing to me, a nice place to live and the kids. Only family and very close friends will be serviced this year."

The team leaves on another trip Monday, but there'll be a lot more days like this one ahead for us.

Chapter 16

Making Arrangements

Dee and the girls are at my house most of the time now, so when Linda called to find Dee, I just handed the phone to her. We were having grilled cheese sandwiches and soup for lunch, and the kids had already finished and left to play.

It seems that the Big Four are coming here to start planning the wedding. Linda, Laura, Mary and Dee have been calling themselves the Big Four lately.

Linda arrived in ten minutes, the others dribbled in later. Dee served them drinks as they each arrived and Linda opened the meeting. She has decided to take charge of the arrangements.

"Alright, let's get started." Linda started the meeting. "We need to decide who is going to do what. Dee all you have to do is make a list of the people you want at the wedding, buy your wedding rings, and get your dress." She said.

"And don't forget this, tell the dressmaker the wedding is a week before it really is or you won't get the dress till you get back from your honeymoon." Mary said.

"That's a laugh, you two have been on one long honeymoon ever since you met." Linda said, with a big grin on her face. The others laughed and made some smart remarks.

"I'll do the church, Laura and Sandy, you do the reception and the cake, Mary you do anything that takes a long time to order, you know, stuff like the invitations." Linda said.

"Is everyone all right with this arrangement?"

They all said it was good with them.

"DJ, where are you staying on the wedding night and what about the honeymoon?" Linda asked.

"You think I'm going to tell you. Not a chance. I know all of you much too well to do that. I've got it all taken care of, and it's Top Secret."

"You don't trust us?" Laura asked.

"Not even for a minute."

She feigned a hurt look and went back to the business at hand.

"Let's get our pencils out and make some notes." Linda said.

They had already written down most of the things that should be done for the wedding, now it was just sorting them out.

"I'll take the church, the minister and the flowers. Since my husband is the best man, I'll take care of his tux. And since I'm going to be the maid of honor, I'll get my dress." Linda said.

"Who are the flower girls and the ring bearer?" Mary asked.

"My girls, Jennifer and Melissa will handle the flowers and little Harry will carry the rings." Dee said.

"We haven't met the girls and Harry yet, Dee." Laura said.

"I'll go get them." I said.

I went back to the bedroom and brought the three of them to meet the women. The four women made a big fuss over the kids with hugs and smooches, but the kids got tired of that pretty fast and they were gone to hide again.

Linda began again, "Laura and Sandy, you take the reception, the cake and the top. Do you think we could have the reception at the Crown?" She asked.

"I don't know, but it sounds good. I'll try." Sandy said.

"Mary, can you get the invitations, they'll probably have to be ordered weeks ahead, and the photographer?" Linda asked.

It seemed like it snowed every other day for the next few weeks, but that didn't stop these girls, they had a wedding to put on and nothing was going to stop them.

Buzz got started on the room addition while I was out of town on this last trip. He has the conversion of the mud room complete and will be starting to dig the basement playroom soon.

Dee called Sandy one day last week, and said she got the feeling that something was wrong with her.

"Something didn't sound right. DJ, would you call her at work tomorrow and talk with her? Her number is here on her card." She said, handing me her card. Dee said.

"Charles Jewelers, may I help you?"

"Hi Sandy, this is DJ, sorry to call you at work, but Dee said she was worried about you."

"Why don't you come to my house tonight? We'll get off by ourselves where you and I can talk." She said.

"OK, what time?"

"I'll look for you at seven." She said.

I arrived at the address on the card at seven and rang the bell. Sandy answered the door and invited me in. She introduced her husband to me.

He seemed very unhappy about something when he asked, "Where's the girl, didn't you bring a girl with you?"

"Dee wasn't feeling very well, she asked me to come and visit by myself."

He went on with his dissertation about how there should be a girl for him and how no one appreciates him. Sandy interrupted him and told him she was going to out get her supper, and we left.

We went to a good restaurant I know, and as soon as the food came the floodgates opened and she began to talk.

"My husband only wants girls to give him sex. He doesn't give a damn about me anymore. I want someone to be good to me, it's a cinch my husband won't. He won't work, he lives off of my salary and it's not enough to make it. I'm in debt up to here." She said. She held her hand up above her head when she said that.

"What do you want to do about it?"

"A divorce sounds like the best idea to me, if I can do it." She said.

"You leave him to me, I'll fix it. You check with a lawyer and get everything started."

We sat and talked after she finished eating for more than an hour and it was time to take her home. It wasn't very far, just on the other side of the little park there.

The team went to Topeka for a week and I couldn't complete a full day without calling her. The guys laughed and made all kinds of noises about it. But when she answered with that wonderful voice of hers and I could see the smile through the phone, it was all worth it.

This time, when I returned home, I found a big hole in the back yard where the basement playroom will be.

March

Getting ready for this wedding doesn't leave much time for silly sexy stunts like we've done in the past, the traveling limits my time, but it certainly doesn't limit her orneriness and inventiveness.

Saturday morning she said she wanted me to take her someplace. It was just ten o'clock when we got into the car. I drove downtown following her directions.

"Park here." Dee said.

We parked in the lot for the office where she works.

As we boarded the bus, she paid for the tickets all the way around the route and back to the spot we got on and took a seat on the back seat of bus. Don't ask me why, but I sat next to her. Once the bus started, I asked where she wanted to go.

"To ecstasy!" She said as she grabbed me.

So naturally, being the obliging kind of guy that I am, I took her there. It was the most unusual city bus ride I ever had.

The team went to Albuquerque for a week and it was the same as the Topeka trip. I couldn't complete a full day without calling her. I don't know what I miss more, that wonderful voice of hers or her smile that I can see through the phone or that fantastic lithe little body. Whatever it is, the phone calls help.

Buzz and his crew have the framing done and have started on the sheathing on the walls and roof.

It was a gloomy Sunday afternoon in March and we were relaxing in the living room together when she began to talk about Sandy.

"We have to help Sandy, she really is in trouble. What can we do, DJ?" Dee asked.

"I have an idea. Call the Big Four and Sandy for a meeting here, right away tonight if they can make it."

Within an hour, all five of them were sitting around the dining room table looking at me with that look that says, "what am I doing here?" on their faces.

It was my meeting, so I started at the beginning.

"We have to help Sandy with her problem. You all know about that, so I won't go into it now. This is what we're going to do, now listen, we're going to do a sting."

"Sandy says that he goes out to bars to pick up women pretty regularly. One of you will be picked up at a bar and taken to a motel for a sexual encounter with him. Who wants to do it?" I asked.

No one raised their hand or gave any evidence that they would like to do it.

"I guess we'll have to draw straws to see who he picks up." Linda said.

Laura drew the short straw. She had a long face, but the other girls tried to cheer her up.

"OK, when he leaves the house on one of these hunting trips, Sandy will call Linda and Linda will start everything in motion. It may not work the first time or the second, but you will get him! I guarantee it."

"When he picks you up, Laura, you'll say something like this. "We can go to my room, it isn't far." And you take him to a room in a motel that you have already paid for. Sandy you'll have to pay for it, but Laura you'll rent it in your name. Make up a name if you want."

"Be sure to get two keys, Laura will have one to let him in. Dee and Mary will have one so they can get set up before the action begins."

"One girl will be in the closet taking pictures while he does Laura."

"I'll do that, I'm pretty good with a camera." Mary said.

"Mary, be sure to use two rolls of film, so we have lots of pictures."

"Do all of you have cellular phones?"

They all answered yes they did.

"Good. Linda will follow him in her car and as soon as he stops at a bar, she'll call Laura to tell her how to find him. Then, she'll tell the others when Laura has made contact."

"When Laura moves in on him, Mary and Dee will take up your positions at the motel. Mary will be in the closet taking pictures. Mary, whatever you do, don't sneeze while you're in that closet!"

"Dee will be in the motel office next to the phone in case she has to rescue you girls."

"Sandy will be at home, the dutiful wife, cooking and cleaning. Don't you leave that house for anything!"

"Linda will stay in her car in case of trouble."

"When Mary calls Dee and tells her that she has the pictures, Dee will beep Laura's pager."

"Laura, as soon as that pager rings, you must now figure how to stop him, and get rid of him and get Mary out of the closet and to the motel office."

"Dee will then call Linda and tell her that you have the pictures and everyone is safe. Dee, Laura and Mary will then get out of the motel as quickly as possible."

"And last, Linda will call Sandy and alert her so she can be ready when he comes home."

"Does everyone understand what they have to do? Are there any questions?"

We had some discussion on the fine points of the plan and they all left smiling and talking.

April

The Team worked a trip to Tucson, and as soon as I got home Friday afternoon, Linda called.

"I'll be right over." She said.

She must have been in her car when she called, she arrived in no time. I haven't seen her this excited since I've known her.

"It all went just as you planned it." She blurted it out and smiled all at the same time. "You are a genius, everything went just as you said it would. Your future wife loves you more each day and I can see why. Sandy has already filed for her divorce, and he has moved out of the house."

Later that week, Denise and I went to a lawyer's office to check on a few small points before the wedding. He is located on the fifteenth floor of a building downtown. We completed our appointment and as we entered the elevator, a light went off in my head.

She said months ago that she wanted to do it in an elevator. When we boarded the elevator I stepped to the back and pulled her back in front of me. There were two people who got off on ten. Now we were the only riders. If this doesn't top her orneriness scale, I don't know what will.

The trip to Fort Riley is always a short one, but I still had to call her every day in order to keep my sanity. You know, it wasn't like this when I was married to Sarah. I wonder what the difference is?

The addition is almost done, the sheetrock is up and the deck is done. All that is left is painting and installing the fixtures in the bathroom and turning on the water.

The bridal shower was held at Dee's house while I was working at Fort Riley. She said all of her friends and the girls were there. She said it was lots of fun. Women must really like that kind of thing. I've been to wedding showers and they always left me cold. It's only two weeks till the wedding now.

The team went to Salt Lake, but I had to be in town for the wedding practice. It's only one more week before the big day.

Chapter 17

The Bachelor Party

It's the day before the big day. The wedding is tomorrow at four in the afternoon. We wanted to have a bachelor party for Denise and I, but they are always done in a bar and now that I've converted Dee, neither one of us drink anymore. Nothing has been done till now, so I guess we'll have our party at home together. And that's not all bad.

I picked up the mail as I came in after work. What's this, an invitation delivered to my house with no stamp on it from an address in the plush northwest side and nothing more.

"Hughes, Ingram and Jessup, Denise speaking."

"Hi future Mrs. McAllister, how's everything going?"

"Hi lover, pretty good." She said.

"I have in my hand and invitation from an anonymous sender for tonight at eight to an address on the northwest side of town for the two of us. Do you know anything about it?"

"No. What's it say?" she asked.

"Your presence is required at the address and time listed below. Be there."

We decided it must be a prank sent by one of our friends so what do we have to lose? We arrived at the address on the invitation at eight and rang the bell. The man who answered the door knew us but neither of us knew him.

"Hi, come on in, we've been expecting you." He said.

There was champagne cooling in a silver bucket, and a cake in the middle of the table. The writing in the icing said, "Congratulations, Dee and DJ"

There were ten people standing around drinking champagne. Obviously, we were the last to arrive. I recognized three of the couples, Bill and Linda and two others from the New Years Eve party. Linda must be the one that set this up.

When we walked in there was a lot of hugging and kissing. I made it a point to kiss Linda and she always helps.

She whispered to me, "You lucky bastard."

"I know it! I know it!"

For most of thirty or forty minutes there was lots of joking around and telling jokes, mostly about weddings and funerals and that kind of thing.

It wasn't long before I noticed that there seemed to be less people there than when we came so I counted. I was right, one couple was missing. Within five minutes more another couple disappeared.

Then there were only four of us standing there talking. We decided to go looking for the others. There they were, undressed in the hot tub, six of them. Three other couples were also in the back yard with croquet mallets in their hands. I never have seen the allure of croquet. But Denise's mom and dad like it.

The hot tub was beautiful, a pale blue with wood all around the outside. It had jets of water shooting into the center.

It was sitting in the middle of a remodeled old porch that gave the look of a room specially built just for the hot tub. The people in the tub looked so relaxed and they were telling us how nice it was.

Linda finally said, "Why don't you give it a try."

"I don't think so, thanks."

One of the girls that went to the back yard to play croquet called to Dee, "Come on and play, Dee."

The back yard is so green and lush, it looks like it was painted on. The grass was soft and freshly cut, and all the flowers and bushes were the same. It looked like a picture out of a magazine.

We went into the back yard to play with them and one of the guys told us how to play. Good thing!

"Here's the rules, if you want to ask a question of anyone playing, you must hit their ball, then ask your question. They must tell the truth as well as they know it." He said.

There were eight of us doing this ridiculous thing. The first girl hit a ball and asked her husband a question, which he answered what sounded like the truth to me.

Soon it's Dee's turn. She took aim and struck the ball with her mallet with a vengeance. Her ball hit mine, to no one's surprise but her own.

She looked up at me and asked, "Do you love me?" Then looked down to hit the ball again, which of course hit my ball again. Then looked up again and asked, "Do you really want to marry me?" Then she took up a pose with her hand on her hip that looked like, "OK, I'm waiting!"

"Let me tell you exactly what I told Linda at the New Years Eve party. In answer to the first question, 'More than I ever thought possible'."

"And in answer to the second. I wouldn't want it any other way. Absolutely, positively, yes, you bet."

"Oh DJ, I love you so much." She said.

She leaped at me, and I grabbed her as she landed on my body. Her legs were around my waist and her arms were around my neck, squeezing the life out of me. I was lucky to get my arms around her waist and keep her from falling.

"Let's go inside." She said into my ear.

I have, as long as I have known her, never even wavered once when she said something like that. I know what it means! She didn't disappoint me this time either.

"Well that's the last we'll see of them tonight."

Chapter 18

I Do, I Do, I Do

Today is the big day. It's finally here, and so is my family from the Springs. They'll all be staying at Dee's house while we are on our honeymoon, but my dad and Harry are here with me this morning.

Dad made breakfast for us. The event is set for four in the afternoon and I have a lot of things to do today. I'm glad Grandpa will be taking care of Harry while I do them.

We moved the girl's bedroom furniture to my house last week, and we have it all set up for them in the new addition. I had to do some final cleaning and vacuuming before they can move in next week.

I had to get the Porsche gassed up and cleaned inside and out. When I did that, I parked it in front of the house and took the van for the same service as the Porsche. After the van was neatly tucked away in the garage, I put the suitcases in it and stocked it up.

After I cut the grass and cleaned up the yard, Dad called me for lunch. It's a good thing he's here doing this, Dee would be extremely upset if I burnt something again today.

We were to be at the church at three p.m., an hour before, to get dressed and ready for this solemn occasion. I drove the little blue Porsche, everyone would be expecting to see it at the church. When I walked into the dressing room, they were all there.

"Come on, you're late." Bill said.

"It's only five after."

"I'll bet the women are all dressed and ready by now." He said.

"OK. OK. I'm hurrying."

Bill, the best man, was nearly ready. My dad was getting Harry ready first, then he would finish. The women would want to see Harry all dressed up as soon as possible.

I got started when my dad asked, "By the way DJ, you didn't say, how was the bachelor party? Bill said you went to one last night."

"Yeah DJ, how was it?" Bill asked with a big grin.

"You wouldn't believe it, I'm not sure I do, and I was there."

Bruce was there getting dressed, listening and not saying anything. "DJ, are you sure about this?"

"Mr. Monroe, there is nothing that I have ever done in my life that I was more sure of than this. I can't even put into words how much I love her. I might not be able to talk when the minister asks me to."

"Do you have the rings?" Bill asked.

"Me? I thought you had them!" My voice must have risen noticeably because they all turned to look at me.

"Yeah I do, I was just checking your excitement level. I'll keep them till the last minute before I give them to little Harry. I've already told him what to do with them." He said.

"We'd better get in there." Dad said.

Bill and I went in the back way to where the minister told us to stand, and took our positions. The left side of the church was filled halfway back, on the right were seated Mom, my brother and sister and the guys from the team.

The minister announced that the reception will be held immediately after the wedding at the Crown Motel, and that a map with the address and phone had been prepared and put on a little table in the foyer.

Pretty soon here came the girls down the aisle. Melissa and Jennifer were smiling so big that you can tell they will have the wonderful smile of their mother when they grow up. Linda was looking more beautiful than I had ever seen her. She winked at me as she stepped up onto the stage across from me.

It seemed like an hour, but it must have been only a minute or two, before the organist began playing.

Mr. Monroe was escorting his beautiful daughter down the aisle toward me and Dad had Harry in tow.

As Dee was walking down the aisle, I noticed some chuckling from the audience. Then I saw Laura and Sandy smiling, with their hands over their mouths and trying to be quiet. Then Carolyn. Then Mary. Here comes the love of my life to stand next to me.

I was looking closely at her to see what the chuckling was about, and as the minister began to talk I saw it.

"You cut your hair!" I guess I blurted it out, because there was an immediate silence throughout the church.

"It's a pixie cut, mister." She said loudly in her little girl voice. "Do you like it? Huh? Do ya?"

I could have died right there. And of course, right on cue, Linda and Bill, who were standing up there with us began to laugh.

Her mother and dad were both laughing. My dad is smiling, but I knew he didn't quite follow what was happening. Soon everyone in the church was laughing.

The minister had to ask for order and began again, but I could tell that he had no idea what was so funny.

By the time he asked me if I took her for my wife, I was beginning to chuckle. "I wouldn't have it any other way."

When it was her turn to answer the question, she grabbed me around the neck. "I do, I do, I do."

I guess the minister had had enough. "I now pronounce you man and wife." He announced with a tone of finality in his voice and threw up his hands.

When she lifted her veil to kiss me, I saw that not only has she cut her hair, but she colored it a lot redder than before. A lot redder!

The minister presented us as Mr. and Mrs. McAllister and everyone applauded and cheered as she kissed me, you'd have thought it was a baseball game instead of a simple wedding.

Each person that came through the line to shake hands with me and hug Dee had something to say about the service, including the minister.

"What was that all about?" The minister asked.

"Some time after all this is over and we can get together, I'll explain it to you."

We shook everyone's hand and talked until the photographer came to get the pictures taken. The whole wedding party stood around posing for photos until there were enough in the camera.

The reception started at four thirty, and we would have been there on time except, getting that gown into the little blue car was quite a trick. Getting it out was a whole lot easier.

The reception went a whole lot smoother than the wedding. Linda and Laura were helping Dee open the gifts. The two of them were writing the names and gifts down as Dee opened them.

There was lots of food and drink for everyone, and it looked like everyone was having a good time. Dee's mom told her it was time to cut the cake. It's a good thing we have all these people taking care of us. We wouldn't get anything done.

I have never had the chance to smear a piece of cake into the face of a pixie before, so I made this one count.

"I'll get you for that!" She screamed.

"I know it, but while you're thinking up new ways to make my life hell, would you dance with me?"

"Yes, but just this once, then I want to dance with two other men." She said.

While we dancing I whispered to her, "I have reservations at the Hilton, your girl friends won't find us tonight. I used another name to register."

"What name?"

"I'll tell you later."

She finished the dance with me and took up with her father and my father after that. Fickle woman!

They announced the money dance, so while she is having all the fun, I walked around and introduced myself and talked to everyone there. I got hugged by every female there including two young girls that I just adore.

"Can we call you 'dad' now, DJ?" Jennifer asked.

"You two can call me anything you like. I love you both"

"Do you think that you will love us as much as you love Mom?" Melissa asked.

"The love I have for your mom is different than the love I have for you, but neither one will ever get smaller than it is right now."

I looked out the window to see someone decorating my car at the reception and smiled. Little do they know that it won't make any difference.

When the money dance was over, we walked around the room once more to greet everyone and then we slipped quietly out the back.

Dee and I went to my house to change before we left. I have already laid out clothes on the bed for both of us.

As I drove up to the garage door, she looked at me funny and wanted to ask something, but decided to wait. I got out and opened the door, and put the little car into the garage.

"Hurry, let's get changed and get going. The van is all ready."

We put on our change of clothes, jumped into the van, closed the garage door behind it and we were finally on our way. We can clean the decorations off the car later.

"You little devil, no one will be looking for the van. I guess that's why I married you, you're so smart." She said.

"That's not why, but I'll accept it." I laughed.

We walked up to the desk at the Hilton and the clerk said "May I help you sir?"

"Yes, Harry Hanson, I have a reservation."

"I used Harry and Moms maiden name, Hanson, to register." I whispered to her. As usual she began to laugh. We had both been laughing all day.

"I bought a bottle of Rose' for tonight, it's in the van with some glasses and the suitcases."

It was a long and cozy night, and to me it seemed to be the best night we had ever spent together.

The next day we drove to a very special motel in Great Bend. During the years of travel with the team, each time we went to Great Bend we would stay at this one motel. It has an indoor pool, the whole inside is like one big atrium, a restaurant, bar, coffee shop and terrific rooms.

The best part is that I didn't tell anyone where we were going, not even Denise. She loved it. She wouldn't even go outside for the first couple of days. It was raining, but I don't think that was the reason.

It warmed up Tuesday and I finally got her outside to walk around in the hot ninety degree sunshine. It was only a week away from the hustle and bustle for us, but it seemed like forever. Just the two of us with no interruptions and no one wanting something from us.

It was a glorious week, but we had to go back to work, so we drove back home on Saturday. The first thing we did was call her mom and my dad and tell him, "We're here." She talked to them for about an hour.

Chapter 19

Moving Day

It's been a month since we were married and I am loving it, I hope she is too. She still does ornery little things but mostly it's been stuff here at home now. Even so, it's really nice falling asleep with her cuddled up in my arms every night.

We moved the girls into the house last month as soon as we came back from Great Bend. We had moved all the necessary furniture out of her their house already, so the girls were happy.

The Monday after the honeymoon we both went back to work and it was tough on both of us. After spending a glorious week with her, then going in to face those guys every day. What a letdown.

They made lots of comments about who runs things at my house. I know who runs things at my house. She does. I must admit that whatever happens is caused by Denise, sometimes I'm the one that does it, but she is always the cause.

No matter how much grief those guys give me, there is always one thing that I remember, and sometimes I remind them of it, too. Every afternoon when we're in town, I get to go home to her. All night with her.

For this last month, she has been showing off some of her cooking ability, she even made a tuna casserole without burning it, and she made sure that I made a note of the event. Yea! Applause! Applause!

She hasn't been normally wearing a bra around the house at night and I really like her new mode of dress. I hope it continues for a long time.

I was sitting on the couch watching something on TV after supper when she just sat down on my lap for no reason and hugged and kissed me. I always welcome a display of affection like that. I reached under her shirt and gently squeezed one of my favorite little bumps.

"Ow, that hurts. Gosh they are really tender. I'd rather you didn't touch them right now." She said.

Having said that, she got up and went to the bedroom and put on her bra. She has been like that for two weeks, it must be that time for her.

The next trip was to Salt Lake, I'll see Paul and he is sure to ask about the wedding and my ornery bride.

I called Paul before the trip and he met us at the airport. On the way in to town, Paul and the guys laughed and joked about the wedding and Denise.

"What was that thing with the funny voice and everyone laughing?" The major asked.

"That's just something she does." I said.

"She sure brought the house down." Gene said.

"I didn't know she was going to do anything like that." I said.

"And this was the one that you said that you didn't know whether you love her. Man, if you don't, you're crazy." Paul said.

"If you remember, I said that more than a year ago." I said.

"I danced with her and we had a chance to talk. I am positive that she is too good for you." George said.

"No disagreement on that one." I said.

The guys on the team were all telling me what a wonderful, if a little crazy, woman she is. Paul and I had a great time while I was there. He was trying to get my goat about Denise the whole time. It was a good trip, but as usual I'm always glad to be home again.

Now, when I go on a trip for four or fourteen days, the return home is much more exciting than before.

She is so hard to describe, there are so many words, I just don't know where to start. If I looked "Denise McAllister" up in the dictionary, I would find, amusing, agitating, arousing, cheerful, enjoyable, giving pleasure, happy, joyful, lively, merriment, pixie, playful and thrilling.

But the one thing that I never forget is this. She loves me. All these months that we have been together and I am still amazed when I say it, and even more amazed when she says it, but I am extremely grateful for it.

After a trip, I usually get home between noon and three in the afternoon, put my clothes away, get the mail and the paper and stretch out on the couch for a few minutes.

She gets off at four thirty, is home by four forty five and pouncing on me and pushing me into bed before five. I hope that goes on for a long time too.

It was Monday morning after the last trip, and time for me to go in to the office. I was getting dressed and shaving when she popped her head into the bathroom.

"I don't think I want to go to work this morning. I'm kind of tired." She said.

"You? You're always the one that jumps up ready to go. Come on, let me help you get ready."

"No, I'll call in and take a little time off this morning."

I wonder what's the matter with her. I hope she isn't coming down with something.

We put her house on the market last month after the wedding, with a real estate agent friend of hers, Laura Lou Williams. Since we wouldn't be living there, she could show it anytime she wanted, so Dee gave LL her keys.

The agent said to leave enough furniture in it to make it look like it could be lived in. Since we had moved all the necessary furniture out of the house already, we left everything else alone. Now here she was with a sales contract from a prospective buyer for us to sell the house.

We set a date to go to the title company for the closing. We were in the middle of the closing and it was going very nicely when Denise got a little light-headed.

I got her a glass of water and we all stopped for a minute and everything was fine. It must be the stress of the closing getting to her.

Denise bought it for $9500, and the contract is for $21,000. With real estate agent fees and other costs, she gets $12,415.86. That's a fair return for just taking care of a house for a few years.

Last week we got her a new savings and checking account at the bank where I do business. She wanted to be able to have her own accounts. Just hers. She dropped the check into her savings on the way home after the closing.

We did the closing on a Friday, and on the next Monday I called my old friend Dick Roland, who also happens to be my stockbroker as well. I made an appointment to see him the next day. On the door it said, "Williams and Randolph Inc."

"Hi Dick."

"Hi, DJ. Who is this beautiful woman with you?" He said in his musical voice.

Dick's voice is the kind that once you hear those melodious baritone sounds, you never forget it. I could walk into a room of a hundred people all talking at the same time and I would recognize his voice.

She said, "Gosh is he good looking, is he married? Maybe I should have waited and picked him instead."

Then she poked me in the ribs and giggled.

"Dick, this is my wife Denise of 6 weeks, she picks on me constantly."

"And with good reason I'm sure. What can I do for you today?" He said.

"We want to open an account for her with the money from the sale of her house."

"I want to put this money somewhere where it will grow." Dee said.

"Let me suggest a new fund that is showing great promise, it's called Future Concepts Fund. I think it will have good growth potential." He said.

"I have $11,558.86 balance from the sale of the house and I want to put it all in the fund. I used $857.00 to pay my bills off. I didn't want to be a burden on our finances." Dee said.

She made it a point to point at me and smile at Dick as she said it. Denise and Dick got along like old friends, I'm sure that we'll have more business together in the future.

We had the rest of her stuff moved to our house right away. She was surprised at all the furniture that we haven't already moved. Now we have to figure out what to do with it.

Chapter 20

The Pickup

Denise comes up with a wild idea every once in a while. We were driving home from an unusually boring PTA meeting, Harry was asleep between the girls in the back seat and Denise was laying with her head on my lap.

"I've got an idea! I think that next Friday we should go out and have a small dinner. Then we could go to a nightclub where we would meet as strangers and steal away into the night, maybe a nearby motel, and make mad passionate love. What do you think?" She said.

"As long as I get to make mad passionate love to you, I'm for it!"

"OK, I'll call you Henry, and you can call me Ann Boleyn." She said.

"I'll drive my car so you won't know what I'm wearing. Besides if I drive it'll seem more like you're picking me up."

She is normally a light eater, she has a salad for lunch at work every day, but for the last week, she has been hungry all the time. She walked in after work tonight and instead of jumping me, she called in an order for a pizza. And I thought I didn't understand her before.

It was a busy week. We took the girls to band practice and Brownies, went grocery shopping, had pizza twice, went to the park and Denise went shopping for a special dress for the occasion Friday night.

She wouldn't let me see the dress saying, "It's special, and if you don't recognize me in it, there won't be any bedtime story for you that night". She said.

Last week she ate all that food and this morning when I was shaving, she stuck her head into the bathroom and said, "I've lost two pounds since Wednesday."

"That's nice."

"No, it's not, I don't feel good about it. I was up to one oh one, and now I'm back to ninety nine." She said.

I don't get it, but I'm not going to say anything, it'll just get me in trouble.

The following Friday we got ready for our little Shakespearean play. I put on my best suit and tie for the occasion.

I parked the car on the street down the block from the club we picked and I have already reserved a room for us at the El Rancho Motel.

She was supposed to park her car around back where it wouldn't draw attention to itself till we can pick it up tomorrow. I walked in and went directly to the bar and ordered a drink.

"May I help you sir?" The bartender said.

"I don't drink alcohol, but if you could give me a Pepsi in a glass like a drink, that's all I need."

"Comin' right up." He said.

She is wearing a fantastic looking dress of pink with little sequin clusters. It's a long dress with a deep thin neckline. She's wearing pink shoes, stockings and gloves, gold earrings and necklace.

It is quite a stunning effect since her hair is still that bright red that she did for the wedding. She's sitting by herself at a table in the middle of the bar.

"Who's the babe in the pink over there?" I asked.

"Don't know, never seen her before." The bartender said.

"Why don't you have the waitress get her a drink?"

"Sure thing." He said.

After the waitress brought her drink and I paid the bartender, I went to the table. "Hi, I'm Henry, would you like to dance?"

The place isn't very full yet and my voice carried around the room. People looked up when she stood up to dance with me.

I told her what has been said at the bar and we laughed about it.

"All the men at the bar are looking at you and talking." You should hear some of it."

"I'd like to, maybe you can get it word for word for me." She said.

"You seem to be attracting attention, my love."

"Yes, isn't it fun?"

We danced to three songs. Her body is so soft and smooth, I ran my hands over her back and her front. I felt her up so the guys at the bar can see, and she smiled as I did it.

When the jukebox went silent, I walked her to her table, thanked her for the dance and went back to my seat at the bar.

The bartender was there to meet me when I sat down.

"Pretty good lookin' chick, how'd you do it?" He said.

"Do what?"

"You know, get her to dance with you. Feel her up."

"Nothing special, I introduced myself and asked her to dance and she stood up. The rest just comes naturally."

"Who is she, anyway?" He asked.

"She said her name is Ann Boleyn."

I started to go again, but another guy is talking to her. It isn't long before he was back at his seat at the bar talking to himself and the bartender. This is going better than I ever thought it would.

The bartender's back standing in front of me. "The guy down there asked her to dance and she turned him down. She said she only likes guys named Henry. What's that all about?"

"I guess Henry gets it tonight." With that I blew on my nails and polished them on my jacket.

I got up and walked to her table.

"Excuse me miss, would you care to dance with me again?"

"Yes Henry, I just love the way you dance." She said.

There's that lilting voice again, and the beaming smile. She's having a lot of fun with this too.

She kissed me on the cheek and nibbled my ear. She told me to feel her up some more and be sure the bartender sees it, so I did. I told her about what had been said and we both laughed about it again.

"I've never been picked up in a bar before. This is very exciting, but if you don't ask me to go to bed with you pretty soon I'm going to explode, let's get out of here!" She whispered in my ear.

One thing about my Pixie, she knows what she wants. I think the curtain has been run down on this play. We danced till the music ran out again.

"One more act and we'll leave, back in a minute."

I left her at the table and went back to the bar again. The bartender has a bewildered look on his face.

"You don't look special, what is it with you?" He said.

"What do you mean?"

"That is the best dressed, best lookin' woman to come into this bar in months. She turned down a really great lookin' guy over there and danced with you. How come?" He asked with a bewildered look on his face.

"Maybe it's my cute smile. There's no accounting for taste, but watch this. I'm going to ask her to go to a motel and spend the night with me."

Here comes the payoff.

"Excuse me miss, would you like to go somewhere with me and make mad passionate love to me?"

Everyone in the club heard me because it got awful quite right then.

"Why thank you, Henry, I'd love to." She said.

She stood up and took my arm. I nodded to the bartender as we walked out. He just shook his head.

We walked out and down the block to my car. I opened the door for her, and she slid in onto the seat like a cat. As I walked around the rear of the car, I noticed a couple of guys standing in front of the club we just left.

I fired the car up and we started toward the motel. We had a short drive to the motel and I let her into the room. I brought our video camera like she said.

"Are you ready with the camera?" She asked.

"Yes, go ahead."

I held the camera at the ready and turned it on and motioned to her. She knocked on the door, I opened it and she came in and faced the camera. She was dressed in that pink outfit and she did a strip to the music on a cassette tape we picked out earlier. "On the road again", Willie said it right.

I knew it! She was wearing pink under the dress too. I would have bet on it! I filmed the whole thing as she did this long sensual strip for the camera - and me.

When she took the last of her clothes off, and with the camera still running, she came to me and said in her little girl voice, "Hi mister, you wanna tango?"

I propped the camera on the dresser and pointed it at the bed and we did the second act of our play. This one was a lot more fun than the first act. We got home late, but we both wanted to play the tape once before we went to bed.

Chapter 21

Feeling Good About You

The first thing this month was a long eleven day trip to Bismarck. The day I returned, Denise was at home when I got there.

"Hi babe, how is the love of my life feeling?"

"I'm terrible, I've been sick all day and I can't see the doctor till tomorrow." She said.

"I'll go with you. Can I do anything for you now?"

I made supper for me and the kids, she didn't feel much like eating, so I made her some chicken noodle soup and seven-up, and helped her get it down. She was still nauseous all night, I did what I could but I didn't know enough about doctoring and nursing to do much good.

I took her to see Dr. Henderson at nine in the morning. When we walked in, Annie the receptionist greeted us with a big smile that faded almost instantly when she saw Denise. Something must be wrong.

"I'll tell the doctor you're here." She said and disappeared into the back.

The nurse came and took Denise back to a room right away. It was only a few minutes before the doctor came out to see me.

"Well doctor, how is she? What's the matter with her?"

"You mean you don't know?" Doc said.

"How would I know? I'm not a doctor!" I said.

"Well DJ, you haven't been paying attention to your wife. I just had a nice little chat with her. She has been sending you signals for months now. I knew it every time my wife was pregnant. Come on with me." He said.

"Pregnant? Pregnant! That's wonderful! How is she? When is it due? Where is she?" My brain went into high speed, and my mouth couldn't keep up.

I went running behind the doctor to the room where she was, but she didn't look very happy to see me. Her face was a sallow color that was not there when she left the house earlier.

"She will have some large mood swings, but she is doing fine. There are many problems a mother may have during pregnancy, and nausea is only one of them. I have given her a list of possible problems and some ways to make them less of a problem to her."

"You two haven't had a baby in several years, so remember, if anything continues on too long, or seems to be hard to handle, you will see me immediately. Bye the way, the baby is due in February, maybe it will be a happy Valentines Day for both of you." The Doc said.

I took her home and by the time we pulled into the driveway in back she was smiling a little smile again and her color was beginning to come back. I was glad of that.

We walked in the back way and she collapsed on the couch in the living room.

"The worst thing about being pregnant is that I'm tired all the time. It was like that the last time and that's the first thing that told me I was pregnant. I just don't want to do anything. Now with all this nausea and constipation to go along with being tired all the time, it's just been a barrel of laughs." She said.

"Do you know when it happened?"

"I know exactly when it happened, I even know which day on our honeymoon it was, that first day in Great Bend. Think about it, do you remember that day?" She said.

"Oh yeah! I remember! That day might go down in history as one of the most memorable days ever. But, how did you get pregnant that night and not before with all the sex we were having?" I said.

"I started using birth control pills when I knew you were the one." She giggled. "I knew that we'd be doing some kinda sexy things and I wanted to be protected if you didn't turn out to be the one."

"You rat."

"I was using a backup every time we did anything. I stopped using anything the morning of the wedding and stopped taking my birth control pills before that." She said.

"You wanted to get pregnant?"

"Yes, I wanted to have your child, this will be something that you can look at every day and see me. One day you can say, 'I made that', and I'll be able to say 'I put the icing on it'." She said.

I thought it might be a good time for a little music, I turned on the stereo and selected a tape. For most of the year, she has been listening to her new tape by The Captain and Tennille.

And her favorite song is "Do that to me one more time". Somehow, I didn't think that was the one she wanted to here right now. I put on some happy sounding country music for her.

September   Month 4

The trips with the team are turning into a blur now, I don't know where we're going or where we've been, I just know when it's time to go home. When the plane landed, I followed the guys down the concourse to the baggage area.

They were all talking and having a good time and all I could think about was Denise and how she must be feeling. About the time I found a spot at the baggage carousel, I felt a hand on my arm and a familiar voice in my ear.

"Hi, need a ride?" The voice asked.

It was Linda dressed in her business clothes. Boy does she look good. She looks good anytime, but she was really exquisite that day. Gene came up next to us and cleared his throat.

"Linda, this is Gene DiAngelo. He is one of the guys on the team and a very good friend of mine. Gene, this is Linda, an old friend of Denise's and mine."

"Nice to meet you, Linda. You sure are stunning, I hope you meet him at the plane again. Oh, darn, here come our bags, see you later." Gene said.

"What are you doing here, I was expecting to take a cab home. There isn't anything wrong is there?"

"No, nothing's wrong.

She dropped me off and went back to work. Normally I'd have been flattered that such a beautiful woman thought enough to do what she did for me today, but I'm kind of in a funk over how bad Dee has been feeling this month.

Denise and I saw the doctor again and he told us the baby is due February fifth. Denise has already picked out names for both the boy and the girl. Her name will be Marion Marie, a little pixie, and his name will be Charles Bruce McAllister.

"Remember last month when you said I could look at her every day and see you. How right you were. Won't it be great if she does look like you?" I said.

"Don't forget, it could be a boy." She said.

"No, I'm convinced that it will be a girl and she will be the exact duplicate of you. And you will teach her all your tricks about how to bewitch and confuse the male population."

I took her car and the van to be serviced for the winter, I don't want something happening to the car and her being stranded or hurt. There are some things you can prevent just by using a little common sense.

Later that night when we were laying in bed and talking, she said. "I don't understand it. After two babies, I should be able to handle this one a lot easier, I've got nausea every day, it was supposed to end last month.

Do you know what that doctor told me? 'Nausea during pregnancy is associated with good fetal health.' It may be good fetal health, but it sure is making me feel bad. More constipation and abdominal pressure and discomfort than the other two put together. And I'm gaining weight like there's no tomorrow." She said.

"Ow! Ow! That hurt! Do you want to feel the baby move? Put your hand right here." She said.

I did, and she kicked me. The baby, not Dee.

It's time for her to go to sleep and the kid decides to do a tap dance on her belly button. That girl is going to be a good dancer.

"Just think how good you'll look after the baby comes and you take all the extra weight off." I said.

I'm trying to make her feel a little better about herself and her pregnancy, but it isn't working.

"I just hope that I don't have trouble with hemorrhoids and varicose veins. I don't think I could handle them right now." She said.

"I suppose that means that you're not interested in sex either."

"Sex? Are you kidding? See me around May sometime, or June, maybe July." She began to laugh, then chuckled till she fell asleep.

I went with the team on another blurred trip at the end of September, we'll be back in early October. I called her every day and every night, the calls help both of us. She has been plagued with everything there is that can go wrong during a pregnancy.

When I call, I usually let her talk the whole time. For the last few days she has had swelling and gas pains. Every so often she would say it's a good thing that I was out of town, because she wanted someone to beat up on, and she couldn't use the kids, they didn't have anything to do with it.

October   Month 5

The flight landed at ten thirty and the four of us did our dance down the concourse to the baggage area again.

As we walked in, Gene said to me, "The beauty in the green dress must be waiting on you DJ, none of us knows anyone that looks that good."

It was Laura dressed in a green suit, blouse, shoes and handbag, standing in the far corner with a big smile on her face. She came over to me as we walked in and I introduced Laura to the guys, they all stood around with their mouths open. Our bags came down the conveyor and we started for the parking lot.

"Hi, how was your trip? Let me help you with your bags." She said.

She picked up my briefcase and we were off.

"OK. How's Denise, is she getting along all right?"

"Yes, but she is having a bout with what the doctor calls 'Breathlessness'. She has trouble getting enough oxygen. He gave her some exercises to do, maybe they will help. She called me last week and asked me to take you home, I took an early lunch so I'd be on time." She said.

Laura dropped me off and went back to work.

When I walked in Denise was on the couch and she wanted to talk, we sat on the couch in the living room and she talked for hours. I don't know why, maybe I'll never know, but I love the sound of her voice and the sight of her smile, they always make me feel good inside.

She wasn't smiling when I arrived, but after she unloaded some of her problems, she began to smile again. It's been three hours, we've had lunch and she's talked the whole time, and now she's smiling that big smile she's known for.

"Quick, feel the baby move again!" Dee said.

I reached where she said, only a little higher, and squeezed gently.

"Not there you clown, here." She laughed, smacked me and moved my hand down to her stomach.

When I got my hand in the right place, I could tell that this baby is dancing again. Harry didn't do all that, he was an easy pregnancy and an easy birth, there weren't many problems before, during or after the birth. From what has been going on with this one, it looks like we were really lucky with him.

We sat on the couch and I held her for another half hour, when out of the blue she began to cry.

"I seem to cry over everything." She said.

"What were you crying over this time?"

"Because I can't make love to you and won't be able to for several months, maybe years." She said and laughed little at her joke.

"That's not something to cry about."

She finally began to smile when I said that. It grew a little and in a few minutes she was chuckling, then even a little laughing after that. She giggled about that for nearly an hour after that. She was feeling pretty good by the time the kids came home from school.

It's fall, and the leaves are turning to all the reds, oranges and yellows you can imagine. I thought there might be a good way to help relieve some of the stress she must be feeling. I brought the van around and the kids, Denise and I took a ride in the country outside of town. About halfway to Haysville, Jennifer turned on the radio and began to sing along with the song, soon the three of them were singing to the radio.

I knew it! Denise was singing too. She was feeling better now and the smile was returning slowly. I know the doctor said 'No junk food!', but a little pizza now and then can't hurt. I stopped in a little place in Mulvane and we all pigged out.

The next day, we were grocery shopping when we ran into Rusty Brown. I introduced Rusty to her.

"He's the maintenance shop chief and a reserve Warrant Officer where I work, I count him as one of my best friends."

He had only heard about her from Gene and I, but hadn't met her yet.

"The worst thing is having to listen to her complain about how fat she is." I said.

"You're not fat Denise, my wife had the same problem as you with our second one, but inside three months she was as thin and beautiful as ever." Rusty said.

He couldn't have done anything better for her. The smile that came over her could have lit up the store.

"Denise, you will never know how lovingly he talks of you at work. I thought he was blowing smoke, so

I asked the guys on the team. Gene described you the same way." He said.

We stood and talked till the standing got to Dee. I said good-bye to Rusty and took her home.

November   Month 6

It was really cold and snowy when the plane landed. We had our heaviest coats and sweaters on as we made our exit. Gene came up beside me as we walked the last mile to the baggage area.

"I want to see what beautiful woman is waiting for you this time, the last two were fantastic. Are they available?" Gene asked.

"I thought you had a girlfriend." I said.

"I did, she said I was always gone and if she was going to have a guy around she wanted him there all the time. She didn't like the traveling. I don't like it either, but it goes with the job." He said.

"I'll find out, but you may not like what you hear."

"I'll take that chance. Ask for me, would you?" He said.

Just then we rounded the last corner and against the far wall was a blonde haired woman dressed in a heavy winter coat and dark blue wool skirt and sweater with snow boots. Gene is still walking next to me although he slowed down considerably when he saw Mary.

"Man! Even in winter clothes she's a knockout, don't you know any ugly women?" He said.

"Sure, would you like me to fix you up with one?"

She moved slowly and deliberately toward us, and as she did, Gene was frozen still next to me. Her voice was soft and soothing as she spoke. "Hi DJ, have a nice trip?" She said.

"Mary, this is Gene, George and Nick. Gene has been admiring the beautiful ladies that met me at the plane the past few months. Mary is a friend of Denise and I know her a little too. These are the guys I travel all over the country with. Boy, it must be cold outside, let's get going to the house and get warmed up."

"Hi guys, nice to meet you, we've all heard so much about you." She said. "Especially Gene."

As we walked out into the cold, I noticed that Gene was still standing there with his bags, staring at us. We moved briskly to her car.

"He's kind of cute." She said.

Well there's an answer to Gene's question and I didn't even have to ask.

"Let me give you his number. I said.

Denise has had so many problems with this pregnancy and put on so much weight that the doctor told her not to go back to work till after the birth and he gave me a letter detailing all of it which I was to deliver to her boss.

I made an appointment with Mr. Hughes for the next day. His office was big and beautifully decorated with wood everywhere. It is "The Boss's Office". Mr. Hughes is a good understanding guy and one of the best guys I've met since I've been here, there won't be any problem with her job.

Mr. Hughes told me, "Really, DJ, I know what it was like for her before she met you, I'll help in any way I can. Tell her to take as long as she needs. She is one of our best workers, we wouldn't want to lose her."

The next day, I hired a maid to come in on Tuesday and Friday to clean the house and cook and freeze meals so Denise doesn't have to stand in the kitchen so much.

I went through an agency, I didn't want to spend a lot of time interviewing women for a job. The agency lady said if there was a problem with the one they sent just call and there would be a different one the next time, she'll start next week.

For the next few days Denise was plagued with backache, heartburn and headaches. She has put on at least twenty pounds, maybe more.

During the weekend and the beginning of the week, Denise complained about the pains being more severe and more frequent, but because she is in the sixth month, we both attributed it to another of the unusual things that have been happening during this pregnancy.

We had been home about four days this time and about five o'clock as I was fixing supper, Denise grabbed me by the arm so hard that she left a bruise and said, "It's time!"

I yelled to Jennifer to feed Harry, "I'll call you as soon as I know something", and I hurried Dee to the van. If it weren't for Jennifer and Melissa taking care of the house and Harry, I'd have already been crazy with this whole thing.

I called the emergency number the doctor gave me and rushed her to the hospital, where he was waiting when we arrived. There was a lot of rushing around and I got out of the way.

I remembered what the doctor told me months ago, "Your job is to notify me and get her to the hospital with time to spare, after that, just get out of the way till I call you." So I got out of the way and went to the waiting room.

I've been going to Doc Henderson since the first day I arrived in town, and when Dee and I were dating, I took her to him just so she could decide if she wanted to change. I sat in the waiting room for thirty or forty minutes waiting for the doctor came out to see me.

"It was pre-term labor, I gave her some labor-inhibiting drugs to stop it. I also administered medicine to hasten the maturation of the infants lungs, the crucial factor in the infants survival is the lungs ability to work."

"If the lungs fully develop in the next few weeks, and this happens again, we shouldn't have as much to worry about as we did this time." Doc said.

"Is the baby going to be OK now?"

"Yes, we're out of the woods on this one. Be sure she gets good nutrition from now on, she doesn't smoke, so that's a plus." He said.

"Is Denise going to be OK now?"

"Yes, she is resting comfortably, but that won't last long. I want her to stay the night and I'll look in on her tomorrow. What about you?" He said.

"I guess I'll stay till she can go home. I have some money and I'll call the kids, so I'll be OK."

"Good, see you in the morning."

He kept her an extra night there and I slept in the chairs in the room and walked the halls and talked to all the doctors and nurses. They all treated me good and tried to explain things about difficult pregnancies in the terms that I could understand.

I took her home about ten in the morning of the second day, put her in bed, and collapsed on the couch for a good solid four hour nap. I awoke to the gentle tunes of the damn phone.

"Hello." I said weakly into the phone.

"Hi, DJ. It's Linda, how is she?"

"It was a close call, but she made it through it. The doctor called it pre-term labor. We could have lost the baby if he hadn't done everything just right. She's asleep in bed now."

"Do you need anything, can anyone help? Does she need anything? Can I do anything?" She asked.

"I don't know enough to ask the right questions, but I'll bet she'd welcome a visit from any of her friends after she gets some sleep."

"OK, I'll take care of it, see ya." She said.

We finished supper around six and I was putting the dishes into the dishwasher when the doorbell rang. When I opened the door, I found the Big Four in the flesh standing there smiling.

"Come on in, she's up and on the couch."

They sat down and all of them began to talk at once. That was my cue to take the kids back to their room and sneak downstairs to my below-ground living room. I turned the TV on and stretched out on the couch for a couple of comedy shows.

The basement had been converted into a large family room, a bedroom and a bathroom. I like the privacy I get down here. Dee and I come down here to get away from the kids. Just as the eight o'clock show was coming on, Linda came down the stairs and sat on the couch next to me.

"How have you been?" She asked.

"Pretty good, I think."

"You liar, you're having a harder time than she is. This is me, remember, the one you can't fool. I've known you for almost ten years, and we've been very close lately, I can tell." She said.

Sure enough, Sandy called at my office the following Tuesday and insisted that I help her move some furniture for her.

I met her at her house at four thirty. She had some trouble with her husband a few months back and since she got rid of him there were some things she wanted to give to Goodwill or somebody. We loaded as much as we could and hauled it away.

December   Month 7

Every December we take our trip to Sixth Army Headquarters in San Francisco, and as always we had a good time. Last year was better, because I had the love of my life with me. It was warm for the time of year when we landed in Wichita this time.

Wait, an idea just hit me! If everything runs according to schedule, there should be another beautiful woman waiting in the baggage area, and I bet I know who it is.

Just like last month, Gene was walking next to me as we rounded the last corner, and I was right. Sandy is standing there dressed in a red coat with black fake fur on the collar.

"Hi DJ, how was your trip?" She said.

Now's my chance!

"Gee Sandy, I must have caught a bug while I was out there, I'd better take a cab straight home, but could you take Gene, here, home with you?"

As I said this, I faked a little cough and nudged her in the side. When she looked at me, I winked at her and she smiled back.

"I'd be glad to, see you later DJ, come on Gene, I'll show you where I parked. Let me help you with your bags." She said.

Gene was dumbfounded, his mouth was open as she grabbed his hand and led him away.

Monday mornings have always been hard for me. I came into the office a little early to make coffee and just sit there with it for a few minutes before the day got started. Gene arrived before the others.

"Morning Gene, how was your weekend?" As if I didn't know. Sandy had called yesterday to confirm that she got the wink.

"That woman, do you know what she did?" She said.

This was beginning to sound like an old movie. "No Ollie, what did she do?" I said, trying to sound like Stan Laurel. I just saw one of their old movies on TV over the weekend.

"She said she had to stop at her house and turn up the heat. So we went in and she got me a drink and she came out of her bedroom dressed in a thin waist length see-through thing and sat on my lap and kissed me. She really turned up my heat." He said.

"What's wrong with that?"

"I never got home yet, I still have my clothes in the car."

"And you're complaining?"

"No, not at all, I just wanted to know what you said to her, you were no more sick than I was." He said.

"You heard me, I didn't say anything. Besides you like a little loving, she likes a little loving, I thought you two might have something in common."

"Man, you don't know. Well thanks, I'm going to stay with her for a few more days. Who knows?" He said.

Sandy called later in the morning and we talked about Gene. "I think I really like him, I'll let you know. Talk to you later. See ya."

During the week Denise complained of headaches, swelling and gas pains. But the one thing that got her the most was, "I have to pee all the time."

The baby is growing very fast and the extra weight and the baby moving around a lot is wreaking havoc on her body. When the baby sits on her bladder just right, Denise winces.

The Saturday after the San Francisco trip, Dee and I were watching the Chiefs play the Steelers on TV when the doorbell rang.

Denise is so big now that she doesn't even try to get up for something like this. I answered the door and showed Linda and Sandy in to a seat on the couch, I took a seat in a chair off to the side while they talked.

"How are you feeling?" Linda asked.

"Feel the baby kicking. He says it's a girl." Dee said.

"Are you going to the party Dee?" Sandy asked.

"Are you joking? Do I look like it? I'm as big as a house, I've put on twenty seven pounds and I've got two more months to go." Dee said.

"We could go together and sit at the same table, you could watch over the guys." Linda said.

"Good idea, maybe some of them would sit and talk to me too." Dee said.

The three of them laughed about that.

"How has he been doing during the pregnancy?" Dee asked.

Sandy began to tell about finding Gene and how well they got along.

"I'd like to invite him to go to the party with me." Sandy said.

"I think it is a good idea. Gene has met all of you and was overwhelmed by each one of you, until he met Sandy. He has talked about her every day since."

"This pregnancy has been tough, I never had so much trouble and I've been a bitch to live with. He has been a rock." Dee said.

Linda laughed and said, "It must be all his fault."
And she pointed her thumb at me.

"No, he's the greatest. I have him put vitamin E on
my skin to keep from getting stretch marks, besides I
like the feel of his warm hands on me. He rubs everything too much, but I still like the feel of it, so I must
not be dead yet." Dee said.

Linda said, "He'll be after you just like before just
as soon as the baby is born and the extra weight goes
away. Don't you worry, if there's one thing I know,
it's that no one can take your place in his life."

"We have a lot of fun with him, but that's all it
is, fun. You are the one! I saw Laura and Mary for
lunch one day this week and when I mentioned his
name they both smiled, so they must like it too."

All three agreed with what she said and that it was
all my fault as well.

January   Month 8

The girls had set up a time for all of them to meet at
the party. I escorted Dee in and two of them met her
at the door and went to a table toward the back of
the ballroom. They had five tables setup in a circle.

They already had Dee a Seven-up to drink. I took
a seat and the girls began to talk. Sandy isn't here
yet. Oh I spoke too soon, here she comes with Gene.
They sat across from us and he looked kind of funny
when he saw me.

"Now I know what she was talking about when Sandy made such a big deal about this party." Gene said.

He looked around and saw Linda, Laura and Mary at the tables next to us and smiled.

"You didn't have to ask for me, did you?" He said.

"No, it was answered before you asked it, but I couldn't tell you."

I watched Denise very carefully, I could tell she was uncomfortable and she was wishing she could do some of what they were doing.

We decided to leave just after midnight, we said our good-byes and they all said they would be around to help if she needed it.

We arrived back from a short driving trip to Hutchinson and Great Bend on Thursday the tenth. Laura was at the house dressed in a maid's uniform, sitting with Dee on the couch.

"Hi DJ, I came to help Dee with her house today, I took a day off." Laura said.

Denise has been so tired this month, I'm beginning to worry about her. I called the doctor, but he said it was normal and watch her carefully for the next few weeks. We're getting close to the date.

The girls put on a baby shower for Denise on the fifteenth. I handled the front door, took their coats, served the refreshments and found extra seating for the late comers.

I counted sixteen women and the place was jumping. Once the doorbell stopped ringing, I went to my hideout downstairs until Linda came down to tell me they were leaving soon.

The doctor's visits seem like they are every day now, and February is right around the corner.

I was talking to Nurse Annie in the waiting room as the doctor examined her.

"The baby will come when they damn well feel like it so don't get too excited about it, just do what Doctor tells you." Doc said.

Chapter 22

Look What I've Got

There was no way that I was going to be traveling all around the country with the team when my darling wife Denise is nine months pregnant and coming up on her due date the next day. I've got lots of leave time so I just took leave till the baby comes, whenever that may be.

It was February in Kansas, and very cold and miserable, I'm trying to get things ready for a run to the hospital and I had made everything as ready as I could.

In October, I put new snow tires on the van and parked it in the garage to use as a ambulance substitute. When we made the trip to the hospital in November, I found out that I had forgotten to pack any clothes for her. Good thinking!

After that scare, I helped her pack a suitcase with whatever she might need for the real thing. I packed everything that I could think of and she checked my work when I was finished.

"You forgot my toiletries, I need a toothbrush, toothpaste, comb and brush and some cologne, get the gold bottle on the second shelf. And I need a pair of small pajamas, better make it two." She said.

I put the suitcase in the van so I didn't have to worry about forgetting it again.

It's Thursday the fifth of February and there is no baby in the cradle with our name on it. There hasn't even been any signs of one. The baby is home, but she's not answering the door or the phone. Denise says there's not much movement, but the doctor doesn't seem to be worried.

For months, each time I was in town, I went with Denise to the hospital twice a week for natural child birth classes, Lamaze classes. When I was gone, one of her friends would go with her.

It's a good thing those women are as close as they are, Denise really needed the help that they all so graciously provided, and not one of them asked anything in return.

I have been calling the doctor or his office every afternoon since the first of the month with a report on her condition. I took leave from work for the duration so I could be there with her.

The weather has been nasty since the middle of last month, but now it seems to be turning colder, it was five degrees yesterday.

Friday afternoon the Big Four arrived one by one from Mary, the earliest at three thirty, to Linda, the latest at five thirty. The talk was the same from each of them.

"OK, you're officially overdue, when's it going to be?" Linda said.

Sandy came up with an idea that made me laugh.

"My grandmother said to drink castor oil to start labor." She said.

"Yuck! Sandy I don't think I could ever get it down, besides I'm sure there's none in the house." Dee said.

"Well, if you don't like that." Mary said. "I know you like Mexican food and they say that it does the same thing. Worse yet try canned sardines in the oil they come in, or vinegar and oil on your salad."

"Have you guys noticed how cold it is outside, I don't really want to go out to eat in this stuff." Dee said.

Linda jumped in. "I have a list, but they won't work now either, but they ought to be good for a laugh, here goes. You could ride a horse, take a ride in a car on a bumpy road, or go walking or jogging."

"The horse thing sounds like it would be dangerous, but you're right, as cold as it is, I can just see me out jogging." Dee said.

"Seriously girls. Dee, why not try something that you can do here at home. You have stairs to the basement, you could walk up the stairs when you felt like it."

"You could take a laxative, that's supposed to work, I don't know personally. Or you could soak your feet in a tub of hot water, it's supposed to make your blood circulate better and get things going." Laura said.

During all of this, we were eating chicken and all the trimmings, they each had each stopped at a fast food chicken place and brought dinner. The party broke up around eight, and as usual Dee was too tired to move.

We slept in, but after breakfast, she decided to try the ideas that Laura had come up with.

"If you'll keep me from falling, I'll try to get up and down the stairs a couple times." She said.

"Sure, hold on."

I helped her downstairs and we were climbing the stairs for the first time when the doorbell rang.

"Who could that be at this time in the morning." She said.

We both stumbled to the door. Who else, her mother and Dad.

"Hi Denise, we came to see if there was anything we could do for you." Her mother said.

"Mom, what I need most is to go to the Post Office and get this delivered."

"She made a joke, I can't believe my ears. Denise made a joke. Maybe there's hope for her after all." Her dad was grinning large.

Her mom and dad stayed all day and fixed dinner for us and the kids and left around seven. We never did get to try any of the ideas Laura mentioned.

Sunday we always go to church, but she said she didn't dare go to church and deliver it in a pew, so we stayed home and played cribbage. Linda and Bill came by about noon with some pizza and we had lunch together.

The cribbage game became four handed and we played the rest of the afternoon. It was the first time I had seen Denise really smile one like she meant it in a long time.

Monday started like most Mondays, the kids get ready for school, make breakfast, lunches, try to get Dee comfortable, TV cartoons and a talk show or two. It started to snow around three, just about the time that everyone is going home from work.

The kids played outside in it till supper time, then they tried to start a snowman, I told them we could finish it tomorrow. It snowed all evening and by the time the news came on at six, the weatherman said there were winter storm warnings out. I knew in my gut it would be tonight, and I thought I'd better call the Doc.

"Hello?" He said.

"Hi Doc, it's DJ. I've been watching the TV weatherman tell about the storm, and I'm betting that tonight is the night. What do you think?"

"I tend to agree with you. I've been in the kid business a long time and they always pick the worst time to come through. Can you get her to the hospital safely in this weather?" Doc said.

"Yeah, I've got everything ready to go."

"You call me! No matter what time it is, it'll be delivered tonight." Doc said.

I knew right then that I should have put on chains, but you can't think of everything.

I put her to bed at nine and stayed up for the news and weather on channel ten. Nothing new here, they're still predicting six to eight inches of snow tonight. I'd better get some sleep, it's going to be a long night.

At one thirty in the morning Dee kicked me out of bed and screamed, "It's time!" I called the doctor and rushed her to the hospital in the van. I thought it would be better if she laid on the floor of the van, the streets are slippery and I didn't want her falling or bumping anything.

It was very tough driving, I slid around almost every corner, some of them felt like I went through the corner twice. Fortunately there were no cars on the streets except me. I did a one-eighty at a corner that looked pretty safe.

I'm taking it really slow at twenty miles per hour, but the wind is blowing hard and the streets are extremely slippery. I executed a very nice three-sixty at the corner of two four-lane streets, and she screamed at me, "Are you trying to kill me?"

I drove up to the door and almost before I could stop, they were outside opening the side doors on the van and taking her inside on a gurney. I managed to park it and find my way back inside. I knew this was the real thing so I just went to the nurses station and identified myself and told them where I'd be waiting.

I found a semi-comfortable chair in the waiting room till I could go back to the labor room. It was only twenty or thirty minutes before a nurse came out to show me where she was. I followed her back to find Denise all smiles. What is this, she's still pregnant and she's smiling?

"The doctor said I was dilated enough to make it a natural birth and the delivery room should be ready in a few minutes. Come and hold my hand. Are you going to be here?" Dee said.

"Of course, all night if necessary. I'll be in to see you as soon as they'll let me."

It only took half an hour in the labor room before they moved her.

"Why don't you find a chair, Mr. McAllister? It could be a couple of hours, someone will find you when we need you." One of the nurses said.

It was just coming up to five in the morning when Doc Henderson found me rereading everything in the waiting room.

"You were right, It's a girl! No wonder there were pains, the baby is 20 inches long and 9 pounds 2 ounces. Come on, you want to see her don't you?" He said.

They had baby Marion cleaned up and Dee was holding her when the Doc and I found her. What a sight! A one hour old baby is something to behold.

With her mother as beautiful as she is, It'll be hard to break the mold, she will be too. Would I like to hold the baby? What I'd like to hold is the mother and she can hold the baby. We held each other for several minutes that way.

"Denise, I love you more than anything in this world."

"I love you too, DJ." She said.

She kissed me! A real kiss, not just one of those pecks on the cheek or lips I've been getting for the last few months. The first time she has done that in a long time. It looks like she'll recuperate just fine. I sure hope so.

I stayed with Denise until they ordered me to go home and get some sleep. It was an adventure going home and by that time I was ready for sleep. I wrote a note to take some warm clothes for Dee and the baby to wear home.

Each time I went to visit, I stopped by the nursery to see baby Marion through the glass. The nurses were very cooperative and would hold her up for me to see.

Dee stayed in the hospital for another couple days and the storm raged on. I left the van at home in the garage until they told me she was ready to go home,

I felt a lot safer driving my little blue car in this snow and ice.

On the morning we were supposed to leave the hospital and take our prize package home, Doc Henderson paid Denise one last visit.

"Denise, you remember to do your exercises regularly, you're already doing the Kegels, aren't you?" He said.

"Yes, and I'll start the others next week." Dee said.

"You don't have to wait that long, I gave you the list of exercises, but let's go through them once more. The leg slide, curl up, pelvic tilt, stretching, bridging, runners exercises and stretching and the tailor position."

"You had a rough pregnancy, but the delivery was pretty easy, but you will need some time to heal. I think you should refrain from sex for eight weeks." Doc said.

"Eight weeks is a long time, don't you think that's too much?" Dee said.

"OK, six weeks if you exercise regularly and lose thirty pounds." He said.

"You can count on it, I haven't had any for nine months and I'm ready to party with this guy." She said.

She looked toward me with that little Pixie smile I hadn't seen for months and said, "That sex you talked about last year, I'll call you when I'm ready, it'll be soon. Be ready!"

"Watch her and watch out for yourself, DJ. She has a list of appointments to bring the baby for check-ups, I'll be seeing you soon." He said.

We came home to an empty house. There was a note on the kitchen table.

"Jennifer called to tell us about the baby, we picked up the kids. Call us when you want them back. Linda."

Chapter 23

Up On The Roof

It has been three months since baby Marion Marie was born. I had forgotten how pretty little babies can be, I also forgot how much trouble they can be. But between the two of us and with a little help from our friends and the kids, we are getting through it.

Denise has been exercising everyday religiously, she weighed one oh eight when she had her six week checkup. She put on forty pounds because of the baby, and took off thirty one of it, but the part that makes her so mad is that with all the naps, snacking, cooking for the whole family and her workout routine all messed up. She's toning up her body, but has put on a little weight as well.

She looks so much better now, I can hardly stand it. She probably doesn't realize that the extra weight has been added in all the right places. I can't see measurements with my eye very good, but everything is more round and firm now and I love it.

I've grabbed things now and then, when I've had the chance, and they feel good to me. I'd say it all went into the right places, but I not going to tell her about it unless she brings it up.

Doctor Henderson said she could begin having sex with me again at six to eight weeks. Just about

241

the time that she thought she was ready, I had to go out of town on a trip for thirteen days, and when I returned, she was caught up with taking care of the baby.

We tried to have a little sex at eight weeks, but it hurt her somehow and we stopped. She decided to lay off for two more weeks and try again. It was a little better but she was still sore, so we still weren't able to finish. Maybe soon.

We are to visit the doctor tomorrow for her last postpartum visit. The big thing that I like about Henderson is that he doesn't pull any punches.

"With exercise, eating right and the contentment that you have told me that you feel he gives you, your weight should remain stable. It is better now for your height, even a few more pounds would be good for you, but don't overdo it."

"Don't go back to work if you don't have to, you are content with the baby, your husband and your family and you look healthier than you did before. I hope I won't need to see you for anything serious for a long time." Doc said.

It has been ten and a half weeks since the birth and she has lost a lot of weight and has been working out with exercises and the weights that we had everyday. She really looks great.

Just as I walked into the bedroom to change my clothes, I found her standing in front of the full-length mirror examining her figure.

She had nothing on and I froze in my tracks as I walked in. It's really hard to sneak up behind someone while they are standing in front of a full-length mirror. Just as I was reaching around her waist to pull her to me, she looked up.

"Hi honey, what do you think? Am I good enough?" Dee said.

"What kind of question is that?" I asked as I caressed her firm body.

"I mean, you saw what I looked like before and now I'm heavier than I was." She said.

"Look that's silly." I said picking her up in my arms and carrying her to the bed.

"No really, I feel like I'm fatter now." She said.

"You weight what, one ten?" I asked as I ripped my clothes off and crawled next to her.

"One fifteen and what do you think you're doing?"

"Making love to you my darling wife. You are so beautiful and have such a fabulous figure, I don't know how I tear myself away from you to go to work in the mornings."

She made love to me like we were on our first date and she wasn't quite sure about everything, but when it was finished, she felt better about herself and her new body.

"I think I love you husband, but you'd better keep reminding me." She said.

For our anniversary, I visited a good friend of mine who happens to own a restaurant, and belongs to the Army Reserves. I explained the whole thing and that our anniversary was coming up soon.

I ordered the meal and paid for it right then, and told him when we would be keeping the reservation. He said that it wouldn't be a problem for a little special service.

On the Friday of our anniversary, we dressed in the best clothes we could find, she wore the pink sequined thing and I rented a Tuxedo. The last time she wore the pink dress, it was a tiny bit loose, and she wore a padded bra, not this time.

We entered the restaurant "Chez Enrie" right on time and Hank, he calls himself Enrie, met us at the maitre d' station.

Hank does a great fake French accent for the customers, none of them know that he isn't really French.

"Good evening sir, I have your reservation, let me escort you and your lady to your table personally." Hank said.

We went out the side door to the elevator and up to the roof.

"What is this? This isn't the restaurant." She said.

Hank had come back to his old American slang when he spoke again.

"Something special for you Denise. DJ is one of the good guys and he wanted a small favor for you. It is my pleasure to help out. Enjoy your evening. Call me if you need anything, I mean anything." And he was gone.

The roof is a finished garden with a patio in the center with flowers and plants on all sides. In the center of the patio there was an umbrella table with tablecloth and candles, two chairs with arms and one without around it, and a chaise lounge and a lounge chair near the table.

I lit the candles and we sat in the chaise and lounge chair and looked out over the city.

It was only a short time until the waiter was bringing food up from the restaurant.

"Your meal madam." He said as he uncovered the dish in front of her. "Pheasant under glass with rice pilaf and steamed broccoli. Enjoy your dinner." The waiter said.

She cried a little, but in a minute she regained her composure and finished every bite of it. The pheasant was delicious and I would make a special effort to tip the waiter a little extra and thank Hank for everything he did.

We ate, we talked, we danced on the patio to the same imaginary music we have danced to before, we kissed and I caressed some of the same things I have caressed before. They seemed to be more firm and round that they were before.

We spent at least an hour dancing and holding each other, but even with all the exercises, she's still not as strong as she was a year ago. We sat in the lounge chairs and talked, I have always enjoyed just talking with her.

"It's funny, I had two kids in my twenties and each time I got my figure back just the same as before. Now here I am with a new baby and thirty and my boobs didn't shrink back down. I had to buy a size bigger bra. I'm wearing a 32B now.

"Great, let's see."

I always say that when she talks about her body and sometimes she shows it to me. To my amazement, she peeled down the top of the dress and bra. She was perfectly round and firm looking. The color is back and they are fabulous.

"Let me see that a little closer." I said as I reached and caressed one in my hand.

"Wait a minute, mister." She said in her little girl voice. "This is how the whole thing got started before."

"Listen who's talking. I seem to remember that it was all your idea in the first place Little Miss Pixie."

"Yes, but wasn't it fun?" She said.

"I loved every minute of it except watching you endure the agony of the past few months."

"Oh, what the hell, let's do it again." She said.

We made love on the chaise lounge and looked out over the city as we were doing it. What an amazingly erotic experience. She loved it and she screamed it out to the city from the chaise lounge.

"I don't know if I can do this kind of thing for each of our anniversaries, but since this one was so special, I spared no embarrassment."

"It looks like we'll be doing this for many years, but from now on, just whisper in my ear - - - sex." She whispered.

"OK, - - - Sex!" I whispered.

We made love again and this time there was no more screaming, just a lot of cooing from both of us.

"Ya know, I've got everything that I could ever want or need. I have a wonderful loving husband and family, a good job, a nice house and car. I just can't imagine, if I had all the money in the world, what I'd spend it on."

THE END?

SYNOPSIS

On the day that DJ was returning from a trip to Denver, his wonderful wife Sarah was hit and killed by a drunk driver. He was devastated by grief and found it hard for him to complete his schooling or anything else in his life, even though the every day demands of a five year old son must be met, but one of his teammates brings him back to reality by talking about income taxes.

An old friend from the church he attends, recommends an accountant that he knows who does taxes on the side at home. He made the necessary appointment and met the accountant, Denise at her office. She is a beautiful caring woman who took him as a client and agreed to help. During the next few months, he met her for lunch at a little cafe, where they talk about his taxes and her work. During these lunches, he noticed what beautiful clothes she wears, including a special gold pendant necklace hanging down the middle of a special outfit. We see that D. J. also noticed bruises that she has tried to cover with makeup on her body and got an indication that she is being beaten on by someone. Since she doesn't wear a ring, he asked her to dinner with him, which she accepts, but she informed him that it must be after work on Friday.

Their first date was in May and he took her to a fancy restaurant for prime rib and all the fixings. It has been so long since anyone has done this kind of thing for her, that she didn't know how to act. She told him through her tears that she is married and her husband gets drunk and beats her up on the weekends. They drove to the Ace of Clubs, a place he knows to have a drink and talk and dance. While they were dancing, she was trying to decide what to do about her abusive husband. DJ drove her home and she decided to see a lawyer about a divorce.

Denise has always been an ornery kid and she grew up to be an even ornerier woman. Ever since she met D. J., she has been pulling small pranks on him, but now she is beginning to blossom, now that she has filed for a divorce and the abuse has stopped. DJ must be falling for her because he has asked her to bring her two girls and pick peaches with him and Harry. She arrived at DJ's house dressed in very tight shorts and a thin shirt. When he opens the door, he is stunned by not only her beauty but what he hadn't seen before. During their peach picking, as he reached for a peach, Denise stepped in front of him and he grabbed something else. We don't know whether this is intentional on her part or not. Later on the ride back to town, she absent-mindedly put her hand on his thigh. He asked her to have dinner with him and she accepted. He picked her up at seven for a light meal and later returned to the Ace of Clubs to dance. While they were dancing she asked him in her "little girl voice" if he would like to play a game with her. Of course he said he would. The game is called "Denise says". Denise says that he should unbuckle his belt and when he did, she lifted the hemline of her dress an inch or so. She plays this game with him for a while till she showed all and he was amazed by the sight.

DJ was awakened at three a.m. by the phone, Denise called because she was scared by a prowler outside. He rushed to her aid dressed only in cutoffs and slippers. He found Denise and her girlfriend Annette dressed in nightgowns and the three of them sat and talked in the living room. With a full moon that night, there was plenty of light for him to see through the nightgowns the girls are wearing. The discussion soon turned to sex as Annette complained of her husbands reluctance to perform his duties. While this kind of talk continued, Denise took matters into her own hands and satisfies a desire that she has had since she first met D. J.

The next day Denise called DJ to tell him that her washing machine had broken down and would he like to go to the laundramat with her. During their return to her house they stopped at a friends house to get the girls. An old and dear friend of DJ, Linda, is the friend of Denise who was watching the girls. She surprised him and invited him to their house to chat, which he does the following day. DJ slipped and said that he loves Denise.

Denise brought the girls to see DJ as he was doing yardwork. He cooked dinner and they all decided that he shouldn't do that again. The kids wanted to play "Hide and seek" and decided that mom was "it". DJ hid in and empty garage at the end of the street and called her into the garage and grabbed her. Denise did something again in her little girl voice and really got him started, but a call for "Mom" from outside stops everything in it's tracks. Just as she was leaving she pulled another ornery prank on him and told him to be sure to call her the next day.

AUTHOR BIOGRAPHY

D. J. McAllister was born in St Francis Hospital in Colorado Springs, Colorado. He lived for several years in Wichita, Kansas and Kansas City and has traveled to many places across the country. He has written many of his unusual experiences over the years.

He is six feet tall and weighs 188 pounds with dark brown hair, hazel eyes and glasses.

He spent two years as a member of the US Army in the Signal Corps, where he learned the skills of an electronics technician.

After his discharge from the army, he attended the University of Colorado at Colorado Springs (UCCS) and earned an Associate Degree in Business Administration, he also holds an FCC 1st Class Radiotelephone License.

For a brief period, he worked as an entry level engineer at a local Colorado Springs radio station. For the next three years, he worked as a technician in the Communications and Electronics shop as Radio Repairer at Fort Carson, Colorado.

He completed his BA in Business at Wichita State University by going to classes nights and weekends while holding a full-time job.

He enjoys hunting in the Rocky Mountains for deer and elk and an occasional predator. He can shoot the eye out of a gnat at 50 yards.

He lived for several years in Wichita, Kansas and Kansas City and has traveled to many other places across the country. He has written many of his and his friend's unusual experiences over the years.

His Dad, Charles, joined the Army and retired as a CW4 after 20 years. He worked for the Santa Fe Railroad from until he died.

He has one brother, Sean and one sister, Doreen.

www.ingramcontent.com/pod-product-compliance
Lightning Source LLC
Chambersburg PA
CBHW072214170626
46813CB00003B/939

Payoff Pitch

Ed McCloskey

Copyright © 2015 Ed McCloskey
All Rights Reserved

ISBN 13: 978-0-9898410-1-6

This is a work of fiction. Characters, organizations, and events portrayed in this novel are products of the author's imagination or used fictitiously. Any resemblance to actual events or locales or persons living or dead is entirely coincidental.

All rights are reserved, including the right to reproduce this book or portions thereof in any form without the author's express written consent.

To my lovely wife Rosi, whose love encouragement, faith and patience makes this book and especially my life joyful.

"Outside of a dog, a book is a man's best friend. Inside of a dog it's too dark to read."

~Groucho Marx

CHAPTER 1

"C'mon, McKenna, get your butt outta bed, breakfast is ready and we gotta lot to do today," came the mellifluous screech from my pretty wife, Hannah.

"Wow, what a joyous way to get roused outta bed, especially on a lazy Saturday morning." I lurched my bleary-eyed way down to breakfast to join my lovely wife. I probably looked like an unmade bed. I know I felt like one. The wall clock said it was 6:45 a.m.

"Your timing is perfect. The French toast is nearly ready," Hannah said.

"I love it when a plan comes together," I said, as I slumped at the breakfast counter. We were joined by our idiosyncratic Black Lab, Riley T. Dog, who had just come back from his morning ablutions with Ivan, our House Manager and friend.

"I do. Now listen up. We're leaving here at eleven to catch the subway, she said in a gentle but still strident tone. You're gonna have to lose the Dagwood hair, my sweet."

"Uh oh, whatcha got us into now?" I asked with arched eyebrows which I hoped etched sufficient curiosity onto my face, my true feelings.

"You'll see soon enough."

Frowning I declared, "C'mon, if you want me to go somewhere—anywhere—after rousting me outta bed on a Saturday, I gotta know the where, okay?"

"You're no fun. If you must know, we're going to the stadium to see the Yankees."

"All right then, that I can do. What's behind the dawn wake up?"

1

"I just thought you might like to join me after reading the papers."

"I'm missin' something... unless..."

"Unless what, Mr. Obtuse?"

"See ya up there," I said with my best ogle.

After an extended foray into the world of erotic behavior, I reflected on how Hannah had bribed me in the past to get me to take part in stuff.

I recalled a persuasive romp last year to get me to help a friend save a car company from ruin. It all worked out well. Company saved, friends helped, handsome profit realized, lots of jobs created, all good things. I especially savored the romp. I bet Hannah hopes this, whatever it is, goes half as well, as do I.

Zero hour arrived. We dashed out the door. Hannah decided now was a good time to pin me down and get answers to the unanswered questions she asked a while ago. She also thought it would be an effective way to dodge my query. It wasn't because she feared telling me, feared negative response, feared no response, what she actually feared was imposing on me again.

Even though the National Motors project was off and running successfully we paid a heavy price in personal grief. Since then, I had done nothing productive in a year. She didn't want to watch me become moldy and stagnant, I suppose. She wasn't about to let that happen.

"Okay, Mr. McKenna, you promised to tell me how your grandfather, Red, got his name. You said it wasn't due to his hair color, so what's the story?"

"I'll tell you later, Mrs. McKenna. I promise." Pointing at my watch I said, "Now we need to hustle to catch the D train if we're gonna get to the Bronx in time for the first pitch."

Off we ran down the crowded street, reminiscent of kids who'd swiped apples from the neighborhood bodega. I ran interference like the tight end I was in college.

"Damn right you will," she said with a stern expression as she followed close behind her personal bulldozer. Down the packed subway entrance, through the stiles, ending on the D train to the Bronx we rode—albeit standing—holding onto a single strap as we jostled along.

I always felt I knew what the inside of a well-used sweat sock smelled like whenever I took the subway. Once again my olfactory memory was refreshed.

We were no sooner seated in our upper deck, right field seats, when a laser-like fly-ball screamed into the second tier seats, over the FOX BUSINESS sign in right field. After a tangle of hands and arms a young fan held the ball up in triumph only to have it snatched from him by some greedy mook. A fight broke out when the boy's father decked the guy to get the ball back for his son. Only in New York!

"Wow, what a shot," I yelled enthusiastically. The homer opened the Yankee scoring in the bottom of the first inning. First baseman, Mark Teixeira's home run drove in the two runners ahead of him for a 3-0 Yankee lead.

I turned to assess Hannah's reaction. I knew she wouldn't have the same appreciation for Yankee success as I did.

As a Red Sox fan—despite hailing from Rochester, New York— she professed an intense dislike for my favorite team, the Yankees. I believed I could read her mind, despite her efforts to conceal her thoughts with a smile.

"Damn Yankees, right?" I said with a twenty-eight piece grin of pearly white Chiclets. We're all supposed to have thirty-two teeth but hockey and football took out four of mine.

"What, now you're a mind reader?" I smiled, fully knowing I nailed it.

Despite my Detroit birth, for some inexplicable reason I never rooted for the Tigers. I didn't hate or dislike them, I just loved the Yanks, always had. I figured it was since the Yankees were my father's favorite. I never knew him, since he was killed in service to his country just a few weeks before I was born. He still has a profound influence over me.

"So I suppose you're happy, huh?"

The stupid grin on my mug told her I was.

"What's not to be happy about? Beautiful day, beautiful ball park, beautiful girl, the Yankees ahead... and watching you squirm. Just beautiful, all of it," I said.

"So you like to see me squirm, huh?"

"Not really, I just thought gloating would be too much."

"I'll tell you what's too much, smug Yankee fans being smug Yankee fans," she said with as much attitude as she could muster, blue eyes flashing and a grim expression of disapproval.

"Twenty-seven world championships will do it to people, ya know."

Basking in the sun, surrounded by nearly 50,000 roaring fans enjoying some of the best players in the world ply their trade was a distinct pleasure. Still I was eager to learn what Hannah had up her sleeve.

After the game, won by the Yankees 9-4 we rode the subway to South Central Park and climbed into a booth with a view of the oil painting of The Mick in the foyer. Mickey Mantle's was a favorite restaurant of mine. Hannah was setting me up for a tough pitch. After we ordered drinks and dinner I looked at my love's baby blues and asked, "How come you didn't root for the Orioles growing up?"

"I did until they dumped their AAA team in Rochester for Norfolk. I just couldn't bring myself to become a *Damn Yankee* fan. My mother's from Boston so I switched allegiance to the Red Sox."

"Well, nobody can ever accuse us of being homers, can they?" We both laughed then I asked, "So what is it you want from me? You never said."

"Can't a wife just take her husband to see his favorite team?"

"Of course, but I've seen this play before, if you recall," I said with feigned indignation.

"Okay, I'll fess up. Remember the call I got from my college friend, Libby Reynolds, a couple of days ago? You know the one in Elmira?"

"Vaguely."

"Her husband, Ted, wants to bring a minor league team back to their home town. They lost their major league affiliation years ago. I just thought you'd like to see a game and..."

"See if I'd be interested in looking into the world of pro baseball. I'm right, huh?"

"You are, damn it," she admitted with an irresistible smile much like Elizabeth Taylor's. Hannah had often been compared to the infamous Liz.

"A very expensive and convoluted way of finding out. I know what those tickets cost these days. You coulda just asked, you know. Did ya have to sell the house to pay for 'em?"

Hannah squirmed then said, "No, just a mortgage. This way you get to see your favorite team, be wined and dined at the Mick's and now I figure you owe me," she said.

"My, my, you are a devious one, aren't you?"

"I know, but effective right?"

I shook my head at the dazzling woman across the table and said, "Right, so what do you think we can do? I don't know anything about running a baseball team, do you?"

"Of course not, but we've proven to be clever and resourceful people. I'm sure we'll figure it out. Plus you need to get off your lazy butt and get involved with something before you turn into a moldy science project," she said.

"Road trip?"

"Precisely," she said looking peacock proud, or more appropriately peahen proud.

At the crack of slumber, we packed up Riley, and enough stuff for a week's stay in the Finger Lake Region of New York State—specifically Elmira. To say I was ambivalent about this idea was on the money. I didn't know these people. I didn't know anything about running a baseball team. But I did know Hannah and I trust her. So here we are on the road. *Nice view,* I thought.

"This area never gets the credit it deserves in the fall," I said gazing at the luxuriant foliage blanketing the rolling foothills of the Appalachian range. "I guess New England has a better PR firm. What've you got to say about it, missy?"

Hannah, a very successful owner of a PR firm herself, took umbrage for a moment but concealed it. However, she didn't fail to be impressed by the surrounding hillsides too. They were resplendent in as many shades as a big box of Crayolas.

"I'm glad to see your razor sharp wit is still honed, dear... misplaced though it is."

"So tell me about your friend. What's going on there?" I said.

"Well, Libby and her husband Ted are natives of Elmira. There was a professional baseball team there some time ago, called the Pioneers. They belonged to the Double-A Eastern League, then a Brooklyn Dodgers affiliate. When the Dodgers moved west they moved their minor league teams to be nearer L.A. Eventually, the Orioles stepped in to fill the void left by the Dodgers' departure." Jutting out her jaw for emphasis and tipping her head back a tad she said, "I did some research after Libby called."

I was paying close attention. "Those first years saw the building of the nucleus for the first Oriole glory days, right?" I said.

"You seem to know your sports history."

"About some stuff," I said.

"To answer, yes. Lots of future stars came through Elmira on their way to Rochester then ultimately to Baltimore. It lasted until Major League Baseball demanded all teams upgrade their minor league facilities to a certain standard. Elmira couldn't afford to do it to MLB's satisfaction at the Double-A level."

"Okay," I said.

"The Red Sox put a Single-A team there for a few years. Twenty years ago, I guess. Then MLB mandated still more upgrades. Once again, Elmira couldn't afford to comply. Ultimately, they lost their affiliation. Now they have a team playing in an amateur collegiate league."

"Why do your friends want to bring back pro ball? More important, why do they think they can?"

"It's why we're going up there. By the way, we're staying up at Justin and Kimberley's cottage on Keuka, where we stayed last year for the race at Watkins Glen."

Hannah was referring to her former college golf teammate and her husband, the president of National Motors. We had worked with them two years ago to help introduce their wildly successful family of hydrogen fueled cars.

"I love their place. Riley will have the best time in the water. I will too, even though I fear this is more of a long shot than the automobile business." I paused to pet Riley and said, "Think mission impossible."

CHAPTER 2

Hank Lewis, seated behind his ornately carved mahogany desk, slowly spun his Super Bowl sized onyx ring, with the full carat diamond in the center around a large finger from what could only be characterized as a paw. It glistened prism-like in the sunlight as he deliberated his next move. Glancing at his gold Rolex his fidgety behavior exhibited annoyance. Rance Butler was late again.

Finally, Butler strode into the opulent office. He paused a moment in admiration of the joint. Glancing at Henry, he shook his head and said, "Sorry I'm late."

Hank recognized the reaction—pure envy—most people had when they entered. Hank figured Butler would be no different. He wasn't wrong.

"Yeah, yeah, whatcha got for me, Rance?"

Butler tried to stretch his wiry, five foot eleven inch frame to meet the six foot four Lewis. Of course, he failed.

"You were right. Reynolds seems to be interested in the Big Flats property. At least he's been inquiring about it."

Hank looked out his window unmindful of the view, leering like a large reptile about to have at his prey and said, "Finally, I've got you, you rat-bastard."

Turning to Butler he said, "All these years of eating his crap is over. I'll finally break the back of the son of a bitch," said Hank. Hank turned his back on Butler and gazed out his window and barely audible said, "Ted Reynolds, you're dead meat. And that goes for your simpering wife too."

"Wow, you really mean it, huh?" asked Butler.

"You bet your sweet ass I mean it. I'll discover his plan and then I'm gonna steal it. Let's see how he likes the meal I'll serve him. You don't know how many times I've gone head to head with Reynolds on a project bid, only to lose."

Hank pounded his right fist into his open left hand repeatedly, finally pounding his desk so hard the knick-knacks on it jumped.

"Somehow he always seems to beat me. I've even lost to him once when I put in a higher bid."

"You're kiddin'," said Rance.

"Do I look like I'm kidding? Do I sound like I'm kidding? Do I give off some vibe that suggests I'm kidding?"

"No, not at all, but if your bid was higher, why didn't you get the job?"

"Yeah, that's the best part. One guy told me the board liked Reynolds better. Can you believe it?"

Crossing his legs stifling a laugh, he said, "Actually I can. You know you're not the easiest man to get along with, Henry. Not too many people like you."

"Then why the hell are you still hanging around?" said Hank spinning to confront Butler with white hot fire in his eyes. "And the name, as you well know, is Hank."

"It's a question I occasionally ask myself. I guess it's habitual. You know it started in seventh grade when you took the blame for spilling the ink on Miss Mueller's purse. You never did tell me why you did it."

"No, I guess I just didn't like the way the nasty bitch was tearing into you," said Hank quietly. There was more to it Hank chose not to reveal.

CHAPTER 3

Hannah's friends, Libby and Ted Reynolds, were headed to their backyard to relax and enjoy the view of the surrounding hills. Strung between two enormous red maple trees, an over-sized L.L. Bean hammock drew them in as surely as a trout to a fly. Ted put a tray of lemonade and ice tea concoction, popularized by the famous golfer Arnold Palmer, on a table near the hammock.

Sipping the drink Ted said, "You know what this Arnold Palmer needs?"

"More lemonade. I didn't put enough in, did I?"

"Some vodka wouldn't hurt either," he said.

"Not with company coming. I want you at your best, not half in the bag."

She added lemonade *sans* vodka. They lay back and enjoyed the much improved drink, even without the hooch, when her cell rang.

"Libby here," she answered.

"It's Hannah. Did I catch you at a good time?"

"Well, if snuggling with my Teddy in the hammock sounds like a good time, yes."

"Bordering on TMI there, missy. Dru and I just got to the lake house and wondered if you guys want to have dinner tonight to discuss your project."

"Hold on a sec, I'll ask Ted. They want to know if we want to sup with them."

"Gee, I don't know, hon, they only spent the whole day driving up here to talk to us. Ya think we should?"

"I heard that, Libby. I see he's still got his dry sense of humor."

"More snarky than dry, I can't seem to break him of it, so be prepared."

"Between Ted and Dru we've got a matched set, don't we?"

"Indeed, where do we want to meet?"

"How about the Harbor Hotel in Watkins? It's not far for you guys and it's just over the hill for us," offered Hannah.

"It's a date. Seven o'clock sound good?"

"Perfect, see you then."

* * *

"We have a date, huh? Feel like a swim?" I asked.

"Water's too cold. Now a boat ride sounds good though, how about it?"

The cottage, more like a full-fledged residence of post and beam construction, sits on the southwestern end of Keuka Lake, near the village of Hammondsport. Tied to the dock was Justin Powell's twenty-five foot wood hulled Thompson powered by twin fifty horse powered Evinrude motors, named *The Deal*. They boarded her and prepared to set off when Riley T. came bounding down the dock and leapt into the boat.

"How'd he get outside? I shut the door," I said.

"He's Wonder Lab. Surprised you didn't know that," said Hannah.

We leisurely cruised up the center of the lake, the three of us. Hannah drove while I hugged Riley.

"Who owns that beauty?" I asked, pointing to a spectacular cottage, more like a full blown estate. The name "Limbo" was written diagonally in black script across the middle one of three large brick chimneys attached to the main house.

Spectacular views of the vineyards, rising like columns of marching soldiers patrolling the mountainsides bracketed both sides of the lake. On the water, a few hearty skiers plied their skills nearby but mostly we had the lake to ourselves.

"Answer the question," I said with mock determination.

Hannah told how liveried servants tended to the needs of the gala party guests held at Limbo in the height of summer, back in the day. It still looked like it could be a magnificent site for such events.

"HELLO, that's not an answer. Who owns that beauty?" I asked.

"I'm not sure anymore. When I was a kid we were told the inventor of the eyelash curler built it. It was claimed the silly invention made him fabulously wealthy, as befitted the owner of such an alluring place," said Hannah.

"Was it true?" I asked.

"Who knows? I hope so," she said.

"Looks like F. Scott and Zelda would be right at home."

We turned back at the base of the bluff which forms the distinctive Y, for which Keuka was famous.

"It's known there are caves beneath the water line here at the bluff. Every once in a while, a disgorged body surfaces to give credence to the belief danger lurks beneath those waters," said Hannah.

"How deep is this lake?" I asked.

"It varies here by the bluff; I believe it's around 190 feet, though some places are only thirty. Its average is about 100."

When we entered the cove, which protected the Powell's cottage from periodic winter storms sweeping down from the north, I encouraged Riley to jump in and swim to shore. Riley beseeched me to join him with his deep throated yowling. I finally acquiesced, rolling into the water and gave out my own yowl.

I gasped, "You weren't kidding about the lake temp!"

"Brisk, isn't it?" she laughed.

"Brisk hell, its FBC. You know . . . freezin' balls cold."

Laughing harder Hannah said, "Welcome to the Finger Lakes."

After making shore, we ate on the dock. Over a simple lunch of tomato, ham and Swiss Panini sandwiches with Caprese salad, fittingly complimented by Bully Hill Growers Red wine from Walter Taylor's winery.

"Fill me in on your friends again," I said.

"The Cliff Notes version is Libby was our housemate at Cornell. She married Ted the summer after graduation. He was an All-Ivy baseball player with professional aspirations."

"What position?" I asked, as tomato juice leaked from my sandwich onto my lap.

"Pitcher, I think. His dream crashed when he tore a muscle in his back, rhomboid or trapeziums, maybe," she said. "Anyway, he went into commercial real estate in and around Elmira, Corning and even over to Binghamton."

"I guess he must be doing all right to think about a thing like this, huh?"

"Very successful, they have two kids at Notre Dame High School, an area private parochial school. I'm sure they're on their way to Cornell if Libby has her way. Ted played sports there—baseball and fall LAX."

"LAX?"

"Lacrosse, but his baseball passion was never fully extinguished. That brings us to the resurrection of the Pioneers which, by the way, is the first hurdle."

"There's a hurdle? We have a hurdle. What hurdle?"

"Libby told me the last owners are reluctant to relinquish the name 'Pioneers'."

"Why?"

"Who knows?" she rolled her eyes.

"We don't seem to know a whole lot," I mused, with what I considered to be the perfect measure of snark.

"Well, duh, what do you think the meeting is for, fool?" she said as she grinned like the Cheshire Cat and gave me a hug.

I thought proudly, Hannah does not take any shit—from me or anyone else.

"I guess I kinda deserved that," I said.

"No kinda about it, Bub," she said rising up to plant a big wet one on me.

"What about Libby? What's her story?" I finished the dripping sandwich and was now attacking the salad.

"Like I said, she was a roommate at Cornell. She had a swimming scholarship, was All-Ivy three years running. She's shortish, pretty enough, I suppose. Blond, blue-eyed and stacked as you guys are wont to say."

"How soon can we leave?"

"Down, boy, she's spoken for. And in case you forgot, SO ARE YOU!"

"Yes, ma'am," I said looking as a chastised one should.

"As I was trying to say, she won everything she ever competed in. She's got the same snarky, irreverent demeanor of all athletes, able to hold her own in any clubhouse. Sound familiar?"

Hearing Hannah's description, my eyebrows rose like two caterpillars crawling across a sidewalk to safety.

"In high school she was All-State in basketball, swimming and track. She can play near scratch golf but doesn't play much now. That's how she met Ted."

"How?"

"Beating the pants off him at an inter-fraternity/sorority golf outing. She was paired with Ted. He shot eighty and she had a seventy-six."

"Not bad," I praised. "Could she take you?"

"With practice maybe, anyway, Ted asked her out and fate took over."

Lunch complete, I decided to roam around the lake with Riley. With more than five acres to explore we set off. I often walked the boy when I wanted to do some thinking, as I did now.

I love getting involved in projects, especially to help people who face uncertainty. Due to family successes—as well as personal achievement—I don't *need* to work. But too young to retire, I like to keep busy.

But there's a catch. With other people's money and dreams riding, it puts me under a ton of pressure. Just like all real diamonds are formed. I'll probably end up in an engagement ring somewhere. It comes at a price. Even though as confident as an unopposed candidate I still fear letting people down. Good thing I can handle it... or at least I think I can, just like the *Little Engine that Could.*

CHAPTER 4

On their way to dinner, Ted pondered what to expect from the meeting. "I know your roomie Hannah's a PR whiz, and god knows we're gonna need one, but what's with her husband?"

"Former roomie, 'Sweet Lips,' you're my roomie now. She told me he's a genius at figuring out how to solve problems before they kill projects."

"Sounds like 'Wonder Woman' found her match."

"Let's hope," Libby said.

***

The newly built hotel, on the south end of Seneca Lake, boasted a fine restaurant with a patio overlooking the picturesque water. At roughly thirty-nine miles it's the longest of the Finger Lakes, with an average depth of 290-some feet. I was entranced by the serenity and beauty of the lake and surrounding hills.

"I guess there'll be snow here before too long, huh," I joked. Or hoped I was joking, it being the end of May. We arrived earlier at the Harbor House hotel hard by the south end of the lake, and after checking out a marina boatyard we made our way to the back patio overlooking said lake.

Just after settling at our table we heard, "Hey there, roomie." A pretty girl and handsome man made their way from the lobby.

"Hey girl," returned Hannah. After the introductions Hannah said, "To answer your first question, you've heard of the turnaround at National Motors, right?"

"Heard of? We bought two of 'em," said Ted.

"Well, you're looking at the man who was the primary reason for it," said Hannah.

I was embarrassed to take sole credit for my contribution to any endeavor.

Ted, looking directly at me, said, "I'm impressed."

"I can't take all the credit. It was truly a team effort and you know it, Hannah," I chastised.

"Go kiss your horse, man. We're not here for a modesty demonstration, Mr. Humble. I gotta offer some of your creds to these people. How else are you to impress 'em?" retorted Hannah.

"Yes, ma'am," I answered.

Ted and Libby looked at each other with a knowing smile.

"Hannah told me about your baseball career, Ted. I guess that's why you want to do this, huh?" I said.

"More like lack of a career. Injury precluded a real career but it didn't kill my love of the game and the desire to be part of it, Dru." I found myself liking Ted already.

"I get the love of the game... but why minor league baseball? Why not sponsor an amateur club?" I asked.

"I know it's a bit out there, but there's more to it than baseball. This area, Elmira, the Heights and all the other small communities around us have really taken it on the economic chin for a lot of years. In the last sixty years the population has decreased by over thirty percent."

"Wow," said Hannah, "that's a lot."

"It is a lot. It's a direct reflection of the economy here and in New York State in general. Companies have moved away, either to the south or offshore, taking their jobs with 'em. New York politics is killing the state. The taxes are punitive and rich people aren't putting up with it. They're moving away, as are the corporations."

I stood up to stretch, nodded my head and said, "Most people are trapped and virtually getting skinned alive. Nothing is being done to address the situation on a long-term basis. Sure there's a ten year no-tax inducement to lure companies to the state on the table. You're all afraid it's phony, right?"

"I figure if I can make a small difference in a small area it's what I want to do," said Ted.

I said, "I'm hearing this more often these days all around the country."

"Yeah it's a recurring theme in small towns. In my graduating class of 160, only about twenty still live here. Those who left did so, not because they wanted to, but because finding good jobs locally was tough."

Hannah nodded at Dru as if to say she agreed with this.

"People who still live here do so because they love the area and their families have deep roots. Many own their businesses. It's a great area to live in, aside from the economic plight."

"Sounds like the question posed to Mrs. Lincoln regarding the play," I said.

"Sure it's reeling but the people and scenic beauty are both positive attractions. I'd like to make a difference in life opportunities, in my small way, for employment and entertainment," said Ted.

"Where do things stand now?" asked Hannah.

"Ted's contacted Major League Baseball in New York to ask permission to contact all thirty clubs to determine if there's an opportunity for us. The response has been tepid, at best," said Libby.

"The most I could glean was a complete overhaul of the facilities and some kind of guarantee of solid profitable attendance would be needed," said Ted.

"The facilities, okay they can be upgraded, but how can you guarantee attendance?" I asked.

"Yeah, that's what I asked 'em," said Ted.

"And the answer is?" Hannah said.

"I'm still waiting for it."

"I heard you mention tax-free zones in New York State?" asked Hannah.

"Oh sure, comes under the heading of barn door closing," said Ted.

Hannah laughed. "As in after the horse already ran away, right?"

"Uh huh," said Ted.

"The ads are real, the state is offering ten years of tax-free status to any company moving or staying here. Sounds good, right?"

"So far," said Hannah.

"Yeah well, what everyone fears is the politicians won't give up revenue up front without a raise in taxes in other areas to cover the shortfall. Like property tax, school tax, sales tax, sin tax or any other despicable tax they can think of. Of course, everyone believes after ten years they'll return to taxing the bejesus out of companies again and send the economy down the tubes."

"Wow, you got some outlook there," said Hannah while she shook her head.

"Accurate though," said Libby.

"I was trying to remember statistics I recently read in a baseball magazine about the rise and fall and current state of minor league baseball. I thought the peak was just after WWII. But with several more leagues and teams back then, the total attendance nationwide was in the thirty million range compared to forty-one mil today. They may be up a bit right now.

"As for the major leagues they're currently enjoying great prosperity due to lucrative TV deals. The future looks bright. So it looks like baseball is stable and a good investment if operated properly. To the best of my recollection, television played a part in both peak and valley of baseball health."

"How do you figure, Dru?" said Hannah.

I explained, "After WWII people had more free time and discretionary income. Minor league baseball was affordable and fun for local people who wanted to spend time enjoying games and the festivities at the park. Every ballpark in small towns across the country put on shows to rival the old vaudeville circuits or circuses. Boxing, wrestling, barnstorming major leaguers in the off season and the like were all big gate attractions.

"Does anybody remember donkey baseball?" I asked.

"Sure," said Libby. "Our kid's school had a fundraiser a few years ago on our athletic field, it was a hoot."

"It used to be a staple at minor league ballparks in the fifties," I said.

"Hold it," said Hannah. "Is this what it sounds like, playing baseball on horseback or . . . donkey back? Musta been some article you read, Dru."

"Do I see wheels turning?" I asked Hannah.

"Maybe, was it one element of gimmicks used to gen up attendance in answer to TV?"

"What's TV got to do with it?" asked Libby.

"We can see almost all games today on TV, in any number of ways. Local stations, cable, satellite links, computers, tablets and smart phones. TV was such a novel idea back then people readily gravitated to it. When they started airing sports, baseball was among the first to be offered. For the first time a choice existed in the minor league towns. Why go to a local game when you could watch the famous stars in your own home, Guess what happened?" I said.

"Okay, so that's what started the decline of popularity, but what about being the solution today? What's changed?" asked Hannah.

"Good question," said Ted. "If I read the times right, people may be getting fed up with Performance Enhancing Drug scandals, greed on both sides of the ball, owners and players."

"And agents, don't forget the agents," said Hannah.

"Ah yes, the bottom feeders of all sports."

"Ted, the popularity is up about two percent over last year but it's been flat growth-wise for ten years. So again, why do you wanna do it now?" I asked.

Ted paused before answering, "I think people still love the game... although football and basketball have supplanted it with kids. The thing we gotta do now is win the kids back. We need to get the texters to rest their thumbs and get into active participation. We gotta make baseball cool. Provide equipment, cool unis, nice fields to play on and sponsors for leagues. Build a better, fan friendly park, bring in fans by having events and attractions and of course, advertise."

"Promotional ideas, special discounts and fundraising events to lure customers can be just the beginning," offered Hannah.

"Don't teams do the same things now?" asked Libby.

"Sure, but do they all have a pro like Hannah?" I said.

"Do I detect a decision to join us?" asked Ted.

"Very astute, new friend, yeah, I think we'd love to get involved in this, if you'll have us?" I said glancing at Hannah for affirmation.

"Okay, great. Thank you. Do you guys really think we can do something?" said Ted.

"We do," said Hannah.

"But how's this gonna work? And why do *you* want to do this?" said Ted.

Hannah answered, "I want to do it to help Libby and you too, Ted. I grew up with baseball in Rochester and loved it. Our family was always going to games and talking baseball all year long. We'd welcome new players to town then follow former Red Wings as their careers progressed. Deserved or not, we took credit for helping launch their careers."

I could see Hannah's thoughts run across her forehead like the news crawl on the New York Times Tower in Times Square.

"When my mother or father and I were at odds, baseball seemed to buffer emotions and get us back on common ground. I'd like to be part of bringing those same buffers to other families. Dru, what do you say?" Hannah asked.

"Here we go again. Does this ring any bells?" I said.

Leaning forward with Ted, Libby asked, "Are we to infer it's good or bad?"

"No, it's good. Dru and I had the National Motors project work out rather well for all parties concerned. This is how it started," said Hannah.

I stood up again to stretch my balky back and said, "She introduced me to the people involved and we were off. So yeah, it's good. I love baseball too, played it, followed it, went to games all the time and I'd love to be part of this. I believe I can help."

"Did you play in college?" asked Ted

"No, I played football, blocking back mostly. The last year of high school I pitched though," I said.

"Not any good, huh?" asked Libby with a bear's shit eatin' grin. I could tell what Hannah meant about holding her own in the locker room and shook my head.

"He was pretty good. A pitcher, fast as snuff makes spit or so I'm told. Tell 'em the tobacco story," prompted Hannah.

"Yeah, okay. I was pretty good just not good enough to go further than high school. And I knew it."

"Don't forget about the tobacco story, Mr. Studly," said Libby.

"Okay, I was pitching against East Malcolm High on the Double-A field in Michigan. Worst locker room I ever was in, filth, mold, no hot water. Nobody showered there. Anyway, my shortstop introduced me to chewing tobacco so I took a chaw. Thought it made me look meaner to the hitters. In the third inning, the E. Mal. batter hit a bullet back at me. Immediately I swallowed the chaw. Oh no. I threw up my glove in self-defense, deflected the ball to our shortstop who threw the guy out at first. Out number three. During the play I went behind the mound and tossed my lunch, breakfast, and what was formerly the chaw on the ground in a pile of nasty. On the way back to the dugout, our shortstop ran up and said to me, 'I'm just tellin' ya, if a ball is hit through that shit I ain't pickin' it up.'"

Laughing hard, Ted and Libby said, "I can just see it."

"Not quite as funny then as it is now, I assure you," I said.

Ted and Libby were smiling and holding hands as I walked over to Hannah and gave her a big hug.

"Here we go again," I said.

She looked up and said, "I bet I know what's next, don't I?"

"Let's put together a murder board," I suggested. "Do we have an office or work space?" he asked.

"What in heaven's name is a murder board?" said Libby.

"I'm working out of my study in the back," said Ted.

I pictured a 12' x 12' room crammed with papers, books, printers, towers, modems, keyboard and supplies, in other words my messy office. Hannah and I exchanged questioning glances.

"It's not a play house or anything," said Libby spotting our reaction.

"Around here everyone is influenced to some degree by Mark Twain, including us. Ted built this replica of Twain's study in the back of our house. We have five acres so we have plenty of room."

"It's a replica with an additional area off to the side for meetings, storage and mini kitchen," said Ted.

"Okay, let's meet there tomorrow," said Hannah.

"Do you happen to have a white board?" I asked.

"Is that your murder board?" asked Ted. "I'll have one tomorrow."

CHAPTER 5

Finding Ted and Libby's house the next morning was easier in theory than actuality. Road signs seemed to vanish or change names for inexplicable reasons, causing our heads to swivel like Linda Blair in confusion.

"Where the hell did the street go?" I shouted with exasperation as we came to an intersection.

"You're still on it. It just changed names, is all," said Hannah exuding calm. "You know how Sixth Avenue becomes Avenue of the Americas at Franklin Street and it drives New York tourist's nuts? Same thing."

"Great, when are they gonna tell us?" I asked. Eventually we arrived no worse for the experience because we enjoyed the scenic countryside, if not so much the confusing signage.

Ted and Libby were waiting on their wrap-around front porch. They warmly greeted Hannah and me. As an added surprise, I introduced Riley T. Dog to the Reynolds.

"What's the T stand for?" asked Ted.

"See what happens?" I said looking at Hannah.

"Answer the man," she said.

"So glad you asked," I answered.

Ted laughed, Libby looked at Hannah and they shook their heads.

"Must be a guy thing," said Hannah.

Riley gave Ted the supreme compliment of accepting Ted's forearm into his mouth with a faux chomp.

"I hope he's not going to escalate this," said Ted.

"Nope, it's his way of including you into his circle," I said.

"How many in this circle?" asked Libby.

"Only everybody he meets, it's a very exclusive club," answered Hannah.

"Yeah, only because he hasn't met everybody yet," I said.

After a short stroll around the house down a flagstone path, we arrived at Ted's office. Hannah and I recognized the building as similar to one we saw last year at Elmira College, the Mark Twain study. From the clutter it was obvious Ted used it as his main office.

"I'll get the dollar tour out of the way, then we can get goin' here," said Ted.

"Dollar? Remember when it was a nickel?" I asked.

"Yeah, and I only charged you fifty cents for the tour of my place," added Hannah.

"But look at the view," offered Ted in his best circus barker's voice as he described the Architectural Digest-like features of the building.

We went into the side meeting room, and I noticed a newly installed white board and smiled.

Exiting a back door we stood on a pool deck surrounding an in-ground swimming pool that would do Hollywood proud. At the far end was a waterfall with boulders in a semi-circle and behind it a barbeque pit, and patio area, complete with dining table and conversation area. The whole of it was beautifully landscaped.

"All right, this'll do fine for our down time," said Hannah.

Libby mentioned they spent a lot of time here. Hannah and I could see why.

Back inside, Ted said, "Dru, you mentioned an agenda. Whadda ya got?"

"I call this the 'murder board' from a cop show on TV we enjoy," I said.

I moved over to the white board, grabbed a green marker and wrote TO DO:

Underneath I began jotting ideas with red bullet points.

- Examine and secure the existing ball park or build a new one.

- secure rights to the team name, if we gotta have it.
- Contact MLB to determine chance of getting a franchise and the hurdles entailed.
- Contact architects for plans and cost estimates for improvements to Dunn Field or designs for a new park if needed.
- Establish budget and secure financing
- Develop Plan B if we need to prove our viability to MLB
- Find out how to get players, staff, equipment, et al.
- Develop marketing plan
- set target dates.
- overcome unknown issues as they arise

"Wow, I believe this might be a record," said Hannah as she grinned at me.

I reacted with embarrassment. "Yeah, 44 minutes from drive in to now."

"What are they talking about?" asked Libby.

"Damned if I know," said Ted.

Hannah and I were both laughing at our friends' consternation.

"The last time he did this at National, it took him forty-eight minutes to come up with a plan," said Hannah.

"Yeah, I see what you mean," said Ted as he examined the list. "I don't see any holes," he continued. "How do you do it that fast? You just got here."

I looked at Hannah, then said, "Years of practice... and it's pretty basic stuff."

"Occam's Razor, right?" said Hannah.

"Yep," I said, leaving Ted and Libby even more perplexed. I explained Occam's razor was a logician's eponymous theory stating when faced with a decision with several choices, the simplest is usually best.

"What's our first step, Mr. Occam?" asked Hannah.

"I'd like to start with the ballpark. Can we get in to look it over?" I asked.

"Sure, I don't think it's locked, all the equipment and stuff is gone. Nobody is permanently assigned to look after it so it's probably open," said Ted.

"Uniform colors," said Libby.

"What about 'em?" asked Hannah.

"He didn't list them?" said Libby. Ted and Hannah stood speechless and I laughed

"Right you are, Libby. We'll let the major league affiliation tell us what we're responsible for," I said.

"Smart ass," said Hanna to Libby as she joined her in laughter.

Ted and I shook our heads and simultaneously said, "Women."

"Let's go," I said.

***

Dunn Field was about ten miles away and was, as Ted predicted, wide open. We entered through a gate between the main grandstands, where a door led us into what looked to be a clubhouse or a broom closet—hard to tell which. The lockers gave it away though. The room led directly to the field through the dugout.

"Wow, this is beautiful," I said admiring the diamond and outfield grasses.

"I know," said Ted. "I played on this in Small Fry, Babe Ruth League, high school and American Legion. That's about ten years altogether. I still get a thrill walking onto the thing."

"I can see why. I've visited Yankee Stadium and the Tiger's Comerica Park and this playing field is on par with them, believe it or not. The stands, no, but the playing area very much so," I said.

Ted filled me in later that Pat Santarone was the groundskeeper in Elmira when Earl Weaver was the manager, before joining the Orioles as a coach for Hank Bauer and later a Hall of Fame manager for the Orioles. He liked Santarone's work so well Weaver took him to Baltimore to transform a bad field into Gold Glove caliber. They carried on the tradition in Elmira for the players.

We walked the entire perimeter. We started down the first base lines past the home team dugout and bullpen in foul territory.

While in the bullpen, Hannah stepped up on the mound, "I didn't realize the slope was this steep," she said.

"It's maybe one of the idiosyncrasies of ball parks. The visitors' bullpen mound is dissimilar to the field mound. Sometimes it can cause a problem for visiting teams," said Ted.

"Why would that be?"

I looked at Ted giving him the okay to take the question sign.

"Well, when the pitchers warm up in the bullpen they sometimes have difficulty transitioning to the field mound. It might give the home team batters a slight advantage until the pitcher adjusts," said Ted.

"Wouldn't the same thing apply to the home team pitchers?" asked Hannah.

"No, because the home team is careful to make their bullpen mound as close to identical as possible to the field mound. The visitors' doesn't receive the same level of precision." I said.

"Doesn't seem fair, isn't that cheating?" asked Hannah.

"All's fair in love, war and baseball," was Ted's reply.

Hannah shrugged, muttering to herself. We continued our patrol around the outfield on the gravel warning track near the twenty-foot tall, wooden fence.

"Needs some paint here," said Libby.

"Needs some advertisers," Hannah and I said almost simultaneously. We noticed there were several unpainted areas where advertisers should be placing ads.

"Yeah, that's another issue, lack of community involvement."

We laughed and Hannah teased, "Carnak again, Mr. Carson?" I laughed and continued the tour. Fittingly, we finished at home plate.

"Let's go over and check out the dugout," I said.

"Watch your heads," cautioned Ted. "I about brained myself when I was in high school. I stood up when a teammate hit a two-run double and smacked my head hard enough to make me woozy." Hannah and Libby looked at each other and laughed.

"What?" said Ted. "You think it's funny?"

"No dear, but it does explain a few things," said Libby grinning like the village idiot.

"Welcome to my world," I said. "I put up with that sort of stuff for two years in Baltimore with the Cornell girls."

"That's right, you were with Kimberley, too," said Libby. "How're she and Justin these days? I've lost track."

"Just great, we'll give her a call tonight," said Hannah.

"I see what you mean about the ceiling, thanks for the warning," said Hannah.

"I'm used to having to duck and stoop in every dugout I was ever in growing up," I said checking out the view. "As usual, worst seat in the house."

"What do you mean?" asked Libby.

"Check it out," I said over my shoulder as I ran out to third base. "Show 'em, Ted."

When I was positioned as a third baseman would be, Ted said, "See how the infield looks like a turtle shell? That's mainly for drainage. The hump, however, makes it impossible to determine fair-foul or safe-out calls, down at third, or first base from either dugout. The manager has to take his players' word for those calls. If a player argues a call, the manager runs out to the ump to make sure his guy doesn't get tossed outta the game."

We went back into the short tunnel which led from the dugout to the small room we were in before. The girls asked what it was used for.

"Back in the day, circa 1940s through 1988, it was the clubhouse," said Ted.

"This? It's so tiny," said Hannah.

"Yeah, that's one of the reasons the club lost its affiliation," said Ted.

"What are the other reasons?" asked Hannah.

"Look around at the stadium, not the field, the stadium. It's small, run down, uncomfortable and just plain ugly. C'mon, I'll show you," answered Ted.

* * *

We made our way past the narrow passage I assumed was the concession area. Close together each section for the various selections was inadequate now—and probably was in 1950, too.

Making our way up the entrance ramp we eschewed the box seats for the middle grandstands behind home plate. Supporting poles limited view to certain parts of the field. Sure to annoy fans. The crumbling platform with its rickety seats made moving down the rows a hazard and screamed for a potential lawsuit. Satisfied, we made our way out the front gates, also open.

"Ted, do we even want to save it?" asked Libby.

Hannah and I looked at each other, and were noncommittal. The overall location served mainly only Elmira. Drawing from surrounding communities without some compelling reasons was problematic.

"Good question, Libby. How about it, Ted?" I asked.

"I've always envisioned it being renovated and brought back to life as it was," he said. "What do you guys think?"

"Since you asked, I gotta be honest. My initial thought is forget Dunn Field," I said.

"My, my, Mr. Blandings is gonna build his dream house, huh?" said Hannah referring to the old Carey Grant, Myrna Loy movie.

I took a moment to consider the downside of this location, facility, and the cost of renovation. "Maybe so. To get this project going we need to think differently than in the past. You said the population, from its heyday in the fifties, is down thirty-some percent. We need to build a state of the art stadium in a location convenient to more of the populi. What's east, Ted?"

"Binghamton's Mets draw from the east, so west or north probably makes more sense. This way we could draw from Corning," said Ted.

"How about Big Flats?" asked Libby. She was referring to the small but growing area west of Elmira. In recent years it had developed slowly with plenty more space to put a park. It could draw from Bath, Watkins Glen, maybe even the other lake areas like Ithaca.

"Maybe," Ted said. "I was looking at it a while back for a commercial development. Or what about north closer to Watkins and Ithaca but still near enough to Corning?"

"I think we need to study some data about the area," said Hannah.

"And land availability," I said.

"Now I see what they bring to the party," said Ted.

"Are we ruling out the south?" said Hannah.

"We're just a couple of miles from Pennsylvania. We could draw from their rural areas but the largest city, Williamsport, is over sixty miles away," said Ted.

"Okay north or west it is," I said.

We turned to face the front of the stadium and continued to be underwhelmed. I would have been surprised if it ever *whelmed* anyone.

"Who's this guy?" asked Hannah. She was standing next to a bust on a white limestone pillar of Edward Dunn who, I assumed, was the namesake for the stadium and said so. Ted knew the answer.

"He donated the land to the city for this place and was an enemy of my father."

"Ooh sounds like a story to me," said Libby.

"Haven't I told you this story, Lib?"

"No, sweetie, I would have remembered. Let's have it."

"To preface, my father knew how to teach stuff to people. All people, that is, unless he was related to them. He could hit the hell out of a baseball, softball, golf ball. You name the ball, he could hit the hell out of it, even when he got older. He tried in vain to teach me. I was a pretty good hitter, not great. I coulda been better but Dad ran outta patience after five minutes. There was yelling involved. But a guy named Dick Edwards learned to hit from my dad, who spent hours with him. He got it, and I asked Dick what the secret was, and from him I got Dad's secret too. Not from Dad but from Dick. So when it came time to teach my mother to drive, Dad decided to ply his teaching technique and skill and again— total lack of patience for family. Job's brother Arnold had more patience than my dad."

"Job had a brother named Arnold? I never heard of him," said Libby.

"Of course not, he had no patience," said Ted. We laughed.

"We were expected to hear it, love it, do it, period from the git-go. My mom was forty-somethin' when she finally got a learner's permit, at my urging. After the third one expired she got the penultimate one. She had it all down but the parallel parking. So Dad got a couple of orange cones and took us out to Dunn Field to practice. The large octagonal curb forming the platform for this statue served as a parking space. Dad placed the cones at either end of a turn and told my mom to fit the car between 'em.

"Dad told her, 'Pull your car up so your steering wheel is even with where the car you're goin' behind's wheel would be. Then slowly reverse while turning the wheel gently to the right until your front bumper is a hair past the imaginary rear bumper and cut the wheel hard to the curb.' All of a sudden she gasses the car. My father yells, 'Cut, cut... STOP!' *Bam!* She didn't cut, she didn't stop. What she did was jump the curb and slam into the monument, taking out the rear bumper. I howled. My father bent over holding his head and shook it back and forth as if a scourge had befallen us. Mom got out of the car and walked home."

"Dad said, 'Get in. I'll take us home.' I shook my head and said, 'I'll go with her.' We didn't see him for a couple of days."

"Did she ever learn?" asked Hannah.

"Yeah, a few years later I had my license, thanks to driver's ed. I taught her. She was forty-eight years old."

Hannah and I smiled and nodded, Ted had enough stuff to see this thing through.

The next day Ted contacted the County Clerk to inquire about land and received disturbing news. The large dormant section of land in Big Flats had recently been looked at by Hank Lewis. Hank and Ted had been rivals for years. Hank, older by a couple of years than Ted, seemed to resent Ted's success—which often seemed to come at Hank's expense.

"What's the story with this Lewis guy? Should we be concerned about him or what?" I asked.

"It goes back a while. When I first started acquiring and developing commercial property, I obtained a section in downtown Elmira. It was mainly because the owner didn't trust Hank and told him so. He always believed I poisoned his reputation to gain advantage. I didn't need to, he did it to himself."

"If you meet Hank you'll get a clearer picture of his personality," said Libby.

"Or lack thereof," said Ted. "The first time I met him, to be polite I asked how he liked to be addressed—Henry or Hank. He said anyway I liked. I chose 'Henry' and failed the first test. Turns out he prefers Hank."

"He mumbles most of the time, too. Says he has a reason," said Libby.

"You're kidding. Whatever could it be?" I asked.

"Get this, he says when he speaks quietly people pay closer attention and it pleases him." said Libby.

"Pleases him? It actually pleases him?" said Hannah.

"That's nuts," I said.

"Uh huh, isn't it? I think he just likes to manipulate people," said Libby.

"Tell us more about this guy," said Hannah.

"You're gonna love this stuff," offered Libby rubbing her hands quickly together.

"Okay, you asked for it. He's in his early forties, tall, skinny but sinewy. He smells like foul tobacco and musty clothes. He's bent over, shuffles along like an aged, infirm geezer and has a nose patterned directly from a John Deere model. His arrogance knows no bounds. He won the gene lottery, due mainly to his successful father, when he was born."

"A familiar story," said Dru as he glanced at Hannah.

"Of course, but it's how he handled it. As Ted often says, Hank was born on third and acts like *he* hit a triple."

"Good use of a baseball metaphor, my compliments," I said.

Hannah and I both chuckled.

"He's both impatient and unreasonable. He was raised with the silver spoon approach, mainly by his socially prominent mother, who really is the exact opposite of his reprobate father. Hank mistrusts everyone and worships at the altar of the almighty dollar. And he's universally disliked. One of the big reasons he distrusts people is a few years ago he invested nearly everything in his daughter's company. Lost it all due to unforeseen economic downturn. Ensuing scandal, similar to Enron—and everyone in town knows it," said Ted.

"Don't forget the wife," said Libby.

"Rumor has it, the love of his life, his college sweetheart at Colgate cheated on him with a fraternity brother after Hank married her. With all the other events, slights, slurs he thinks he's encountered through the years, it's molded him into the malevolent man you'll see," said Libby.

"Wow, I can't wait for the day to arrive. Does that mean he's going up against you if we want the Big Flats parcel?" asked Dru.

"I guess so, if the rumors are true," said Ted.

"If so, what's plan B?"

"I'm not sure that's plan A. It was just the first place I thought of. I'll do some more research. If I can help it I'd just as soon keep away from Whisperin' Willie—that's what I call him."

"If we find another place I may have an idea of how to out-fox Mr. Lewis when the time comes," I said.

CHAPTER 6

"Next order of business, let's contact the owner of the name 'Pioneers.' "

"Who owns it, do you know?"

"Oh yeah."

"So we'll talk to him," I said.

"I already did a few months ago. His name is Rance Butler. Insisted he wants to preserve the Pioneer heritage, so I don't think he'll sell," said Ted. "After making the call, I wondered how someone like Butler could become such a pompous asshole." Libby laughed at the memory.

"I've known him since we were eleven. Played Small Fry football with him for three years, played a little bit against him in high school football, even though he didn't play much."

"What's Small Fry?" I asked.

"It's like Little League but with real basketball, baseball and football rules. In Small Fry baseball a good catcher is vital because you can steal. That's the major difference from Little League. It's a local thing. We had a Little League in West Elmira but Small Fry had the best players—or so we thought. When it came time to pick the team to vie for the Little League tournament team to represent the area not many from the Little League teams made it but Small Fry's best players all did."

"Was Butler any good at football?" asked Hannah.

"Good? He was great, a real star. He maxed out there though. Oh, he played a little in high school but wasn't as great as when he was twelve."

"Why is he so arrogant then?"

"To make up for the last twenty-eight years, is my guess."

"So what's your real opinion?" said Hannah.

"Schmuck comes to mind. Did you buy that crap about wanting to save the heritage?" I said.

"I take it you don't," said Ted.

"Ted, if you offered him some cash he'd sell out the heritage in a heartbeat," said Hannah.

"So let's offer, whadda ya think is fair, Dru?" said Ted.

"That we let him live with it, that's it. Screw the name. We're gonna start our own new heritage, blow his outta the water, we'll make people forget all about the Pioneers," I said.

"I don't know, let me think about it."

"Ted, why is the name so important to you?" I asked.

"It's gonna sound silly but when I was a kid I had severe scoliosis. My mother and uncle, who lived with us, would rub my back and legs every night to relieve the ache. Uncle Bud, just got out of the army and stayed with us until he got married a year later.

"When I got better, after a chiropractor literally straightened me out over the next five years, my uncle took me to ball games to see the Pioneers. Later that summer he got me a uniform jersey from the visiting Binghamton Triplets, a Yankee affiliate. At the time, uniforms were handed down the chain of minor league teams from the major league clubs to save money. So I had a real gray Yankee away uniform. It was number six, my first number in baseball in Babe Ruth League ball... we didn't have numbers in Small Fry. So I guess I'm hung up on the memory of that as much as anything."

"That's sweet. Who was number six for the Yankees?" asked Hannah.

"Most prominently my all-time favorite, Mickey Mantle," said Ted.

"I thought he was number seven, and you're too young for him to be your favorite," said Libby.

"That was his number in 1952, his second year. The first year, 1951, he was issued number six. He got to wear seven the next year, that's the one he made famous and the one, after his All-World career, the Yankees retired. Mickey was my dad's favorite and he used to tell me stories of his exploits, so I just adopted him," said Ted.

"Dru, did you know that?" asked Hannah.

"Of course, he was my all-time favorite, even though I only saw him play on film. He was my dad's favorite too," I said.

"Okay, you guys I get all the history and memory stuff, but if we're moving the venue don't you think we need a new name?" asked Hannah.

Ted thought a bit and nodded his head. "I guess it does make more sense. We'll create new memories for kids, huh?"

"I think so. Now let's come up with a new name." They agreed to all think, but I had one in mind already. Hannah had her own ideas.

Next item on the list was contacting Major League Baseball but the pennant races were winding down and playoffs would soon be in full swing. I thought it would be wise to hold off contacting them at such a busy time.

Horse before the cart should be a simple concept but rarely seems to work out that way. Team first, then place to play. Recent baseball history though has favored place before team. To move a team you obviously need a place to go, or somewhere to build. The where is what makes it possible.

"I think we need to focus on land. I don't want to deal with Mr. Lewis either," I said.

"Ted, what about that land near the Domes of Elmira College? You know, the old farm land?" said Libby.

"It's worth looking into. If the college owns it they may want to dump it for cash. I'll check tomorrow."

"Who's hungry?" asked Libby. We agreed it was time for food... off to Morretti's for a relaxing uneventful meal. After dinner Hannah and I drove back to Keuka each with our own thoughts. The nighttime provided no distractions. I'm not sure what Hannah was mulling over, though I'd guess promotional ideas were crashing around her brain cells like ping pong balls in a mouse trap filled room. The ensuing explosion emptied every trap.

For myself, I couldn't help but fear letting these nice people down. I include Hannah, of course. My heart would deflate like a poorly constructed soufflé if I disappointed her. I was also wondering if I bit off more than I could swallow. Chewing was easy... getting it down would be easy. Ah... but keeping it down? Aye, there's the bitch.

I'd feel like a jerk if the plan failed after my forty-four minute murder board concoction. I'd made this plan comparable with a walk in the park. But they weren't. And I knew it.

CHAPTER 7

The next morning at breakfast, Hanna put in a call to Kimberley Powell in Baltimore. She told Libby they'd do it last night, but things ran longer than planned. Neither Hannah nor I could abide night driving, especially on dark winding hillsides so we drove carefully. Arriving at the cottage we decided to put off the call 'til morning and filled the void with other activities that seemed to disturb Riley. But we didn't care. Like I said, let 'im get his own girls.

"Kimberley Powell," answered Kimberley Powell.

"Hello, Mrs. Powell, this is your maid-of-honor. How ya doin', old married lady?"

"As well as can be expected, what with a wonderful husband, great friends and a thriving business. Whom did you say this was again?"

"Droll, dearie, very droll."

"How's the lake, Mrs. McKenna?"

"Couldn't be better unless we owned this house."

"Cottage, Hannah, cottage," chided Kimberley.

"Oh that's right, I forget you Lake Folk have your affectations. By the way, you're out of bread."

"That's it, eat us out of house and home."

"So you admit it's a home and not a cottage?"

"Yeah, yeah, yeah, I talked to Libby last night so I was ready for this morning's onslaught. I hear Dru's doin' his thing again?"

"Set a record too. Forty-four minutes before the bullets came out."

"I know, Libby and Ted were flummoxed. Does he really have a handle on it?"

"He does, or at least the complete outline of the plan." They chatted for a few more minutes and Hannah invited them up to their own house, but Justin was going out of town so they took a rain check.

***

I checked the murder board, solidifying the decision regarding the Pioneer name. At the M/T office, Ted and I figured, since he'd already been rebuffed by Butler, I'd take a turn at bat... so to speak.

"Why do I feel like a teenager calling for his first date?" I asked.

"Yeah, I'm sure you had lots of trouble getting dates," said Hannah over her shoulder as she left to join Libby in the kitchen.

"I noticed she didn't even try to hide her snark," said Ted, while a grin spread over his chiseled visage.

"Okay, might as well get this show on the road." I dialed the number Ted gave me. We sat in Ted's study for this epic moment. *He's right, this view is somethin'.*

"It's ringing," I said.

"Hello," answered someone.

"Mr. Butler?"

His mellow voice filled the office since I'd put him on speaker. "All day long, who is this? And by the way I'm not in the market for anything."

Ted stifled a chuckle as he brought his hands together in a silent clap.

I said, "No, no, Mr. Butler. I'm not selling anything. I'm the one who may be in the market for something you have though."

"Call me Rance. I don't believe I have anything for sale but you've got my attention."

"Okay, Rance, what I'm talking about is the Pioneers. Or to be precise, the name Elmira Pioneers."

"The baseball Pioneers? We went down in flames years ago. Right after Baltimore threw us away."

"I know, but you retained the rights to the name, I hear." Detecting an edge to Rance's attitude, I let it slide, for now.

"Until the day I leave this mortal coil, as they say."

There it is, I thought. *Edge confirmed.* "But why?" I asked.

"Young fella, I don't see what business it's of yours. Now if you'll excuse me I'm going to hang up."

I looked at Ted with a bemused expression and said, "He hung up."

Hannah and Libby came in with a coffee service complete with Danish and stayed to eavesdrop.

"How about that," said Ted shaking his head. Picking up his phone again I hit redial.

"Hello, for crissakes," the now familiar voice answered. I put him on speaker again.

"Rance, before you hang up on me would you please tell me why won't you sell the Pioneer name to me?"

Libby and Hannah moved closer to the speaker Dru was holding up to hear both sides.

"I can see I'm not going to get rid of you until I do, so here it is. My family was involved with the Pioneers ever since we were affiliated with the Brooklyn Dodgers back in the forties and fifties. Like Tommy Lasorda, we all bled Dodger blue. Then the traitorous, bastard, O'Malley chose to chase the almighty buck out to LaLa land. We built Dunn Field for them and they left us holding our dicks."

I rolled my eyes toward the others as Butler rattled on.

"He's giving a history lesson, Butler loves to do it to everyone," whispered Ted to the women.

"My dad died in those stands. I thought I'd go the same way, you know, watching the Dodgers farm club at Dunn Field. But that boat sailed on O'Malley's yacht. So I'm not going to sell for any price to anybody, got it?"

"Yes sir, Mr. Butler, have a good day and thank you," I said.

"What for?"

"For making my decision a no-brainer. Now I don't have to feel bad about not having the Pioneer name."

"What did you want it for?"

"Well, Mr. Butler, I don't see what possible business it is of yours, and I'm the one who's gonna hang up now."

"I guess that's that, huh?" said Ted after I'd disconnected.

"I should have realized when he said his name was Butler," I said. I looked over at Ted's quizzical expression and said, "It's a long story, I'll tell you some time."

"The funny thing is, you seemed to predict his reaction, didn't you, Dru?" asked Ted.

Hannah countered, "Don't be too surprised, guys. That's another arrow Dru seems to have in his quiver."

"You caught that, did ya? I'm going to start looking out for them from now on. I wonder if they're related?" I asked.

"Okay, fill me in on what I'm missing," said Libby.

"Yeah, me too," said Ted.

"Good luck getting him to tell ya, guys. I've been trying for two years to get him to tell me about something else," said Hannah.

"It's not a secret. Years ago I was helping a friend when a shit-bird named Butler tried to steal my friend's business away. Reminded me a lot of this Butler, only his name was Blake, not Rancid," I said.

"That's it?" asked Libby.

"More or less," I said as Hannah shook her head while I grinned.

"So do you still think we've gotta have the Pioneer name, Ted?"

"Dru, I just liked the tradition of it, I suppose. But the more I think of it, what with Dunn Field's stadium condition and location, I think a clean break with the past does work better. What do you think, Lib?"

"Yeah, I think a new name would be a good way to start this thing off, how about you, Hannah?"

"I think a new name would add significant promotional value as soon as we get the project off the ground," said Hannah.

Ted looked at Libby and said, "I see what you meant when you said they make quite a team, hon."

"Kimberley told me what you guys did for her and Justin at National Motors and quite frankly they're in awe of you both."

"Libby, nice to hear but you know how Kimberley is prone to hyperbole," said Hannah.

"Sounds like you told Libby what've you got in mind," I said.

"I promise I'll let you know when it's time, big guy. Unlike some I could name, I keep my promises."

CHAPTER 8

"Before we talk to the MLB people we need to get our local geese in a row," I suggested.

"That would be ducks, dear," corrected Hannah.

"Just as long as it's not a 'fowl ball,' " I said.

"That's a punishing remark, even for you, Mr. McKenna," chastised Hannah.

"As my aim was true, my goal just and my heart pure, I'm pleased with the outcome," I said, grinning like a happy chimpanzee with a banana.

Hannah groaned as Libby and Ted shook their heads, neither for the first time nor the last. We realized this project would be complicated, fraught with twists, turns and pitfalls. Hannah and I had been through similar last year with our National Motors project and were confident of success. Ted and Libby less so.

"Dru, you were saying you had a plan for dealing with Hank Lewis. Wanna fill us in?"

"It's quite simple, really. Let's call it the old misdirection play. Your old friend, Hank, doesn't know me from Adam's off ox so it's better if you confirm you're interested in the Big Flats property. After all it's you he wants to thwart."

"By thwart you mean have my head on a pike, right?"

"Couldn't have put it better my own self," I said.

"Meanwhile with your guidance, Hanna and I will look into the college land on Route 14."

"Yeah, I get it," said Ted.

"I've been in the auto parts distribution business for years, done rather well too. The name McKenna carries some weight there. I'll employ McKenna Automotive as my cover for the interest in the land, but make sure the owners know I'm not desperate, just exploring a number of options, Route 14 being one of several."

"So while Hank is focused on my interest in Big Flats, you'll get things moving up north, right?" said Ted.

"Clever, Dru. You think it'll work?" asked Libby.

"I do, but both of you must stay completely away from there and the deal. We can't let Hank or Butler tie us together, let alone the details of the baseball part. And yes, you can trust me on this," I said.

Ted and Libby both laughed, "Kimberley said you could read minds, Dru," said Libby.

"I never doubted it," said Ted a little sheepishly, "at least, not now."

"Let's get moving on our land deals, folks," I said.

After a few phone calls to the records people and a trip down to the records bureau it was ascertained Elmira College did indeed own the property just north of an existing distribution area known as the Holding Point. I scheduled a meeting with the college administrators for the next week.

Meanwhile, Ted contacted the town of Big Flats to inquire about a parcel large enough for their needs. Those included space for a ball park, amusement center, picnic area, hiking trails, horseback riding, and a dog park. It took a bit of time but the town found some land they could cobble together from parcels already up for sale by four different owners, none of whom were Hank. *So far so good,* I thought.

***

That night, back in our borrowed cottage, Hannah and I discussed what we were getting into.

"How do you feel about this thing?" I asked.

"A lot like I did last year. I like the people we're involved with, I think the overall plan is sound and worthwhile. There's doubt galore, caused by enemies known and unknown. There's bound to be hurdles ahead but I can't wait to get my hands on promoting this deal."

"So, you're up for it, huh?" I said.

"You bet I am. Until last year, for me, business was all about other people's success or failure. Me, I got paid either way. A successful campaign added glory and earned me a solid reputation but it wasn't like I had skin in the game."

"And now you do," I said.

"And now I do. I like this feeling of being involved with the outcome on a gut level. I think I better understand why you do this."

"You're right. I do get a sense of satisfaction and take pride in my part of it, but I genuinely like helping good people overcome the odds."

"What about the bad guys?" she said.

"Yeah you got me. I especially like sticking it to the bad guys. Arrogance is the most heinous sin a person can commit."

The next day Ted went to see the honchos in Big Flats. When he returned he gave me the run down.

"Dru, he was a shade over five feet, smelled like Cherry Blend pipe tobacco and Bay Rum."

"Sounds like the shortest honcho ever, maybe a honchlet, or maybe one of the Keebler elves, but he was very helpful, huh?" I said. "Greatsinger seemed to already know about our plan even though he wanted Ted to spell it out."

"Did you stick to the script?" I asked.

"Yep, played it close to the vest. Said I'd check with my financial people and get back to him." Ted smirked like he was holding something back.

I refilled his whiskey glass and urged him to continue.

"Guess who was parked across the street when I left?"

"Arnold Palmer," I retorted.

"More like Benedict Arnold. I circled back around the block to see Hank Lewis sneaking in the building I'd just left."

"So Hank's on to us," I said.

"Apparently, Dru, you called this one on the nose."

"So *Henry* bought it?" I grinned.

"Like the proverbial bridge in Brooklyn."

* * *

The next couple of days Hannah and I hung out at the cottage. She liaised with her New York staff, while I fished and went into Hammondsport to shop for our next few days' meals. While in town, I picked up a 'Things to do in the Finger Lakes' magazine. *We might do some of this stuff,* I thought.

While strolling around the quaint village I found myself standing at the marina as if drawn by a spirit force, Indian perhaps. Looking out toward the bluff, a random thought rocketed through my consciousness, quickly disappearing into the recesses of my mind. Immersed in the retrieval process, I fished for the gist of the thought when suddenly it broke the surface. Tangentially, I thought, *A fitting analogy in this place, where many a fishing expedition was launched.*

Did I think this project could be accomplished, or were unseen forces lying in the weeds waiting to pounce, thereby thwarting us? I didn't often search deep within myself but when I did it usually brought more help than hindrance. *I only wish I knew Ted and Libby better,* I mused. I think we're in for a bigger battle than it initially appeared. I thought of Hannah and was comforted by the thought, *I'm so lucky she's in my life. I need to ask her for her take on this deal.*

Turning from the lake and walking up a slight incline I gazed back at the lake and town below. This could have been captured in a Christmas snow globe from Thomas Kincaid, so quaint and old fashioned.

Back home, I found Hannah in her commandeered office. It was actually a spare bedroom overlooking the pool and lake in the distance, a beautiful view. I find it hard to focus for long before the vista would steal my attention.

"I had a thought walking around town. This thing is going to get more complicated. I know we can do it but it's going to be a lot harder than Ted and Libby fully understand," I said to Hannah.

"Sounds to me like you're asking if they can play *hard ball?*"

"How well you think you know me," I answered shaking my head.

"Well, am I right or what?" she demanded.

"Of course, you're right. I'm thinking Hank and Butler and maybe Greatsinger are all in cahoots. Small towns all have movers and doers. I wouldn't be surprised if these guys are those guys."

"What's that mean for us, Dru?" said Hannah.

"I always think it's better to have information than not to. I'm not ready to worry about how to combat these bozos until we know what we need. At this point just knowing where enemy positions are can help us outflank them down the road. My concern is Libby and Ted may not be up for trench warfare. These small towns can be enclaves of intertwined labyrinths of self-serving ego trips full of malevolent evil."

"Wow, that's some rant you got goin' on there. Where's it coming from?" asked Hannah.

"From a long line of family lore and personal experience. You saw it firsthand last year with Ian Steele and the oil folks," I reminded her.

"Yeah, I guess I did, huh? But we handled it okay."

"Yeah, I know but if you recall, we got very, very lucky, Mrs. McKenna."

" 'Luck,' a baseball man said, 'is the residue of design,' " said Hannah.

"Branch Rickey, GM of the St. Louis Cardinals and Brooklyn Dodgers, back in the day of Jackie Robinson," I said.

"I just knew you'd know that. The fact remains we did get lucky, persevered and won. We'll do it again, I can feel it," said Hannah.

"In your bones?" I said.

"You betcha, big guy."

I hope you're right, but we might share with Libby and Ted what we may be in for," I warned.

"We can do that. I think it's a good idea to get 'em accustomed to the way you think, plan and act in the heat of the fray," offered Hannah.

CHAPTER 9

We began the next day with breakfast at the Reynolds' hacienda at eight a.m.

"So you really think this is going to get down and dirty?" said Libby.

"If money is an issue I'm sure it will. Small town or megalopolis, it doesn't matter. People always want to win. Money is how they keep score," I said.

"I suppose you're right, especially with Hank. I just didn't figure on the others," said Ted.

"Start figuring. I'll be surprised if our boy Hank isn't the leader of this group but don't be shocked if there aren't others. In the end though it's Hank who'll be calling the shots," I cautioned.

"What's next?" asked Libby.

"I think we should inquire about more land in Big Flats to add extra diversion to the scheme. We need to stall while we move on the north property," I said. "In the meantime, I want to find out about successful small town franchises. We need to make plans for the size of the ballpark. Too small is no good. We never want to turn away fans. Too large and the place will seem empty and unsuccessful. We don't want to appear unpopular. Let's do some research."

"Libby and I can handle that," said Hannah.

"Murder board says we need to go to MLB next to get some info," I said.

"I'll take care of that," offered Ted.

I agreed. It was only fitting he should be the face of the project to MLB. After all I had no desire to stick around after it becomes real. It'll be Ted and Libby's baby to run.

The newly formed team got down to business.

"Hold it, we all have something to do except you, Dru McKenna. What's up with that?" asked Hannah.

"No flies on you, are there, dear?"

"I should say not, and don't try that sleight of tongue with me, Buster. What're you going to be doing?"

"Me, I'm going to play with my dog," I answered over my shoulder and headed for the car and back to the lake house to play with Riley, and most important... to think.

* * *

After spending the afternoon exploring the hills above the lake, Riley and I left to meet the team at Morretti's in Elmira. Calling Hannah's cell I told her we were on our way.

"Are you sure they'll let Riley in?" she asked.

"If they want..."

"Yeah I forgot McKenna's immutable law: 'Take me and my dog or neither of us,' right?"

"Right, Kiddo."

Over dinner Ted said, "You guys aren't gonna believe this. There's a team in Las Vegas up for sale."

"What league?" asked Hannah.

"Pacific Coast," replied Ted.

"Whoa, Ted. That's Triple-A," I said with a pronounced frown.

"I know, isn't it great?"

I looked at all of them then said, "You know the buy-in for a Triple-A team is about twenty mil, right?"

"Yeah, but with that we get instant affiliation, support for player and coaches' salaries and half the equipment costs," said Ted.

"Who's the parent club?" asked Libby.

"That's the best part, Hon. It's the New York Mets," Ted announced proudly.

"Wow, that would mean we'd be at a higher rank than Binghamton," said Libby with an ear-to-ear grin.

"Hold on, folks, we gotta work this out. Doesn't final approval of a sale and move need the Mets approval?" I said.

"Probably, not to mention MLB," said Ted.

"How the hell are we going to get that?" said Libby turning toward Hannah.

"Who knows? I've ridden this wagon before and all I know is we'll figure out somethin'," said Hannah. "Right, Dru?"

"Sure, lay it all on me," I answered with a smile replacing the frown.

Riley, who had been quietly lying next to me seemed to sense the meal was finished. He roused to see if he'd get his customary "last bites." He did and we returned to Ted's study to make plans for a bid on the Las Vegas 51s.

* * *

The next morning, I harbored a worrisome notion. I think if I put my brain on the edge of a razor it would resemble a BB on a four-lane highway. I need an idea but looks like I'll have to steal one.

I knew Hannah could tell I was worried, mainly because she said, "Dru, I know you're worried."

No flies on her or me, I thought.

She let me off the hook... for the moment. I took Riley out for his morning ablutions and asked the spirit guides for an answer. With coffee in hand I stood on the dock and stared out at the lake. I was still agonizing over what in God's name we could do to pull this off. *Maybe nothing*, was my fear.

Triple-A, how did I get involved in a business like this? I was fairly certain we couldn't get approval from either the Mets or MLB, but we'd soldier on and try. Helping out friends, sure I can do that. Overcoming small town petty grudges, conspiracies and the potential to fail beautifully, I'm pretty sure I can't do THAT too! Come on. Just let me come out of this thing with a scalp on my belt that's not my own.

On the drive to the Reynolds' Hannah knew I was still troubled. I was waitin' for her to nail me on it soon. True to form, I didn't have long to wait.

When we settled down in Ted's office, Hannah brought out her hammer.

"What is it, Dru? Something's bothering you and before you go Clint Eastwood on me with the tall, strong, silent bit I'm here to tell ya', Pilgrim, it ain't gonna fly, so don't try it."

I laughed. "You do know John Wayne said that, not Clint, right? Besides, he looked nothin' like a dame."

"Are we mixing movie references here or what? And don't think you're getting away with a patented McKenna distraction ploy, Bucko."

"I was thinking about Bloody Mary, hon," I said trying yet another distraction ploy using *South Pacific,* which she wasn't buying.

"I just bet you were. C'mon, what gives, or do I tell one of the most embarrassing moments of Dru McKenna's life?" she threatened.

"Wow! Okay, I was thinking today we really need to finesse this gambit of misdirection perfectly or we'll blow Ted's dream out of the water. I'm not gonna dismiss Hank as a small town yokel. I don't fear him but I respect him as the malevolent evil rat bastard I know he'll turn out to be. Revenge is a dish best served cold... but freezing him out might trigger some vengeful plot to thwart us. It's a delicate balance."

"Come up with a plan of your own, did we?" she asked.

"I believe I have, Mrs. McKenna."

"My hero," she sighed while gazing upon me with moon-calf eyes. "Whatcha got?"

With the unexplained plan in the middle of the room, we were joined by Ted and Libby who were finished seeing their kids off to school. Based on the looks of them, executing the plan for D-Day was easier than getting a seventh and eighth-grader off to school.

"What'd we miss?" asked Libby.

"Dru was about to share an idea," said Hannah.

"How does this sound? First we hide in plain sight," I said having received an answer from spirits, guardian angels or from somewhere out there.

"Like a needle in a haystack?" she asked.

"More like in a stack of needles," I answered.

"What exactly does that mean?"

"Well, the idea of the diversion is sound but I want Hank to think like a Steele-type hump might think."

"What's a steel hump?" said Ted.

Ignoring him for the moment so as to not lose my brain train o' thought, I continued, "In fact I'm counting on him to do exactly what I hope he'll do."

"Why do you hope he acts like Steele?" asked Hannah.

Perplexed, Libby turned to Ted with eyebrows about to threaten her hairline. "What's steel got to do with this?"

"Here's the deal. I just don't believe subterfuge will be fool proof in a town this size. There's too many accidental contacts, where a word here or there may jog someone's memory... and poof, the plan is up in smoke."

"As in the jig is up, Mr. Holmes?" said Hannah.

"Exactly, Mrs. Watson, just like that," I said.

"You believe Hank'll catch on?"

"Maybe not right away but when he ponders a while he could put the pieces together even if he doesn't know about us. He knows Ted is up to something, just not the whole agenda. People like Hank and Ian Steele believe they're the smartest most clever person in any room they're in."

"Who's Ian Steele? What the hell is going on here, Ted?" said Libby.

"Libby, I have no idea. They won't tell me. How about it, Dru? What are you guys talkin' about and who's this Steele guy?"

"Sorry, last year in Baltimore, one of the malevolent creatures we had to deal with was Ian Steele. He betrayed my godfather, Jon

Fallon, and was directly responsible for his death," I said, bringing them somewhat up to date.

"Wow! Jon Fallon was like a Warren Buffet type guy, wasn't he?" asked Ted.

"He was, even advised Warren from time to time," I answered.

Ted looked at Libby and said, "We are in rarefied air here, hon."

"And you're hoping Hank acts like Steele?" questioned Libby with a perplexed look still in place.

"Not the dangerous part but the treachery. I, er, we can deal with that," I assured them.

"We can?" said Ted.

"Here's my idea. What say we go to Hank and bring him in on part of the deal? Not the baseball part but the amusement park part. Ask him to join in the project financially. I don't think Hank will accept Ted's overture at face value, still it may keep him preoccupied enough to keep him away from the Elmira College land and keep our baseball deal secure."

"Okay, but how do we conceal the baseball part?" Libby asked.

"I've got an idea for that too. We do what any self-respecting man does when faced with a troublesome situation. We come up with an expedient lie."

"I knew it. I've always felt that believing everything a man says is dangerous. So what's the lie?" asked Libby as she cast an evil eye toward Ted.

"We tell 'em we went to Butler for the Pioneer name because we want to use it for the amusement park as a connection to a popular time in the area. I know we talked about calling it Eldridge Park but they've already started to resuscitate Eldridge in its original location on a small scale so that's out. We found we couldn't buy the Eldridge or Pioneer names so we'll need to change it."

"What if Butler, since he's in cahoots with Hank on other deals around town, offers to sell the Pioneer name after all?"

"We'll let him, but not to us. If Hank really wants to stick it to Ted, he'll end up with the name, the land, the whole enchilada."

"So it's not really a lie after all," said Libby.

"Not entirely, but it serves a purpose."

"How's that gonna happen, if Butler is the one selling the Pioneer name?"

"I'm sure Hank will instruct him to sell to Ted, which he will. After all, how much could he ask? Ted in turn will give it to Hank as the first step in the offer of an olive branch," I said.

"What if Hank turns the gesture down?"

"Then we go to step two," I said.

"What's step two?"

"Offering Hank a piece of the Big Flats land deal to go with the name."

"Holy cow! You've got Ian Steele down pat. You worry me," said a grinning Hannah.

"As well I should, dearie. I've been through it before."

"Doesn't Butler know it was you calling about the Pioneer name?" she asked.

"I never gave a name. I only said I was calling on behalf of Ted. Caller ID will show Ted's office number since I called from here. So as far as Butler knows the call was made by some minion of Ted's."

"It sounds audacious enough to work. What better way to keep your enemy close, eh, Sun Tzu?" said Hannah.

"Precisely. In addition, even though Hank ends up holding the bag, so to speak, nothing prevents him from profiting from a development program of his own. The whole idea is not to hurt Hank and his crew necessarily—but to prevent him from hurting Ted, which, I'm sure, is Hank's main goal."

"It's amazing how your mind processes these problems," said Hannah.

"Yeah, how do you do it, Dru?" asked Libby.

"Someday I promise to share the whole of it."

"Including how Red got his name?" asked Hannah.

"That and much more. I think you'll find it as fascinating as I do."

The rest of the day was spent mapping out responsibilities: the amusement park for the women, baseball for the men, and where Team McKenna's mascot dog would go on his next walk.

Back at the lake and after Mr. R.T. Dog's nighttime ablutions, the boys joined Hannah in the cave.

"How was the perambulation?" she asked.

"Quite satisfactory and you'll be glad to know the hood is secure, and we can all sleep in tomorrow. He's had a busy day."

"As we all have," she said, trying unsuccessfully to stifle a yawn.

* * *

Awakening to the delightful aroma of fresh brewed coffee and biscotti straight from the oven, I rolled over and soon was accosted by a leaping hundred-pound Lab who proclaimed it was the best day ever. Riley offered a morning faux chomp on my arm by way of a greeting. We horsed around until Hannah entered with a tray of goodies and the papers.

"What's going on in here? It sounds like you were fighting."

"Riley was just telling me what a great day this is, and alerting me to your arrival."

"Yeah, as if the delightful aromas emanating from the kitchen didn't already deliver that message," she said.

"You're right, it does smell scrumptious. Let's eat."

"And good morning to you too, fine sir."

I laughed as Hannah placed the tray on the nightstand and pulled her down to me. Seems breakfast would be delayed a bit.

* * *

After a bit of fooling around, we were in the middle of breakfast and the papers when the strains of *The Good, the Bad and the Ugly* signaled an incoming call. A wave of dread washed over me. The number of times a phone call informed me of disaster looming was legion. I looked at Hannah with fearful eyes, as if to say, 'Not again.' In spite of myself, I took the call.

CHAPTER 10

In Hank Lewis' office the phone rang, he answered and said, "What?"

"It's me, Hank. I was talking to Bob Crandall at the college and according to him some big deal auto parts company is investigating building a regional distribution center over by the Holding Point," said Rance Butler into his cell as he drove.

"Really, who did he say it was?" said Hank.

"McKenna Associates, ever hear of 'em?"

"Holy shit, this could be huge. They're the largest and most successful aftermarket auto parts business on the planet. Who contacted Crandall, did he say?"

"A guy named... hold on, I wrote it down. Here it is, Dru McKenna."

Hank was lost in thought trying to figure out how to use this info to his best advantage.

"What chance does Crandall think this has of happening?"

"He's not sure yet. He's checking with the college now to see what's available. He knows the school needs funding for expansion so he's confident they'd love to do it."

Hank was lost in thought again. He sat mulling over ideas when he realized Rance was still there.

"Rance, I need a favor."

"What is it?"

"Go check with the college about any land in that area and see if we can buy it up now for cash on the barrel head."

"We?" asked Reynolds.

"Of course, you brought this to me so naturally I'd include you," said Hank. "I'll even overlook you calling me Henry. You know I hate that."

"Sorry, Hen... er, I keep forgetting. I'll get right on that and get back to you. Are you thinking of grabbing some land and selling it to McKenna?"

"Rance, sometimes you surprise me. That's exactly what I'm thinking. I've dealt with these kinds of hot shots before. If they want something bad enough they don't let anything stand in their way. It helps that I know of him but he's clueless about me."

"Good thing," muttered Reynolds.

After getting the news from Butler, Hank put in a call to his banker, Austin Coleman.

"Austin, how you doin'? Hank here."

"As if I didn't know. I put the volume on high after caller ID warned me," said Coleman laughing. "Doin' great, what's up?"

"I'm not sure, but I may be buying some land soon and wondered what I could comfortably commit to."

"Hank, you have enough collateral to float a loan for the whole county," Coleman exaggerated. "How much are we talking about here?"

"Not exactly sure yet, I'm just covering my bases. But I may have a figure in mind soon, maybe even today."

"Just let me know and we'll work it out, Hank."

"Thanks, Austin."

Later that day, Hank's cell intoned the theme from *The Godfather*.

"It's me, Rance. Looks like Reynolds has no interest in the college land."

"We already know it's the McKenna guy, so why are you calling?" asked a surly Hank.

"Just confirming. The good news is there's forty-five to fifty acres that's privately owned but the owners may want to sell. Crandall can't promise it but he thinks it's likely. It wouldn't block the sale of the parcel but its value might go up significantly being adjacent to a project of this apparent scope.

Hank rose and began to pace as Butler continued, "Crandall also mentioned an overlooked piece of land right at the entrance of the plots he forgot to tell McKenna about. It's an old piece that ran in front of Brown's Pharmacy—you know they had the best lemon ice cream when I was growin' up. Anyway when train tracks were laid years ago Brown's never sold this plot and it's been overlooked for decades. Crandall didn't think to tell McKenna about it. If you want to move now you could buy it. The Browns have no use for it and since the college really needs the money you can get the forty-five acres from Crandall. It's not sure McKenna will go through with the deal anyway, so for him it's a bird in the hand."

"Sorry I snapped, Rance. That was good thinking about Reynolds and terrific news about the Brown's land."

"Thanks, Hen, er ah, Hank. Are you willing to go on a flyer and buy this tract?"

"Yeah, land is never a bad buy. Even if the deal folds we may be able to do something later, and I have another idea in mind," said Hank.

"Anything more I can do, Hank?"

"Indeed, Rance, I want you to buy that land today. I'll call Coleman and authorize a check made out to the college to be picked up by you and delivered to Crandall."

"For how much, Hank?"

"That's for you to find out from Crandall. I'll meet his price. I gotta move fast."

CHAPTER 11

"Ted, what's wrong? You sound awful," I said.

"He found out about the college land," said Ted.

"Ouch! I knew small towns were tight knit but this is tighter than a duck's ass—and that's waterproof. How'd you find out?" I asked.

"I got a call from Steve Greatsinger. He's worried I'm gonna be more interested in the land up there than Big Flats. He sees our project as being a real boon to his area."

"Why did he think you were interested in that other land?"

"I'm not sure, but I know somebody was checking. Maybe it was Butler or maybe Greatsinger himself being squirrely," said Ted.

"Well, no matter, it sounds like we have you firmly entrenched as being interested in Big Flats," I said.

"So now it's time to contact Hank with an offer to join me, right?"

"Soon, but not yet," I said. "First, we need to get the ballpark plans together, investigate the Las Vegas deal, and get a firm quote on the land in both places."

"You guys comin' over tomorrow?" asked Ted.

"I'm sure we can, but I'll check with Hannah and call ya."

Over dinner, I filled Hannah in on the happenings of the day.

"Seems you were right about small town intrigue, huh?"

"I expected no less, Hank and Butler so reminded me of Steele. I couldn't help but be on guard."

"Anything we can't handle?"

"No, don't forget we're clever and resourceful people."

"I couldn't if I tried. You keep telling me every day."

At that point, Riley, who had finished his last bites, instructed me it was time for a walk. And so we did.

* * *

While the boys were walking Hannah called Libby and invited them up for the weekend for an old fashioned New England clambake.

"We were going to have you guys down, but I love the lake and a clambake tips it. We'll be up. Hannah, what do you think of this whole Hank deal?"

"Libby, I know I keep saying how good Dru is at this stuff but it's really true. I've never been around or even heard about someone with his instincts for solving issues that pop up in any project. It's like a sixth sense for finding the correct path in strange woods. It's uncanny how he always senses true north. We won't get lost in this mess, believe me."

"Funny, that's what Kimberley said. I can't wait to see how it unfolds," said Libby.

"You ain't seen nothin' yet. Wait 'til it really gets hairy," said Hannah.

"You mean more than it already is?"

"Oh yeah, probably as hairy as Chewbacca's butt."

* * *

On Saturday, Ted and Libby rode up to the cottage to visit Hannah and me. Of course, Riley, who greeted them as long lost friends with mock chomps and wagging tail, was assured he was the true reason behind their visit.

I was holding sway at the grill on the patio. I'd pre-cooked the chicken thighs and downed a Sam Adams Ale while waiting for the charcoal to heat. After greetings were out of the way, I brought out my version of a New England clambake.

"What's a Michigander know from New England clambakes?"

"I'm from a long line of New Englanders. I grew up on this stuff."

As we sipped our beers, Ted asked me how much baseball I played.

"I started in Little League, went to Babe Ruth League, then high school and American Legion. I played one year in college but wasn't good enough to go any further."

"What's your greatest day?" asked Ted.

"It happened in Little League. We had a terrific red-haired pitcher, Rusty Hatch, who threw hard and most times had good control."

"That usually means wins at that level," said Ted.

"Right, but we also had other very good players. We had Joe Kostelnek at first, Skip Johnson behind the plate, Gary Leak at second, George Olivetti at short, and me at third. Those were the All-Stars. Our outfielders were good hitters and fair to middling fielders."

"You got some memory. Are you still in contact with those guys?"

"Not a one," I said.

"I bet they didn't have many chances with that fireballer on the mound, did they?"

"Not many, usually weak grounder balls or pop-ups to boot. We were playing the other undefeated team in the league for the championship. In the bottom of the seventh we held a 2-1 lead. I remember this like yesterday. Three more outs and we'd celebrate at Lovell's ice cream parlor. Their leadoff hitter inexplicably walked on a bad call. Next guy, a lefty, hit it down the third base line swinging late on Rusty's heater. I was shaded over there because not many got around on Rusty. I easily scooped it up and threw to Leak for the start of a 5-4-3 DP."

"Not bad for kids, what thirteen?"

"I know, right."

"This sounds like it might not end well," said Libby.

"Very prescient, there are two outs, none on. I could see the trophy in our hands and was as excited as Christmas mornin'. Next guy got a perfect bunt base-hit down first, a tough play, base-hit. The next guy got walked on two of the worst called pitches I've ever seen. I know how that sounds but after all these years I still believe it. During the game I got three hits and drove in both our runs. Now I was thinking of the MVP but knew Rusty would probably get it... mostly because he deserved it."

"What happened?" asked Libby excitedly.

"Well, the rest was in slow motion. Our best outfielder was in right field over toward the right field line. 'Cause a right-handed batter was up and they swung late too."

"Did he?" asked Libby unable to stifle her enthusiasm.

"Just as if we planned it, which we did, the batter popped up the first pitch right to Corky Kramer, just a can of corn. We all watched the arc as we inched toward the second base side of the mound for the upcoming celebration. We never took our eyes off the ball. Corky yelling 'I got, I got it,' as we were taught to do on all fly balls. He didn't *got it*."

Ted laughed and Hannah rolled her eyes at Libby who also laughed. I didn't find this painful memory all that amusing,

Hannah asked, "What happened?"

"The ball hit him right on top of the head and stunned him. He promptly fell like a wounded buffalo. The ball rolled a few feet away and the runners ran like they'd stole something. Corky just sat there dumbfounded. The rest of us were jumping up and down yelling 'pick it up!' He remained inert. Gary Leak ran out to retrieve the ball and threw home but way too late. Both runners scored. Corky later said he lost the ball in the sun but when we looked up all we saw were clouds. I'll never forget that moment, we lost 3-2. End of story."

"If that was your best day, what was your worst?" asked Ted.

"Same day."

We sat silent a moment as if grieving the loss of a loved one. Then laughter rang out and doubled them over. Each apologizing, but I too joined them in glee. I guess it was funny, after all.

"That's some memory, hubby dear," said Hannah.

"I think anybody who has competed in anything at any level has similar memories. Some can handle 'em and others not so much," said Libby.

"You're right on the money, Libby. As I recall, someone blew a short putt for a team victory in college golf," I teased.

"Never mind, Bub, now I know your underbelly, so watch what you say, Mister Loser," said Hannah.

After the tale of my disappointment I resumed assembling the next ingredients to go in the bake: corn on the bone, lobsters, sausage, potatoes, all on the grill carefully watched until done. Accompanied by Naylor Wine's Gris, it was a veritable feast.

They all loved it and complimented the less than humble chef.

"Where did you get this recipe? It's delicious," said Libby.

"I stole it from Bobby Flay, courtesy of the *Food Channel*," I said.

"What about the authentic New England Clambake from generations of McKennas?" asked Hannah with an impish smile.

"Perhaps I embellished a tad," I said.

After dinner, while we wallowed around the pool Ted asked, "Where do we stand with the ballpark designs?"

"Hannah and I did some research on attendance levels and the size of successful Triple-A clubs and there's a study by the Economics Department of a Maryland college that said the size recommended for Triple-A stadiums be a 10,000-seat capacity. That's probably optimal. Only twenty percent of teams of that level sell out so they concluded that smaller parks may be better than some current ones."

"There are a number of variables to consider like population pool, positive promotional activity, team's playing ability, and the new-stadium honeymoon among them. I think we need to think about our chances of being approved by MLB first and foremost. I believe there's a good chance if we don't meet the minimum it will be held against us," said Hannah.

"I can see what you're sayin', but what can we do to convince the Mets and MLB to take a chance on us?" said Ted.

"I think I have an answer. We build a pro forma to detail our C.V. including financial position, our business acumen and our promotional plans including the entire entertainment facilities, and past success," I said. "Also I think we should size the thing to be a 12,500-seat facility with twenty-five to fifty luxury suites and sky boxes—some not all, on season ticket basis, but we'll figure all that out later."

Discussion turned to cost of land, building the field and stadium, scoreboard, sound, team acquisition and operational expenses. We adjourned to the cottage, since the nights were getting chillier.

"How about the money, Ted? What's your plan?" asked Hannah.

"Well, we need to delve into the costs Dru just mentioned and get some numbers together so we can figure out the financing."

"Okay, some of us have marching orders, right, ladies?" I said. "I have a standing walking order from my dog. Tomorrow I'll return to the college to move the land deal forward. Ted, you can touch base with Hank and put that part of the plan in motion."

With that we bade goodnight and looked forward to the next steps.

When R.T. Dog and I returned from securing the 'hood, Hannah asked if I thought this project was doable.

"Providing we get approval from the Mets and MLB we should be A-OK. I have a feeling Triple-A may be one A or two beyond our reach and therefore hard to get acceptance for... but if we put a plan together that impresses them enough we may be in line for a lower classification. I believe it's a more realistic goal, given this population pool and all the variables like demographics connected with something like this. We may be better off at the Double-A level but we'll see how it shakes out. In any event we'll be able to swing it. Hell, I can swing it myself. Or I should say *we* can swing it."

"Are you sure you want to get that deeply involved?"

"Remember your husband and his family has done pretty well for ourselves over the years. Don't forget the inheritance from Jon Fallon. Actually, we'll use Fallon's money for this, but I want Ted to chip in up front and as always in these deals, I'll structure it as an internal loan he'll pay back. I have no intention of full time team management."

I stood up to give me time to mull this over. Am I sure I wouldn't mind running this show? It was appealing but there'd be a lot of tension and dealing with disagreeable humps that would turn me into a hump my ownself. Who the hell wants to be a hump this side of a camel on Wednesday? After my quick bit of introspection I answered, "Guess whose name will be on the stadium?"

"Ian Steele?" guessed Hannah.

"You really are a wise-ass, aren't ya, sweetheart?"

"Always and forever. Why don't you tell me whose name now?"

"Jon Fallon Stadium. I want to pay tribute, and I figure invoking his name with the powers that be in MLB won't hurt us either."

"You have more angles than a pool table and my geometry classes," she said, "and remember I went to Cornell not Ohio State," chided Hannah.

"But Michigan is where the donkeys go."

"Oh ya, I forgot. Goodnight, dearie," she said kissing me goodnight.

CHAPTER 12

"Are you sure we can handle this, Ted?" said Libby.

"Sure? No. But, I haven't been this amped for anything in my life. Have you noticed how everything seems to be falling in place? And I believe, in Dru, we are associated with the most skillful project architect in the world."

"He is amazing. I can't wait for what Hannah has in store for us. According to Kimberley, she's the Princess of promotion."

"What, the 'queen' was busy?" Ted snarked.

"You know you share a lot of the same qualities as Dru. For one there's the smart ass side to both of ya."

"Thank you dear, I live for recognition."

***

"How surprised will the little piss-ant be when he finds out it's me going up against him?" asked Hank. He and Rance Butler were sitting in Hank's office enjoying the Irish whiskey Hank favored.

"He's bigger than you, Hank, and I'm not sure he doesn't already know," answered Butler.

"Only by size," grumbled Hank.

"Steve seemed to think he knows about your interest," said Rance completing his update.

"Yeah, but Steve wouldn't tell him anything. He plays his cards close to those paisley vests of his. He ain't that sharp either. Oh, he may wonder a bit because of our past run-ins but we haven't crossed swords in a while. I know what he's up to but I'm betting he has no clue what I'm up to."

"What exactly is that, Hank?"

"First I want that Big Flats land, then I want to rub Reynolds' nose in it. Then I can be free to develop the thing any way I want."

"So you don't really have a plan."

"Yeah, I do, it's to stick it in Reynolds' ear, smart ass. You're being pretty smart-mouthed today. What's got into you, Butler?"

"I'm not sure it's a good idea to underestimate Reynolds. After all, he did eat your lunch quite a few times in Binghamton, and every time you two have competed."

"Yeah, sure, but I was distracted with the lawsuit with the Ex. I'm going to meet with Steve on Friday and get this deal movin'."

Ted answered his cell and was mildly surprised to hear from Steve Greatsinger.

"Hi, Steve, what's up?"

"Ted, I just wanted to let you know Hank is coming in on Friday to discuss the land you're lookin' at."

"I'm surprised he's looking at it. Did you mention I too was lookin' at it, Steve?"

"I wouldn't last too long if I spread intel like that around, Ted. No, I didn't." Ted thought about it. Since Steve was telling him about Hank's interest, he concluded Steve didn't much care for Hank either. No surprise, not many did.

"The reason I called is to say, if you really want this land, you better move soon."

"Thanks, Steve, I appreciate that. And I am interested but I haven't got the financing in place yet. What did you decide the freight is?"

"Thirty mil, Ted."

"Yeah, that seems okay but I can't make an offer until my ducks are rounded up. I'll commit to thirty mil to discourage others, but if you get a better offer, take it. Thirty is probably my limit."

"Okay, if you're sure. I'd give you last look if you wanted, but you'd have to beat the high card, Ted."

"I understand, and thanks for the heads up, Steve."